Run

By

Jackie McLean

ThunderPoint Publishing Ltd.

Run

by

Jackie McLean

TP

ThunderPoint Publishing Ltd.

First Published in Great Britain in 2019 by
ThunderPoint Publishing Limited
Summit House
4-5 Mitchell Street
Edinburgh
Scotland EH6 7BD

Cover Images © Eky Studio / Shutterstock.com
Cover Design © Huw Francis

ISBN: 978-1-910946-64-0 (Paperback)
ISBN: 978-1-910946-65-7 (eBook)
Printed and bound in Great Britain by Clays Ltd, Elcograf S.p.A

www.thunderpoint.scot

Dedication

To Simon, Stephanie, Brooke and Mia
My anchors in life

Toxic killer loose on the streets of Dundee

A Weekend Special report by Lindsey Forsyth

In this weekend special, we can exclusively reveal a catalogue of incompetence at the heart of Police Scotland in Dundee, and we'll be asking why crazed killer Jonas Evanton has been allowed to roam free among the city's unsuspecting citizens for the last two years.

We can provide the inside story about how the former Detective Inspector – arrested two years ago as the mastermind behind a smuggling operation that resulted in eleven horrific deaths across Tayside – was sent to Belmarsh Prison as part of a deal. He became the only person ever to escape from the high security facility, and has evaded police ever since. Coincidence? We let you decide.

A source close to Police Scotland told us how Evanton, despite being the subject of the police force's biggest manhunt in its entire history, managed to sit right under their noses in Bell Street for months. The brutal murderer remains at large, and we will be demanding to know why no warning has been issued to the public.

In further revelations, we have learned that lead detective DI Donna Davenport, who recently spent several months in a psychiatric hospital, has been given her own armed protection. We understand blunders made by Davenport were responsible for Evanton's escape following his most recent sighting. We will be asking questions about Davenport's role in the disastrous investigation, and we'll be looking at concerns about her state of mind and fitness to be on duty.

Local Councillor Hugh Finnie has expressed

1

alarm at the revelations, and has confirmed that a number of vigilante groups have begun to patrol parts of Dundee. "People need to protect themselves," he told us, "if they can't trust the police to do it."

Turn to the centre pages for full story

Run the gauntlet
Saturday
Chapter 1

Thud.

The team room at Police HQ in Bell Street was unusually quiet today. Even though there were plenty of officers about, most of them were getting on with the laborious task of sifting through the details of the gazillion phone calls and emails that had come in in response to their investigation into an illegal adoptions scam that had recently been exposed.

Thud.

Every contact had to be logged into HOLMES, indexed and cross-referenced so that it could be shared in what was a massive international operation. An operation that was being led and coordinated right here in Bell Street by Detective Inspector Donna Davenport.

Thud.

"Will you quit that?" Sergeant Alice Moone yelled across the large room.

Several pairs of eyes flickered towards her, but mostly her outburst received little attention. Least of all was the attention given by the target of her outburst, DI Davenport.

Donna was sitting alone, casual in faded blue jeans, at a desk on the opposite end of the room from Alice. On the desk in front of her lay open Lindsey Forsyth's Weekend Special. Donna let her head drop onto the open pages, *thud*, sat back upright, and let her head drop back onto the newsprint, *thud*.

Alice got up and crossed the room, sitting back down next to Donna. She squinted at the headline and moved the paper a little so she could look at it properly.

"They're accurate about the crazed killer bit," she said.

Donna stopped and looked at her. "I'm fit for duty, aren't I?" she asked.

3

"Fit as a fruit loop, boss," said Alice.

Donna couldn't help but chuckle. "So, while my *state of mind* is under a cloud," she began, "I might not be held fully responsible for my actions if I hunt Lindsey Forsyth down and wring her neck."

"Hmm," Alice responded. "That would be a bit of a gamble, but I'd pay to watch."

They scanned the report's details again for a moment.

"Boy, you've really pissed her off big time," said Alice. "What did you do?"

"We've got a bigger problem than a pissed off journalist," said Donna, stabbing a finger at the line referring to the source close to Police Scotland. "Somebody in here has been leaking sensitive information – the deal with Belmarsh, my armed protection, my fecking medical history – none of this was ever made public."

Alice frowned. Just then, DC Fran Woods emerged from under the pile of paperwork she'd been ferreting through, and Donna called her to join her and Alice.

"Where are we at?" Donna asked her.

"We've eighteen sets of parents who've come forward," said Fran. Donna chewed on the end of a pen, taking in the details of each sorry case as Fran rhymed them off.

They were spread all over the country, these families. It was going to be one hell of a task to untangle the details and decide whether a crime had been committed in each case, and if it had, how on earth to deal with it.

A radio in the background played an array of current hits and 80s classics, interspersed by the build up to the day's cup games, with particular attention being focused on the expected battle between nearby local rivals Arbroath and Montrose. Donna kept half an ear cocked whenever it was mentioned. Her brother-in-law Danny was at the game.

The door creaked open, and DCI Angus Ross entered the room, balancing plastic cups of steaming coffee.

"To keep the Saturday crew awake," he said. He and Donna exchanged a smile.

Donna pushed her chair back from the desk, and she, Alice and Fran each grabbed a cup from Ross. He looked down at the empty cup holder, shook his head, then nodded at Fran's open case file.

"The adoptions?"

Donna grunted and Fran nodded.

"I take it by your eager responses there's not much to report there?"

They shook their heads and Alice slurped noisily at her coffee.

"Anything on Evanton, then?" Ross asked, flopping onto a nearby seat.

Donna sighed. "About 300 apparent sightings over the past fortnight," she said, the misery obvious in her voice. "All randomly scattered between Land's End and John O'Groats."

"And one in Spain," added Alice.

"Spain, yes," said Donna. "So we're down to next to nobody in here while all of those are being checked out."

"What's this?" he asked, craning his neck to look at the newspaper in front of Donna. Then he groaned. "Oh, that! Look, don't let it get to you…"

"It's not getting to me," said Donna.

"It's getting to her," said Alice.

"We're going to have to issue a response," said Donna. "We can't just let them get away with this, especially when it's affecting public confidence in our abilities. I mean, we need to at least let the public know the lengths Evanton went to to alter his appearance, so there was no way we could have known it was him."

"That's a tricky one," said Ross. "It's the sort of information that could spark even more public alarm. But maybe you're right. Maybe it's time now to get the information out." He scanned the rest of the article and rolled his eyes in frustration.

"As if we don't have enough to deal with," he muttered. Then he sat up, and his expression softened. "You're both going to have to take a break, before all of this kicks off. You haven't stopped since you came back from Turkey…"

"Actually, I'm just about to finish for the day," Donna said, stopping Ross in his tracks and eliciting surprised eyes. "We're off up to Arbroath to have a look at a couple of houses."

"Well good," said Ross, looking at her coffee cup with longing. "That's good. It'll stop you whingeing about living in that cramped mansion on Claypotts Place…"

Donna fired her empty cup at him and chuckled.

"And I've booked my tickets," Alice announced. "I hope you haven't forgotten you'll be without me for the next couple of weeks."

"That's great," said Donna, glad that Alice was flying back to Turkey, this time on holiday rather than business. "Make sure you don't get Efe into any more trouble."

Alice huffed a pantomime huff, a twinkle in her eye. Donna felt a glow of pleasure in her stomach for her friend. Their recent ordeal had had a silver lining, with Alice and Efe forming a bond that went beyond their policing relationship.

Chapter 2

Archie McKinnes ran for his life. The freezing December air knifed into his lungs, and he found it hard to catch a breath. But it would be suicide to stop now. Looking over his shoulder, he felt the first stab of anxiety.

He tried to shut out the insults and the threats that were flying at him thick and fast. Then, from his blind side, the big guy in the navy top barged into him, almost sending him flying.

"Fuckin book that prick, ref!" screamed a block of fans to his right.

"Get him off!" from the stand directly ahead of him.

Archie stumbled then quickly regained his balance, but the moment was gone, and his apparent decision to allow play to go on sent a roar of fury up from the home support.

Howls of rage ripped into the air.

Taunting chants erupted from the away fans, and an object was lobbed onto the pitch.

More roaring from the home support, then a harbinger of trouble as a trio broke from the away end and leaped over the railing into the home crowd.

Archie's eyes bulged as he scanned the pitch and the stands. These lower league local derbies could be unpredictable and could turn nasty at any moment. He felt things were getting close to the bone now, but there was no way he was going to call the game off before half time. He flicked his eyes to his watch, a gesture that didn't go unnoticed by the home support, who began to whistle with vigour.

Three more minutes.

Archie kept running, and kept trying to block out the abuse being hurled at him and to concentrate on the game.

The last minute arrived, and finally Archie McKinnes could call half time. He fingered the whistle, ready to bring it to his lips the instant the second hand touched twelve. Then he could do it. He didn't realise his eyes had closed momentarily, picturing what he was going to do next, until an almighty roar assaulted his eardrums. Startled, he looked towards the away goal, and his heart sank when he saw two opposing players lying in the penalty area. Before he could move a muscle, two of the Arbroath players rushed to where they lay, bouldering into a posse of Montrose players as they went.

The shoving began amongst the players.

Then punches began to fly.

Now the home support and the away fans were all shrieking for the referee's blood.

Archie looked towards the linesman to his left, but his colleague drew him a dirty look, and slowly shook his head. The other linesman was standing with his hands over his face.

By the sound of the reaction, Archie surmised the Arbroath player must have been fouled. He drew out the red card. He would get one of the Montrose players off the field, award the penalty to the home side, and then at least one half of the crowd would shut up.

The Arbroath player took the penalty, hit the top bar, and Archie blew the whistle on half time as fast as he could.

The players continued scuffling as they filed off the pitch towards their respective changing rooms. The linesmen didn't look surprised when Archie made his excuses to leave them to go to their locker room without him. Then he made his way nimbly towards the office he'd been told contained the cash. It was a fair amount, by all accounts, and Archie wasn't about to question why a drugs middle man would hide it here at Gayfield park – must know somebody who worked here, he reckoned. The main thing was, Archie was tipped off and knew where to find it. In all the hustle bustle of half time, nobody would be stopping to chat. By the time anyone ever figured out what had happened to the money, Archie would be long gone. A new start, away from this dead-end life of his.

He didn't notice the large figure in the black bomber jacket who followed him from outside the locker room, and who kept on his tail along the club building and on into the office.

As the minutes ticked by after the end of half time, the linesmen stood scratching their heads. The players were jostling in front of the Directors' stand, trying to keep warm in the face of the icy blasts coming off the North Sea that billowed next to the park. The fans were getting restless. Things had calmed down over pies and Bovril, following the outbreak of near anarchy during the disastrous handling of the penalty situation, but tensions were resurfacing as the demands to know what the delay was grew louder. Where the hell was the referee?

One of the stewards was dispatched into the building to look for Archie McKinnes. He scurried along corridors and up stairs, looking into each room that he passed, and calling out the referee's name.

Puzzled, he re-traced his steps back towards the pitch, and realised there was one room he hadn't checked – the old disused office beside the changing rooms. With a sweat forming across his brow, he placed a light hand on the door and went in. It had lain unused for a long time, this office, which probably explained the odd smell, he thought.

The office was L-shaped, and he just had to check the part that he couldn't see from the door.

The hairs on the back of his neck prickled. Something didn't seem right. He glanced around, and felt his skin grow clammy. He grasped the two-way radio in his pocket, and tentatively peeked around the corner.

There on the floor lay what looked like…His eyes seemed to be deceiving him…*My God!*…it really was…The sight before him made him gag, and he rushed from the room, with a yell of anguish.

Chapter 3

Donna stood shivering outside the main gates of Bell Street, wondering if she would have time for a sneaky fag before Libby arrived. Watching the traffic snake along the road, scanning for Libby's Fiesta, she plucked a cigarette from her pocket and quickly lit it. She glanced at her mobile, saw that Natesh wasn't online, and put it away again. She was blowing out a stream of smoke, when the *toot toot* of a car horn made her turn.

Puzzled, she still saw no sign of the Fiesta.

Toot toot.

A white Mondeo pulled up in front of her, a taxi, and she took a wary step backwards. Instinctively she glanced over her shoulder, and saw that the two armed officers who'd been assigned to her protection were watching, discreet as always.

The door opened, and Donna's eyes grew wide in surprise when the driver got out. She threw down her cigarette end and stamped on it, and took a step towards him.

"Natesh!" she said, a smile spreading across her face.

Natesh leaned with his elbow on top of the driver door, and held up the car key, jingling it in the air. "Time I got back behind the wheel," he said casually, with a lopsided grin. Then a whoosh of freezing air ran under his shirt and he made a face like *The Scream*, squeaked, and wrapped his arms around his slender torso.

Donna couldn't help but laugh as the pair embraced.

Then she caught sight of Libby in the passenger seat, and immediately kicked the stubbed-out cigarette under the car. Too late. Libby rolled her eyes.

"Surprise!" said Natesh. "Like it?"

"You kept that one quiet," Donna said. "Both of you."

She knew how much it would have taken for him to drive here, not having driven in the eighteen months since his terrible accident. If it had been an accident. Still, she snapped her thoughts out of the disturbing possibility of what could have been, glad to see her old friend and pleased that his healing journey seemed to be complete at last.

She clambered into the taxi behind Libby, and the two briefly entwined fingers.

As Natesh started up the engine, Donna noticed his familiar ID badge and his Japa Mala beads that hung from the rear view mirror, just like they had in his old taxi. It made this one feel familiar.

Donna watched him check carefully around before pulling out onto West Marketgait to begin the approach towards the roundabout-fest that was the A92. Twenty minutes later, its red tarmac took them cross country past a patchwork quilt of fields towards Arbroath.

Donna peered between the two front seats, reading the particulars of a house on Keptie Road that were contained in a brochure on Libby's knee. She could see the brochures for the other two houses they'd decided to view were neatly piled beneath it.

As they came into Arbroath, passing the caravan park, Natesh took a left before the railway bridge onto Dundee Road then along Addison Place until they reached the first of the houses to be viewed, on Keptie Road.

Checking the street number on the brochure, they pulled up outside the house, and Donna took a look around, taking an instant liking to the area and the view from the house directly onto the pond across the road.

"I like it," said Libby, standing back and taking in the front

10

garden of the house.

"Me too," Donna nodded appreciatively. The brochure actually hadn't done the house justice.

A man in a smart suit opened the door and he welcomed them in with a Cheshire-cat smile, introducing himself as the estate agent.

The first impression continued as soon as they stepped inside. Donna could tell Libby felt the same instant at-home warmth that she did, and at the estate agent's

invitation, they took a walk around without him before getting the official tour.

"I bags the room looking onto the koi pond," said Natesh, staring out of a back bedroom window on the second of three floors.

"You got it," said Donna, "but don't you think Erin will be a bit annoyed if you move in with us?"

Natesh laughed. A little too quickly. Donna caught the stiffening of his back and wondered just how much grief he was still taking for their friendship. If he was going to be getting married, then his bride to be was going to have to melt the ice at some point. If Erin were to give an ultimatum, Donna wasn't sure that Natesh would choose to go ahead with the wedding.

"You do realise it's within walking distance of Danny's place?" Donna said. She momentarily wondered how the game was going.

"I think we'll be hearing from him plenty once the baby arrives," said Libby.

"Auntie Libby," Donna tried out the new title.

"Auntie Donna is worse," said Libby.

"Uncle Natesh," piped in Natesh. Donna and Libby exchanged a look.

"Erm, is everything okay with you and Erin?" Donna ventured.

"Oh look," said Natesh, dashing towards another window, "you can see the pond from here, too."

By the time they left the house, there was little doubt in Donna's mind that this was the place for them. Libby grinned as she put her mobile away.

"That's our interest formally noted," she announced, indicating that stage in the house buying process where you were considered a serious potential buyer. She and Donna high-fived as they got back into Natesh's taxi.

"We should still go and look at the other ones," said Donna. She saw Libby's eye lingering over the front garden, and knew her heart was set on this one, no matter how many more houses they went to view. It was fine by Donna. She was happy with it, too. Nice area, near Danny, and far enough away from Libby's parents to keep everyone happy.

Her phone trilled, and she answered without checking who it was.

"Donna?" She recognised PC Aiden Moore's voice. "Your office said you're in Arbroath at the minute. We need a DI over at Gayfield. There's been a murder."

Chapter 4

Donna pulled up outside the main gates of the football club, and took in the scene around her. Flecks of snow peppered the air, and the previous night's gale had blown the Christmas lights off the high fence that surrounded the club grounds. They lay in a heap of wire, broken light bulbs and brightly coloured plastic moulding on the grassy verge, with Santa grinning maniacally up at the sky.

Inside the club gates, she saw groups of fans standing or milling around on the concourse. High-vis vested stewards were buzzing around, responding to a barrage of questions and calls.

Several marked police cars were already parked there, along with the club's mini bus and a coach, probably for the visiting supporters. Donna decided to continue on down the narrow lane that ran along the western edge of the ground and that separated the football park from Pleasureland, the neighbouring amusement arcade.

She parked half-way along the lane, and sat for a moment looking across at the shore and the brooding North Sea, only 100 meters in front of her. It gave Gayfield its reputation as the coldest football ground in the country.

Snippets of the morning's discussion in Bell Street about the fall-out from the Moira Cowan and Eleanor Wallace murder cases floated through her mind. The shore that lay ahead of her was where Moira's body had washed up, sparking off the investigation that became linked to Eleanor's murder and eventually led to the revelation about the illegal adoptions. She couldn't help but wonder if there might be a connection with today's incident. But as she chewed the possibility over, she didn't feel it.

Archie bloody McKinnes, she thought. He could start a fight in an empty room. She could hardly believe he was actually a football referee, as if there wouldn't already be enough people with reason to see him gone. This was going to have scarce police resources diverted from the real priority – finding cop killer Jonas Evanton.

She parked up and walked back around to the main gates, where a uniformed officer stood. As he stepped towards her, Donna saw him tense his shoulders, an attempt to stop shivering in the cold. His skin was pale, his nose red, and eyes watery. Then she suddenly became aware of the biting cold herself, and felt sorry for the young PC.

"How long have you been standing out here?" she asked him, holding out her warrant card for him to check. His eyes glanced over it briefly. He knew who she was, alright.

"Couple of hours, Ma'am," he said. Her two armed guards slid into the club ground, and the PC eyed them with obvious discomfort. Then an involuntary shudder jerked his jaw, the freezing cold gaining the upper hand against his attempt to appear unaffected by it.

"Who did you piss off?" Donna asked. The grin twitching at the corner of her mouth elicited a smile from the PC. "I'll send one of the boys in there to swap places with you." She indicated through the gates with her thumb, and noticed again how busy it looked in there.

13

"Thanks, Ma'am," said the PC, a grunt of relief finding its way into his voice.

A small man in his sixties and wearing an over-sized donkey jacket with a hi viz vest draped over it scurried towards Donna as she made her way past the turnstiles. Groups of fans, colour co-ordinated by two sets of hats and scarves, loitered around the concourse. Several of them looked at Donna, some holding their stare.

"Are you the police?" the small man asked her.

She showed him her warrant card, and he introduced himself as Frank, one of the stewards on duty for the game today. "Come round this way," he said, leading her past the club building and onto the park itself. She could see several stewards standing in front of the building's entrance in what appeared to be a barricade. Her armed guards melted into the throng.

"It was me that found the body," Frank went on.

Donna looked at him in surprise as he cackled nervously and led her past assorted groups of people and onto the ground's seated stand.

Several men and women, dressed somberly in dark suits, appeared to be waiting for her arrival, and one – a tall man with short grey hair – stood forward and introduced himself as Niall, one of the club Directors. All of them, Donna could see, looked shocked.

"The police are inside," said Niall, "where the… the… where it happened." He swallowed nervously. "They said to keep everyone out here, but there's just too many people everywhere. We can't…"

"Don't worry," said Donna. "We'll get everything under control." Running a football club usually wouldn't extend to managing a murder scene, she sympathised. "Can you show me where?"

She followed Niall into the club building, where a group of fans surrounded them, firing questions at them.

"What's happening?"

"Is it true the referee's been killed?"

"I've got kids with me, we need to get out of here…"

The bewildered and disgruntled fans tried to follow Donna and

Niall as they walked on, but were soon held back by the arrival of more stewards.

Walking across the passageway that contained the changing rooms, Niall led Donna into a small lobby. A staircase rose to her right, and ahead of her was the exit back onto the concourse. To her immediate right was a room whose door stood ajar. Another uniformed officer stood outside this door, and he nodded an acknowledgement to Donna.

"Detective Inspector," he said.

"Morning, Davie."

"Not nice in there, Ma'am," he warned, thumbing in towards the room. Then he turned a glare at two football fans who were heading towards it. He placed a hand up and told them, "Out of bounds, lads." The pair looked at one another, exchanged worried glances, then headed back in the direction from which they'd come.

Donna thanked Niall and allowed him to return to the Directors' stand, when she became aware of a racket that was coming from the top of the staircase. Shouting. Lots of voices, by the sound of it. She walked to the foot of the stairs and looked up. A large group of people appeared to be tussling with a sole steward. Davie came to her side.

"Are forensics here?" she asked.

Davie shook his head. "Not yet."

"And is everyone who's making a noise up there supposed to be there?" she asked.

He shrugged an apology. "It's pure chaos. I've requested back-up, should be here any time."

"This is going to be a forensics nightmare," Donna muttered. "Who's with the body just now?"

"Ehm, Sergeant Scott Dexter and DC Wilma Cornton," said Davie, reading from his notebook. "And I've started collecting details of everyone who's been in there since the body was found." Donna nodded approval, although she didn't like the sound of *everyone*.

Another group of fans barged through the exit door into the

lobby, and again Davie sent them back out.

Donna looked back up the staircase, and spotted a couple of uniformed officers, before remembering her promise at the club gates. "Who's the poor bugger standing guard out front?"

Davie made a face while he searched his memory. "Stewie McClure," he said. "He drew the short straw."

"Bring him in here, will you?" said Donna. "He's about to snap like ice with the cold. Get one of the guys up there to take a turn outside."

"Ma'am," said Davie, following her line of vision, and making his way towards the foot of the stairs. She watched as he instructed one of the officers, and ignored the look of disdain he threw her as he lumbered outside to swap places with PC McClure.

Pulling on a pair of latex gloves, Donna pushed the room door fully open, and took a step inside. Although not like the usual murder scenes, the familiar ferrous smell of blood was in the air. The shouting that was going on all around became muted in here.

Her eyes quickly adjusted to the gloom, and she saw that the room turned in an L-shape to her left, from where a harassed looking uniformed officer hurried. He held out his hand to Donna. She saw that he was wearing latex gloves, too, and his shirt sleeves were rolled up, despite the chill in the air.

"Sergeant Scott Dexter," he said, sounding out of breath. "And this…" as a young woman in a suit appeared at his back, "is DC Wilma Cornton."

Donna could tell right away that neither of them looked particularly overjoyed to be there.

"I was the first attending officer," Dexter went on, "but it's been like herding ferrets since I got here. Back-up's been taking its time."

"Alright then," said Donna, following Dexter and Cornton back around the L-shape. "Let's go and have a look at what we've got."

The body lay the length of the office floor, on its front and in a pool of blood around the head area. His feet were closest to the door. Donna's eyes took in the worn black trainers, the black socks and shorts, the bright yellow top with black trim and blood-stained shoulders, the grey face lying side-on with its grey eyes staring at the opposite wall. And the wooden-handled axe planted firmly into the back of his shockingly crimson skull.

She glanced up at the surrounding walls, and wondered what story the blood spatter she saw there would tell.

Archie McKinnes is dead, she thought, leaning in to take a closer look at the all too familiar face. The world was a better place. She caught the look that passed between Dexter and Cornton, and wondered if she'd said it out loud. Not that it mattered. She was pretty sure they were thinking the same thing.

"Don't waste your time trying to find out who killed the useless fucker," came a woman's voice. "There'll be a queue a mile long."

Donna flinched as much in annoyance as in surprise that someone else was here at the murder scene. The newly widowed Agnes McKinnes stood in a corner of the office, staring at her husband's cleaved head, with her arms folded firmly across her bosom, and an expression on her face that could stop a train in its tracks.

"There *is* a queue a mile long," said Donna, picturing the 780 fans who'd been at the game.

Agnes drew a cigarette from her pocket and went for her lighter.

"Put that away," said Donna, "this is a crime scene." She turned to Dexter. "And what the hell is she still doing in here, anyway?" There were too many McKinneses in here. Even if one of them was dead. "Get her out of here."

Dexter mumbled something about the imminent arrival of the FLO.

"She's hardly shocked or upset," Donna told him. "It's not family liaison she needs."

Dexter's cheeks flushed, but he dutifully began to usher Agnes away from the crime scene.

As they were leaving, Agnes seemed to have a change of heart, and she broke free of Dexter's steer, hurrying back to Donna's side.

In a small voice she asked, "Is it you that's going to lead the investigation?"

In that moment, Donna saw the version of Agnes that she'd seen many times before. The Agnes with the fire belted out of her guts. The Agnes with her life in pieces, who endured the sting of failure and the bitter taste of self loathing over and over as she would let the words of some ludicrous excuse cross her lips – an excuse that would make an arrest pointless.

Donna saw the stock reaction in Agnes's eyes, even now when the brute lay dead and could never lay a finger on her again. Even now, the woman felt she might have to come up with an excuse for him. For her own repeated suffering.

Donna glanced back down at Archie's body. "I've got paperwork to do now, because of this," she said. Agnes chortled. "But since you ask, do you know what Archie was doing in here, anyway? He should have been with the linesmen along at the changing rooms."

"How should I know?" Agnes said. "He never consulted with me about anything, did he? Anyway, if I can't have a fag in here, I'm going outside."

She stomped towards the door, making Dexter jump to attention in an attempt to look as though he was escorting her out as he'd been instructed to do in the first place. He was about to open the door, when Agnes looked back towards Archie's axe-embedded head again. An anxious twitch took hold of the corner of her mouth. "Is he definitely dead, then? You're sure?"

"We'll have a better idea when we cut him open down the mortuary," said Donna.

"Ha bloody ha," said Agnes, pulling together her act of bravado. It didn't fool Donna, though, and she watched Agnes's eye linger a split second too long over her deceased husband's body, as though terrified he might suddenly spring up, snatching away her chance of freedom. Watching her finally leave with Dexter, Donna just hoped to God the woman's fingerprints wouldn't be on the axe handle.

Chapter 5

The forest loomed ahead, threatening to swallow the silver Audi as it left the A97 and crept onto a rough woodland track that led towards Loch Kinord. Jonas Evanton liked his Audis, and he grimaced as the track overwhelmed the suspension momentarily. Taking the speed right down, he manoeuvred the potholes that had appeared over the course of this unusually harsh early winter.

Despite the trees having hardly any leaves left, the sun barely penetrated this part of the birchwood, and Evanton found himself straining to make out the way ahead. He'd only been this way once before, and he remembered how tricky the track was to navigate. That was part of the appeal, though. It wouldn't be easy for anybody to come looking for him out here.

Up ahead and tucked into an enclave near the loch was a small stone cottage with an outhouse. The cottage belonged to an older couple, Mr and Mrs Marr, who'd lived there for the best part of their 40 years of marriage. No family, the couple kept pretty much to themselves and were rarely seen in any of the surrounding village shops. When the police had visited during their sweep of Deeside properties in a desperate attempt to find Evanton's bolthole, the Marrs had little to tell them. There were no visitors, and walkers rarely came around this side of the loch. They would certainly have noticed anything out of the ordinary. The cottage was logged in a file with all the rest, being of no further interest in the investigation.

A week after the police had been, Evanton paid the Marrs a visit. Now the Marrs lay side by side in a shallow grave amongst the trees, and the cottage was free of attention for Evanton to use as he pleased.

A clunk and a muffled torrent of incoherent words suddenly came from the boot of the car, and almost made Evanton swerve off the track. A flash of anger brought him back to the present. His unwilling passenger had better not cause him any trouble.

Eventually, the track curved round and down towards the enclave, and the cottage came into view. Evanton brought the Audi to the rear of the building and killed the engine. He sat for a moment, savouring the silence and catching a ripple of reflection off the loch through the trees. This was a truly spectacular spot, he appreciated. It was a pity he wasn't here for the view, he thought, before his attention was drawn again to more thuds from the car boot.

He opened it up, and yanked out the cuffed and gagged youngster who lay there. He set her onto the ground roughly, and loosened the ligatures as she stumbled to maintain her balance.

"Let go of me, you pervert!" she yelled, taking an unsteady step back from him.

"Just get a move on," Evanton growled back, shoving her away from the car.

She swayed on her feet, and put her hands out in a reflex to hold onto something. Evanton saw her eyes grow wide, probably in fear, as she took in the surrounds and the total silence that engulfed them. She seemed pretty streetwise, and must realise something of the predicament she was in.

Righting herself, and flicking a stray strand of hair from her eyes, she took in the low white cottage.

"Where are we?" she demanded.

"Shut up." Evanton overtook her and began to walk around to the front of the cottage, not even checking to see if she was following him.

"Pervert!" she yelled after him again. "You'd better not touch me, you filthy bastard."

He spun on his heel, and he saw her face blanch in fear at the expression on his.

"You're a fucking child," he spat. "What do you think I am?"

"I'm sixteen," she retorted, then bit her lip.

She should think twice before putting up an argument that could backfire on her, Evanton thought, letting his eye slip over her body.

"A child," he repeated, and disappeared round the side of the cottage.

He knew she would follow him. And so would her father, Abrim Kozel – the country's most wanted gangster – just as soon as he found out his daughter was being held by its most wanted killer. Evanton knew now that, with Kozel in his pocket, he would have the manpower he needed to begin his revenge on that bitch, Davenport.

Chapter 6

Donna turned to DC Cornton. The newbie detective was leaning over the body, a frown of concentration on her face.

"Your verdict?" Donna asked.

Cornton looked up quickly and stared like a startled rabbit. "Erm, murdered fairly recently," she blustered.

"Murdered?" Donna held up a cautionary finger. "First rule of detective work: never assume. Other potential causes of death?"

Cornton turned her stare back on to Archie McKinnes's axed skull. Her mouth formed several words, but none came out. Then she jumped at Donna's explosion of laughter.

"Sorry," spluttered Donna, "couldn't resist."

Cornton laughed, too. "You had me there, Ma'am," she said.

"Look, what's with all the *Ma'am* stuff today?" Donna said. At that moment, a wall of noise erupted into the office as the door opened and PC McClure hurried inside, bringing with him a remnant of the icy air from outside.

"I really appreciate this, Ma'am," he said.

"For crying out loud, my name is Donna!" She threw her hands in the air. "I hate being called *Ma'am*. Just stop it! It's Donna."

McClure and Cornton glanced at one another.

"Ogilvie will be here shortly," Donna told them. "But in the meantime, what are your observations on the crime scene?"

"Well, obviously it was a murder," said Cornton. "He couldn't have axed himself in the head."

"He'd have been too vain to have done a thing like that, anyway," said Donna. "Anything else?"

"The blood is fairly fresh," said Cornton, reverting to her first comment. "So it must have happened recently."

"Which means?…" coached Donna.

Cornton hesitated.

"Which means the killer won't be far away," said Donna. "Unless they have a getaway helicopter. But we'd have noticed that, and it's a tad windy today for a helicopter, anyway." She caught herself, suddenly aware that she was beginning to witter.

"We need to focus our efforts on identifying the radius of where the killer could be now," said Cornton, "in case he poses a danger to others."

Donna nodded her head, deciding on this occasion not to add, *or she*. "I've seen more splatter on the walls of a murder scene; most of the blood is under the wound," she said.

"He died very quickly where he fell," Cornton guessed. "So, probably a very heavy blow, delivered by somebody with a lot of strength."

"Upper body strength, at that," said Donna. "It would be difficult otherwise to strike a blow like that to somebody as tall as Archie McKinnes."

"Couldn't he have been knocked down first?" PC McClure piped in.

"It's possible," Donna said. "Ogilvie will be looking for signs of other injuries or a struggle when he does the PM. So maybe, although there aren't any obvious signs in here of a struggle." She saw McClure's cheeks flush with pleasure at having been taken seriously by a DI.

"He could have been leaning down looking for something," Cornton suggested.

"So, let's see what Ogilvie can tell us," said Donna. "See if we got any of that right. You two can babysit Archie. I'll be back in a minute."

She made her way through the building and onto the dug-out by the side of the pitch, where she spotted one of her armed guards. Scanning the Directors' stand, she found Niall and beckoned to him.

"Ehm, how does it seem in there?" he asked.

22

"It's going to take a while for us to get organised," Donna told him. "But I'd appreciate if you could walk me around the premises, show me where everything is and where you would have expected Archie to go during half time."

Niall seemed relieved to be given a role in what must have looked to him like a scene from a horror movie. He pointed out the track going from the pitch into the building.

"This is where we last saw him," he said. "He would have gone in there and to the right, to sit with the linesmen during half time. Well, he would have done if, you know…"

He walked Donna along the corridor, showing her where the linesmen had waited. Then back out to the lobby, studiously avoiding the old office, and on up the stairs. A large group of fans from both teams were at the top of the landing, with some heated discussion and jostling going on. A command roared from beyond the group made the activity stop, and several of the fans looked at the cop who was shouting at them. Others stared at Donna and Niall as they made their way upstairs.

Pushing past the group in the tight space at the top of the stairs, Niall pointed out the hospitality room to the right, where two long tables sat, still bedecked with white tablecloths and the remnants of dinner. Through to their left, Niall brought Donna into a bar, "The Directors' bar," he told her, and showed her how it led onto the top row of the Directors' stand.

"This is it, really," he told her, sweeping his hand around. "Do you want to see around outside?"

"Yes," said Donna. "I need an idea of where the killer might have escaped. If he did escape."

"My God, could he still be in here?" Niall gasped.

"We're not taking any chances," said Donna. "Referee killed at a football game, everyone's a suspect."

A shade paler still, Niall led Donna back outside and onto the concourse. There, she saw that more police vans had arrived, a traffic diversion was being set up, and the forensics team were here.

Niall pointed out a row of cabins to their right, which housed the club merchandise shop and the stewards' rest areas. All of these would have to be searched and sampled, Donna thought, as she watched a team of officers make their way towards them to do just that.

She followed Niall past more groups of agitated fans towards the ground's perimeter overlooking Pleasureland. Here the tarmac rose in a steep slope, and the wall that ran along this part was only around a meter high. Easy to jump over, she thought, except for the long drop on the other side onto the lane where her own car was parked. She looked down over the wall, and found she was looking onto the roof of the club minivan. It would be a simple matter of running out here via the concourse during half time, she thought, then jumping over this wall and onto the van roof. There would hardly be anyone around over here at that time, and the killer could easily have vanished into Pleasureland and never be seen again.

A cough behind her made her turn round, and there was DC Cornton.

"Needed out of there for a bit of fresh air, Ma'am. Er, Donna."

"Look at this," said Donna, pointing to the wall. "We're going to have to establish exactly who was out here during half time and might have seen someone running away. We'll get forensics to have a look at the roof of that van, and now we're also going to have to find and interview everyone who's been in Pleasureland over there this afternoon. As if that's not bad enough, we can't let anyone out of the ground until we've taken their details and a brief statement, and we need to get a detailed search of the premises underway."

"Waste of our bloody time," Donna heard Cornton mutter under her breath.

"Couldn't have said it better myself," she said, smiling at Cornton's flushed cheeks. "Listen," she went on, "you get back to the locus, and I'll join you there in five minutes."

She dismissed Niall and made her way to the turnstiles, where she stopped and lit a cigarette. She could feel her thoughts begin to race, and it worried her. Only three weeks ago she'd come face

24

to face with Jonas Evanton. The police psychologist had warned her about the risks of an emotional upset like that, and she found herself tapping her pocket to check the tub of lithium pills was still there. She breathed slowly. They were there if she needed them. In the meantime, a smoke would calm things down.

She waved to PC McClure's replacement at the gates as she wandered to and fro. The officer glared at her. She could see that, even from where she was standing, and made a mental note to never ask him to make her a coffee. Colleagues with a grudge, and all that.

Inhaling deeply, she studied the file of incoming personnel. Police back-up and forensics were here at last. The ratio of police to civilians was finally getting better, she thought.

A sharp wind whipped up from out of nowhere, blasted her hair and made her shudder. She began to pace along the fence, and caught sight of a white private hire coming towards the ground. It slowed near the gate, then swung round abruptly and began to head straight towards her. Donna glanced at the steel fence posts, a reflex to check how well they might withstand the impact of a car ploughing into them. Just in case. She also noticed the armed guards appearing out of nowhere at the arrival of the vehicle, and tensed.

Then she stopped and smiled. Natesh's face stared out of the driver-side window. It was going to take a while to get used to seeing him behind the wheel again, like old times.

"You okay?" he called to her. She sprinted through a turnstile and leaned in to talk.

"I'd rather be picking out wallpaper for the new house," she said, blowing smoke away from his direction.

"Is it true it's Archie McKinnes?" asked Natesh.

Donna grunted, a non-committal sound. "Jungle drums are quick off the mark this time," she said.

"Social media," said Natesh. "Lots of folk who were at the game have been posting, speculating that the referee died, and Burly McKinnes has been telling them he was murdered."

Burly McKinnes, thought Donna. Spawn of Agnes and the late

Archie. "He's telling people his father was killed?" she asked. "But he wasn't here at the game?"

Natesh nodded, *yes*, then shook his head vigorously, *no*, then looked confused.

"Great," sighed Donna. "I'm going to have to bring him in, now, too."

"How come?"

"We haven't released any details about what happened," said Donna.

He looked shocked, and she knew why. In all the time she'd been a cop, she'd never allowed herself to divulge any information about a murder investigation, despite all of his pleading.

Donna could tell that Natesh was biting his lip, afraid to say more in case it made her suddenly realise she was confiding in him.

"Should you have told me that?" Natesh finally cracked.

"Probably not," said Donna. "But I'm this close…" she pinched her thumb and forefinger almost together, "…this close to throwing in the towel."

Natesh glanced at her quickly, then out towards the road. He unhooked the Japa Mala beads from the driver mirror and began to fidget with them. "Man, I don't know how you handle it," he said.

"I'm not handling it," she said, her voice rising by an octave. "I need to be out there looking for Evanton."

She looked around and caught sight of Agnes trotting back inside the clubhouse at Dexter's back. Davie was guarding the door, and was now sipping from a mug of steaming liquid. "That's the pathologist arrived," she told Natesh, spotting the familiar transit. "Once I've had a word with him, I can clear off and do something useful."

"Can I come and watch?" Natesh made big eyes at her.

"Don't push your luck," Donna laughed. "You already know too much."

"Damn!"

She saw officers placing groups of fans into lines on the

concourse. *Finally*, she thought. *It's beginning to look like a respectable crime scene.* Then she spotted Danny standing in one of the lines.

"Wait here a moment," she told Natesh, and she darted off to where Danny stood.

"Oh, thank God you're here," said Danny, looking anxious. "What's going on? Is it true there's been a murder?"

"I'm afraid so," said Donna. "But I'll get you out of here as quickly as possible. We don't need you turning up in another investigation." Danny didn't appreciate the humour, she saw.

She showed her warrant card to the officer in charge of Danny's line. Not that she needed to. Although she didn't know him, he certainly knew who she was.

"Take his details and get him out of here as priority," she told the officer.

"Ma'am," he obeyed, though sounding uncertain.

"He's my brother-in-law," Donna said, and she saw recognition dawn on the officer's face. "I think we owe him, don't you?"

The officer nodded, and quickly took Danny's details, then let him move away from the line with Donna. She led him to the turnstile, where Natesh was waiting.

The two men grunted a stilted greeting at one another. Donna wasn't sure what had gone on between them when they'd joined forces to look for her when she'd gone missing back then – she shuddered at the memory of being held captive by Evanton – but she could tell they hadn't exactly hit it off. They hadn't seen each other much since those awful days, but she didn't have time to hang around dwelling on it, and she sent Danny away with Natesh, then made her way back to the murder scene.

She pulled on the fresh set of coveralls that Davie handed to her, and followed the scent. Inside the old office she counted six white-suited forensics personnel who were standing at various angles around Archie's body, stepping around it to avoid contaminating their shoes, all shouting information or instructions to one another. All in a hurry, with somewhere better to be.

Then she saw the familiar tuft of blond hair.

"Morning, lass," said John Ogilvie, the pathologist. He gently pulled her aside, and whispered into her ear, "Is the victim's widow meant to be in here with us?"

"These are interesting times," said Donna.

Ogilvie hesitated. "I know what you're thinking," he said. His words unnerved her. "But I still need to do the same job I would do with anyone else."

Donna grunted. "We're way over-stretched just now. For me, this just isn't the priority it might once have been. I'll only need a summary report."

"I get the picture, lass," said Ogilvie. He smiled. "But it's still business as usual for me. I take it you don't want to sit in on the post mortem, then?"

"I'll meet you over there," she said, her tone flat. "Just in case there's any hassle."

"From what I've been hearing, nobody's particularly upset," said Ogilvie.

"They're not," said Donna, "but where the McKinnesses are concerned, they don't need to be upset to cause trouble. If they think there might be something in it for them, they'll turn up and kick up."

Ogilvie turned to get back to his examination. "It's not a complicated one," he called to her over his shoulder. "We'll have plenty of time, if you're still on for dinner?"

"As long as you wash your hands first," Donna laughed.

Walking back to her car, Donna was surprised by a harsh shout of her name. She looked around, to see Agnes McKinnes hurrying towards her.

"What's happening?" Agnes hissed at her. "Where are you going?"

"The pathologist is in charge for now," Donna told her. "He'll arrange to get Archie's body moved to the mortuary."

Agnes continued to stare at her.

"Just you go home," Donna told her. "Why don't you get Burly to come and pick you up? Here, you can use my phone." She held it out, but Agnes frowned at it.

"I don't know his number," she said. "It's just a mobile he's got, those numbers are too long to memorise."

Noted, thought Donna. *So Burly didn't get his information from you.*

"Is there somewhere in Arbroath I can drop you off, then?" she said. "I need to go into the station here, so I won't be going back to Dundee for a while."

Agnes breathed out a sharp release of nerves, and shook her head. "I'm going over the road to Tuttie's for a drink. Or two."

Chapter 7

Libby was curled up on the settee, marking student end of term assessments, when Donna finally got home. She glanced up and smiled, keeping her attention for a moment longer on the paper she was marking.

"How was your day?" she asked once she'd finished the section she'd been on.

Donna stretched and yawned, and threw herself down beside Libby, burrowing her head into Libby's fleece.

"Pfft," she said in reply. "The referee at the Arbroath game got killed, so we've a football park full of suspects. I've just spent the last few hours talking a station full of coppers through the most labour intensive investigation they'll ever have been involved in. They're going to need to interview about 800 potential suspects!"

"Bet they loved you."

"They always do," said Donna. She paused, as if suddenly remembering something, and her tone was lighter when she went on, "Danny was at the game, did you know?"

A brief flicker of alarm crossed Libby's face.

"It's okay," Donna was quick to reassure her. "I made sure he got out as quickly as possible."

"That would be all he'd need," said Libby, "getting caught up in one of your…"

"Well, he isn't," said Donna, realising too late that she'd snapped.

Libby sighed and put the student papers down.

"And there's nothing sinister about this one," Donna went on, eager to avoid the onset of an icy atmosphere. "Just a straightforward clobber over the head by any one of several hundred people who hated him." She sliced her hand through the air. "Dead."

"Urgh, I hate your job," said Libby, beginning to smile despite herself.

Donna hated it too, right now, especially knowing there were armed officers following her every move.

She floated into a daydream about the moment, two weeks ago, when she was told she was to get the armed protection. It had been right after she'd made eye contact with Evanton, given chase, and – as Lindsey Forsyth had broadcast in her Weekend Special – lost him.

She had been in many a situation since joining the Force, including being nearly killed by Evanton, but she never imagined this. Suddenly the danger felt like a living thing there in the room with her, squeezing the life from her, and she became aware of her own breathing becoming rapid. She had to work hard to push away her fears for Libby. For Natesh. For Danny, and now for Sally, too. How far did it reach, this ongoing threat?

"Listen to me, Donna," she remembered Ross saying, grabbing her by the shoulders. *"It's a precaution. We're dealing with a high profile missing person who's known to have a personal vendetta against you. You've known for a long time this has been risky for you. At least now there's going to be some protection."*

She came out of her trance, relieved to hear Libby in mid flow about what it was going to be like in the new house, how much babysitting they might end up doing, and wondering if Sally was going to make it to Arbroath before the baby was actually born.

"I mean, she's only due in a few weeks," Libby went on, making Donna smile and forget about the day's events.

Run riot
Sunday
Chapter 8

The next morning, Donna was sitting in the line of traffic that snaked its way slowly across Dundee and wondering which car contained her armed guards. The Christmas shoppers were out in force, she mused, while she idly surfed the radio channels. Snow was forecast for later on that day, explaining the unexpectedly high turnout at such an early hour on a Sunday. She turned the car heater up another notch.

Her mind drifted back to the previous evening, when she had briefed a station full of coppers in Arbroath, outlining to them the massive scale of this murder investigation. They'd never had to deal with anything this big before – 780 football fans, all potentially with a motive to kill the referee.

Then she thought about the house on Keptie Road. They would have to decide soon about making an offer, and they would have to think about selling Libby's bungalow on Claypotts Place. She wondered whether all the extra security they'd had fitted a couple of months ago would be off-putting to potential buyers. Or would it be a selling point? In and out of second gear, she mulled the question for some time, before deciding it would probably put normal people off. She made a note to herself to arrange to have it removed as soon as the place was on the market.

She yawned and rubbed her eyes when she eventually made it to Bell Street. The journey had been torturously slow, and she was desperate to be around the buzz of her team's real focus, the hunt for Jonas Evanton. The investigation into Archie McKinnes's death was going to take a while, with all those witnesses and potential suspects to interview. While she was sure there would be nobody breathing down her neck for results, it did mean she wouldn't be able to count on support from the Arbroath office for the foreseeable future. And there was only so much they could stretch to without that support. Here in Dundee they'd already had to make the decision to stop responding to reports of drugs deals going on, to free up resources. Just as she stepped from her car, sure enough, her armed guards appeared at her side. They nodded a tight-lipped greeting without saying actual words.

She walked into the team room and dropped her bag and jacket onto an empty desk. Fran, who of course was already there bright and early, called out a good morning.

"I'm just ploughing on with these adoption cases," she said. "Oh, and DCI Ross was in a couple of minutes ago, wants an update on yesterday."

Making her way to Ross's office, Donna hoped she could swap information about yesterday for anything Ross might have on progress in the hunt for Evanton. But she could tell as soon as she saw the expression on his face, that there would be no news about that.

She launched into her own update for him. "Archie McKinnes, refereeing yesterday's game at Gayfield Park, didn't come back after half time, and one of the stewards found his body in a disused office," she told him. "By all accounts it was a bad tempered game, fans on both sides unhappy with the referee's decisions, so everyone's a suspect."

Ross raised his eyes to the ceiling and sighed. "As if we don't have enough on our bloody plate," he muttered. "But at least Archie McKinnes won't be causing us any more trouble."

"You always see the bright side," said Donna, sitting down opposite him. "In the meantime, Arbroath are handling the interviews, poor sods, and I'll remain as acting DI on the case. But I'm not pushing for a quick result, if I'm honest."

She saw Ross contemplate arguing back, then saw the resignation in his face. "Alright," he concurred. "But I need everything you've got to pin down where Evanton went that day, and where he is now."

"Well, you know my thoughts on that," said Donna. "The only way he could remain under the radar, what with everything we've thrown into this investigation, is for him to have help on the inside."

"I know, I know," said Ross. "I've finally got the ACC in Glasgow to agree to set up an internal investigation. I think that newspaper article actually did us a favour in the end. Made them realise we've got a problem in here. Though they did ask a few questions about your armed protection…"

Donna scowled, and then consoled herself with the fact that at least the possibility of a mole was being entertained at long last. "Okay," she said, standing up and heading back out.

She checked her watch as she walked towards the main doors. Her armed shadows melted into her wake. She would have time for a quick smoke, then she would phone Aiden Moore in Arbroath for an update there, before getting on with the real work.

She stood outside and took a cigarette from her pocket, watching the first of the snowflakes begin to float towards the ground as the weak sun began its morning climb from the horizon.

Her thoughts drifted to John Ogilvie. She'd known the pathologist for around three years now, and had worked with him on more cases during the past 18 months than she cared to count. Far too many.

She inhaled deeply, and coughed as the freezing air gripped her lungs. She had taken to Ogilvie right away, with his gentle manner and off-beat sense of humour, and the two of them had formed a friendship very quickly. She remembered being astonished, therefore, when it took him several months to reveal to her that he was married. During that time, despite their friendship, he'd divulged very little about his home life. But as time went on, and Ogilvie grew more comfortable talking to Donna about things that were more personal than the contents of the latest victim's stomach, she soon realised why he hadn't talked about his wife before. Now she felt a little uncomfortable about meeting Cerys tonight over dinner – it would be the first time. Libby hadn't been as fazed about it as Donna had been when Ogilvie had suggested it to her.

She went to fetch her mobile from her pocket to give Libby a call, when the doors towards the rear of the building crashed open, pouring out a stream of uniformed officers. Her two armed guards bolted into defensive positions while she watched, with raised eye brows, as their uniformed colleagues flooded into a fleet of squad cars that then screamed out of the complex.

Donna immediately threw down her cigarette, stamped on it as a reflex, and ran inside. Officers were charging along corridors and down stairs, out of the building, and she ran on against the flow of them and the deafening noise they made.

There was only one thing that would elicit a response like that, she knew, and it sure as hell wasn't a breakthrough in the Archie McKinnes case.

Chapter 9

Donna took the stairs two at a time, raced along the corridor, and flew into the team room, closely followed by one of the armed guards. The room seemed larger than usual now that it was almost empty.

Sergeant Alice Moone looked up, stopping mid-sentence in what Donna thought looked to have been a heated discussion with DCI Angus Ross. The scars on Alice's face stood out like a white labyrinth on skin that was still tanned a month on from her ordeal in Turkey.

Ross's phone began to ring, its tone shrill and piercing above the din of ringing landline phones around the large office. The noise gave the room the sci-fi feel of being the only inhabited place in a post-apocalyptic world. Each of the ringing phones sat on a desk that had been vacated in a hurry.

"Is it a lead on Evanton?" Donna called to them both as she came into the room.

Ross turned to look at her and nodded his head quickly, his flame red hair falling across his eyes as he did so. He brushed it aside with a flick of his finger.

"Could be," he said, bringing his phone to his ear. "Word just in." Donna noticed the strain showing in his features.

She reached for his mobile in an attempt to stop him from

answering it. "Tell me," she demanded.

Ross shot her a glare and turned away to take the call.

Alice moved so that she stood in between the two of them, and addressed Donna.

"We've had a call for all units to attend a firearms situation in Arbroath," she said. "They received a phone call from a woman who said she was being held at gunpoint by a man whose description matches Evanton, although the details are very sketchy at the moment."

Donna thought this over briefly, before asking, "The hostage phoned?"

Alice nodded her head. "She did, yes. She was following his instructions. For some reason, he didn't make the call himself." She paused and looked at Donna as if wondering what the DI was thinking, then went on, "But it's as near as damn a positive ID from what I can tell. We have him cornered."

Donna felt her heart rate spike, to the point where she felt almost dizzy. She walked across the room towards the windows and looked out, consciously slowing down her breathing. She had almost lost her life at the hands of Jonas Evanton's brutality. He had murdered two of her colleagues. He'd been making a mockery of them all for so long, despite everything they'd thrown into this operation. She could barely believe he might finally be within their grasp.

But she smelled a rat.

Something about this didn't feel right. Evanton would never allow himself to be backed into a corner, she knew that much. And why would he get the hostage to make the phone call, instead of doing it himself?

She glanced at Ross, who was still on his phone, and turned back to Alice.

"What exactly did the woman say?" she asked.

"I don't know yet," the sergeant admitted. "We literally just got a frantic message from Aiden two minutes before you came through the door." She nodded towards Ross. "We're going to have to wait to find out more."

Ross ended his call and bid Donna and Alice to sit at one of the desks with him. They took their places around a heap of files that were scattered across its surface, and ignored its ringing landline. At the far end of the room, two uniformed officers were frantically trying to answer and log all the calls that were coming in. Aside from Donna's two armed guards, nobody else was in the room.

"No more information to add," Ross said. Addressing Alice, he added, "You've told Donna the details we already had?"

Alice nodded, *yes*.

Ross looked to the ceiling, as though seeking inspiration. One of the strip lights began to flicker, and Donna saw annoyance cross his face.

"We've to wait for another phone call, but probably not imminent," he said. "Looks like we're in the very early stages of what could be quite a protracted hostage situation." He glanced again at Alice. "And despite the similarity of the description, we can't jump the gun and assume we're dealing with Evanton."

My arse, Donna wanted to say, but didn't. Again she had that niggle that something didn't seem right, wasn't Evanton's style.

"So," Ross went on, catching her eye with an expression that Donna recognised as anticipation that she might start arguing with him, "it's not very likely that Arbroath are going to be interviewing many of their 800 suspects in the Archie McKinnes case today, not with an armed hostage situation going on in their patch."

"Silver lining," Alice muttered.

Ross glanced at his phone, a gesture of impatience. The three of them sat at the desk, and during the split second of silence when the office phones seemed to suddenly pause, Donna was sure Alice and Ross felt just as impotent right now as she did.

If there had been a clock on the wall, it would have been ticking very loudly.

Ross broke the silence. "What's the story with the post mortem?"

"Ogilvie's doing it this afternoon," Donna said. Ross was going for diversion, she knew. But he was right – there was nothing they could do for now about the hostage situation. Talking about Archie

36

McKinnes's murder would at least be an easy way to fill the time.

She brought her mind again to the McKinnes murder, and to her last conversation with Agnes.

"He was murdered during half time," she said, "and we informed Agnes McKinnes in person at her cleaning job in Arbroath around 4.30pm."

"The wife?" asked Ross.

"Yes. But around the same time, here in Dundee, Burly McKinnes was blabbing to all and sundry that his father was dead."

Ross narrowed his eyes. In common with just about every other cop in Dundee, he knew the McKinneses alright, but Burly himself wasn't so well known to him.

Donna continued, "The odd thing about that is, Agnes doesn't have a mobile, and when I checked with her, she told me she didn't know Burly's number."

"So, how did Burly know," said Alice. It wasn't a question.

Ross picked up a pen and began to tap it on the surface of the desk. "Would he have time to murder his father in Arbroath and be back in Dundee within the timeframe?" he asked.

"If he was in a hurry, yes," Donna confirmed. "And he fits the bill. We're looking for a bit of muscle, and he's a regular at the gym, by all accounts."

"We'd better get him in, then," said Ross, but without much enthusiasm. He glanced up, and seemed to realise there was no-one around to go and pick Burly up. All of their officers, it appeared, were attending the hostage situation. Or enjoying their Sunday off. "On second thoughts," he went on, "you'd be best getting over to the mortuary. Alice will call you as soon as we have anything more on the hostage situation." He stood up to go. "There'll be plenty of time later to talk to Burly McKinnes."

As Ross left the room, Alice turned to Donna. "Enjoy," she said, picking up a sheaf of papers from the desk, as though ready to read through them. "Like he says, I'll keep you posted."

"Just what Sunday afternoons are for," said Donna, fetching her jacket. "A lovely trip to the latest post mortem."

She ran almost headlong into her two armed guards when she opened the door to leave.

Chapter 10

Archie McKinnes didn't look any less grey lying on the mortuary table. And his skull was no less shocking than it had been at the football club, even though it was now minus the axe.

Donna stood behind the viewing window, and held a paper tissue over her mouth and nose. An instinct. She hated post mortems. Still, it was a distraction from waiting for news about the firearms situation in Arbroath.

John Ogilvie glanced across at her from time to time while he prepared his instruments for the first cut. He walked around the body with an almost apologetic air, as though sorry that he was about to invade and expose the inner parts that were never meant to be seen by another human.

John's methodical actions and his reverential demeanour helped to calm Donna. She found herself looking afresh at Archie McKinnes.

Thug. Lout. Wife beater.

All round nuisance and waste of space.

Then, for the first time, a glimmer of sympathy.

Donna had known the McKinneses all her life, but she'd never known anything of Archie's own beginnings. In all probability he had simply grown into the mould that he'd come from, unable to see beyond it to break free of it. A bit like Agnes, it struck her.

A buzzing from her pocket jolted her from her thoughts.

"Armed response unit's in place," Alice reported as soon as she answered the phone. "It could be a long stand off. No more information and we're not aware of any demands being made. We've put the call out for Burly McKinnes, and we managed to get hold of a couple of PCs to check known places for him. I'll let you know as soon as we pick him up."

"Thanks," said Donna. "Any media attention yet?"

"A trickle of reporters turning up outside," Alice confirmed. "Word's got out about the situation, but most of them will have gone up to Arbroath."

"Let's just hope Evanton isn't waiting for an audience before springing something on us," said Donna.

"Feck, I hadn't thought of that," said Alice. "Do you think that could be his game plan?"

"Who knows?" Donna sighed as she ended the call.

Ogilvie's technician, Robbie, arrived at the table, ready to jot down all of the pathologist's observations. *Bert and Ernie*, Donna found herself thinking as she watched the pair of them. Robbie was even wearing a striped shirt just like Ernie's. John had a monobrow like Bert's.

"I thought Chinese," Ogilvie was saying. He stared at Donna for a second.

"What?" she answered, caught by surprise. "You're really talking about food?"

Ogilvie shrugged. "Just another day in the office."

"Chinese is fine," said Donna, then she felt her stomach lurch. "Excuse me," she managed, before rushing from the viewing room. She lunged through the door of the Ladies, only just reaching the bowl before throwing up.

Panting and clammy, she leaned against the cubicle wall, and wondered what the hell had just happened. During all of the times she'd watched Ogilvie slice open murder victims, she had never been comfortable, but she'd never reacted like this.

She washed her face and rinsed her mouth, and wondered how to put Ogilvie off for tonight. He had talked about this meal endlessly for the last two weeks. It was a big deal for him, a cry for help. Donna's heart softened at the memory of him, just last week, struggling to confide in her. But she was going to have to be at the station now that they had this hostage situation going on. Ogilvie would understand that.

Slowly she made her way back to the viewing room, but when

she got there, Robbie was alone with the late Archie McKinnes.

Robbie looked up at Donna's arrival. "John had to take an urgent call," he shrugged.

Odd, thought Donna. She glanced at her phone. No message. Ogilvie couldn't be taking a call about a murder, otherwise she would have been told about it, too. And it wasn't like him to stop in the middle of something like this for anything else.

She pondered the situation while she watched Robbie continue his boss's ritual. She looked again at Archie McKinnes's grey face and found herself speculating about what it must have felt like to have been him. What had gone on inside his mind? What reference points shaped the reasoning for his actions? Was a police officer really meant to think about these things, she wondered? Then that nagging voice came, telling her to jack it all in, this job, that it wasn't worth it, not for the pressure it was putting on her and Libby.

The sound of the circular saw revving up brought her attention back to the here and now.

Just then, John Ogilvie returned. The mortuary grew suddenly silent as Robbie switched off the saw. From where Donna was standing, Ogilvie's face seemed noticeably paler than it had been earlier. He walked past Robbie, barely acknowledging him, and walked straight across to the viewing room. Donna's heart rate quickened. Something very unusual was going on here today.

"I'm sorry," said Ogilvie. Donna noted the strain in his voice, as well as the way he turned his eyes away, refusing to look at her. "But could we...er...take a rain check on tonight?"

Donna opened her mouth to reply, but before she managed to think of something suitable to say, Ogilvie turned to go back to the body.

She watched the pathologist, now more keenly interested in what Ogilvie's body was saying about him, rather than what the dead one was saying about the circumstances of the murder. But Ogilvie was giving nothing away, other than that something serious had happened when he'd taken that phone call.

She watched as Ogilvie took the circular saw from Robbie, and flinched when it whined to life once more. The harsh shrill of metalwork vibrated through Donna's stomach, making her feel queasy again. She stood up and called through the door from the viewing room.

"Doesn't look as though there's going to be any trouble here, after all." She was speaking to Ogilvie's back. "At least, not from the McKinneses," she muttered as, unnoticed, she turned and walked briskly from the mortuary. She decided to put John's mood down to perhaps an incident at home. From what she'd learned, going out for dinner was never going to be an easy thing for his wife, and maybe she'd bottled it at the last minute. Still, she was relieved to be gone from the post mortem and to be getting back to her own environment.

When she reached the bottom of the stairs leading out of the building, her mobile buzzed in her pocket again. Puzzled, she saw that it was Ross calling, not Alice. This was more than a routine update, then, she realised.

She began to answer, when Ross's voice cut in, urgent and serious.

"You're not going to like this," he said.

Chapter 11

When Donna hurried back into the team room at Bell Street, there were a couple more officers sitting at the desks, ferreting through files and on phone calls. Alice was sitting alone at the top end near the evidence board, and listening to a running commentary that was coming from the local radio station. She glanced up at Donna's arrival.

"Updates are a fraction ahead of what we're getting directly from the scene," she said, indicating the radio on her desk.

Donna sat beside her and tuned into the news reporter's speculation about what might be going through the minds of any one of the armed officers surrounding the flat.

"Do they know it's Rory Thomson's flat?" she asked.

41

Ross had been right when he'd phoned to tell her – she didn't like it one bit. During her faster-than-the-speed-limit drive from the morgue, she had replayed all of her previous dealings with Rory Thomson, beginning with the first time she'd met him when he had turned up at Bell Street to confess to a murder he'd had nothing to do with. Then there was the interview when she had been so convinced – was even more convinced now – that Evanton was using him. Then finding him covered in blood in his flat, and his living room wall that was adorned with pictures of herself.

As soon as Ross had phoned to tell her this was where the hostage was being held, she knew it had nothing to do with Rory Thompson himself. She knew he was currently in a secure psychiatric ward and would be there for some time yet. Still, she found herself shuddering involuntarily at the thought of all those photos he had of her on his wall, and of the times when she had had a feeling she was being watched. Knowing now that it had been Rory Thomson watching her.

There was only one reason, Donna knew, why Thomson's flat was the scene of the current situation: Evanton was goading her. He was sending out a clear challenge directly to her.

"We haven't released that information," Alice broke into her thoughts.

Just then, Ross came into the room carrying two mugs of coffee and a large bag full of fast food. He did a double take when he saw Donna, and said, "You're not telling me you stayed within the speed limit to get here."

"Don't ask, then," said Donna, taking the food from him. "But if I did, then so did my two knights in shining armour." She glanced behind her, and caught the expression of discomfort the armed guards quickly shared.

Ross sighed. "Did you miss much of the PM?"

"The part I saw was very strange," said Donna before she could stop her mouth. At Ross's arched eyebrow, she went on to give a brief account of John Ogilvie's uncharacteristic behaviour.

Ross frowned. "You didn't press for an explanation?"

42

Donna hesitated, aware that it was what Ross would have expected her to do. But Ogilvie's problems with his wife – which most likely explained the pathologist's odd behaviour – had been shared with her in confidence.

"We've all got better things to be getting on with," she finally said. "What's the next plan of action in the Arbroath situation? Are there any more details?"

The pit of dread in Donna's stomach grew, swelling like her hunch about this entire situation.

"Okay," said Ross, sitting down and frowning as Alice and Donna each took a coffee, leaving him with none. "I had a fuller chat with Aiden Moore just after I spoke to you. When the hostage phoned at 3pm, she gave her name as Marnie Whyte. She sounded distressed, confirmed she was the woman who'd made the call to Arbroath police this morning, and said she was still being held at gunpoint in a flat in Arbroath. We confirmed, as I told you, that it's Rory Thomson's flat. She said that the man with the gun had told her to phone with those details, along with his description, and a message that we would receive another call in an hour. Then the call ended, and Aiden phoned me straight away with the update."

"Marnie Whyte?" Donna repeated. "Is she known to us?"

Ross shrugged. "Too early to say. The guys over there..." he indicated to the officers at the other end of the room, "...are doing their best to dig out as much background as we can get. But to be honest, we're down to the bare bones of staffing in here."

"We need to go up there," said Donna, rising from her chair.

"Arbroath are handling it," said Ross. "And we've no more to go on until the next phone call at four."

"Aye, right," said Donna, heading for the door.

"I said, we're staying here," said Ross. Donna kept going. The armed guards looked unsure as to what they should do. Ross called after her, "That's an order. Get back in here." His face was pale, but his eyes were blazing with anger. "The three of us are staying here until Evanton gets brought in."

Donna opened her mouth to protest.

"Orders from up high," said Ross, holding up an open palm.

Donna spun round to look at him. She heard the wheeze in his voice, the tell-tale sign that he was scared. Then the penny dropped.

"They suspect an ambush, don't they?" she asked. "They think it could be a set up."

Ross lowered his eyes and studied his hands. Then he slowly nodded his head.

"It seems the Chief Super thinks if we attend, we could be walking into a trap," he said finally. "That this might be Evanton's way of luring us to where he wants us to be – and in front of all that media attention."

Donna thought it over, conceding the possibility. But another one jumped into her mind. "Arbroath police station will be crammed full of cops while we wait for this next phone call," she said. "Don't you think that would be a much bigger target?"

Without replying to her, Ross took his mobile back out of his pocket and made a call, asking for Superintendent Brodie, station commander at Arbroath.

Alice shifted closer to Donna's side as the two of them listened to Ross plead with Brodie to disperse the officers around the town rather than allow them to congregate at the station.

The longer it seemed to take for Brodie to accept Ross's advice, the stronger Donna's unease grew, until she found herself contemplating the unthinkable.

"Was it Brodie who gave the order for us to stay here in Dundee?" she asked Ross as soon as he was off the phone. Ross nodded that it was. The unthinkable, she now decided, had to be spoken out loud. "What if it isn't a station full of coppers in Arbroath who are being set up?" she said. Ross and Alice gave her their full attention. "What if it's us *here*, when we're not expecting anything?"

There was a moment of silence, and even the desk phones paused their ringing. Then Ross sighed again.

"Are you really suggesting Brodie – Superintendent Brodie – is collaborating with Jonas Evanton in some scheme to ambush the three of us?"

"Just one of us," said Donna. "Let's be realistic here."

"She's got a point," said Alice.

"I don't buy it," said Ross. "Not Brodie." But the way he shifted in his seat as he spoke, so as to allow himself a glance towards the window said otherwise. He was certainly tempted to buy it. Then, "Listen, there's nothing we can do until the next phone call. We've got thirty minutes."

Chapter 12

The thirty minutes dragged by. Officers came and went from the room, carrying out various tasks, while Donna, Alice and Ross sat listening to the running commentary on the radio.

Ross had just begun to speak, when his mobile rang. His glance at Donna and Alice told them it was an update from Aiden. Donna watched intently as she saw Ross shift uncomfortably in his seat. She could hear Aiden's voice, but was frustrated that she couldn't make out his words.

"Thanks for that, Aiden," Ross said, ending the call, and letting his shoulders slump.

"Well?" Donna and Alice demanded in unison.

"That's the call just come in from Marnie Whyte," Ross said. "She still can't confirm her captor's name, but says he'll have something to tell us at 5pm."

"Keeping us waiting, just where he wants us," said Donna, thumping her fist on the desk.

"There's more," said Ross, catching her eye. "He gave her instructions to read out a note. It said, *You're not going to know what's hit you.*"

Donna sprang to her feet. "He's playing with us! It'll all end if I just go up there. That's what he wants."

"No," said Ross, his voice uncompromising.

"We know only a fraction of what he's capable of," said Donna,

45

"and we've no idea how far his reach is. I'm going. That's the way to stop him."

"He must have help on the inside," said Alice. "She's right – playing this by the book isn't going to get us anywhere."

"Don't encourage her," said Ross. He gave Donna a warning look. "Under no circumstances am I letting you go up there."

"Well, have you got any other bright ideas?" Donna challenged, a flash of anger raising her voice. "He's just issued a warning, telling us we won't know what's hit us. You need to let me go up there *now*."

"No," said Ross. "We don't know what risk we'd be putting the hostage in. ARU are in charge of the situation. We need to be smarter than this. I've been thinking it over, and at the risk of sounding like you…" he looked at Donna, "…I think we need to try and get into his mind set, see if there's a way to get ahead of him."

There was a brief moment of silence between the three officers, only serving to amplify the phones that were ringing out on the empty desks around them. The few officers working in the room were doing their best to handle all the calls.

"There is one person who knows his mind," said Donna. "And she's the one person Evanton might actually listen to."

"You mean Mo Skinner, don't you?" said Ross. "I'd been thinking the same thing."

"Oh, no, we can't put a member of the public in danger," Alice cut in. "I know Mo is perfectly capable of holding her own, but you're not seriously suggesting we let her talk to him?"

"He's got our police resources tied in knots, and he knows it," said Ross. "I want Mo brought in. At least to get her thoughts on what he might do next."

"She's not a fecking mind reader," said Alice. Donna looked at her, surprised at the harshness in her voice.

"She does know him," said Donna. Then she flinched at the look Alice gave her.

"Are you being serious?" Alice hissed. "We can't bring her into

46

the investigation. It's too risky. And anyway, we haven't even confirmed that it is Evanton."

"Are *you* the one being serious now?" Donna retorted. "We've a maniac who just happens to meet Evanton's description, holding a hostage in a flat full of photographs of me, and who's just issued a warning that he's got something planned. Of course it's Evanton – and remember he is the one who put a bullet through two of our own colleagues. It makes total sense to try and second guess him, before we start getting casualties, or worse."

"You're talking about letting a civilian talk to him, for God's sake," Alice said, her voice gathering anger.

The argument over whether to bring Mo Skinner into the situation went on for some time. Finally, Ross stood up and picked up one of the desk phones. He made the call to have Mo picked up from her home in Arbroath and brought to Bell Street.

"My decision," he said, putting an end to Alice's protests. "Now, why don't we bring Burly McKinnes in for a chat while we wait for her? Find out how he knew about his father's murder before the information was released?"

Donna checked her watch, feeling uncomfortable at having argued with Alice. They'd never had a serious disagreement before, and she was taken aback by Alice's strength of feeling on the matter.

"It's not the best time for us to be interviewing a suspect," Donna replied to Ross. "By the time he gets here, we'll be getting the next update from Arbroath. We should focus on that."

Ross took in a sharp breath, but before it could turn into words, Donna went on. "You know as well as I do…"

Her thought for the day was cut short by Alice, who suddenly waved her hands in the air. "Listen, quick," she urged them, sounding much more like her usual self again and turning up the volume on the radio.

The reporter's voice had risen by several decibels and at least another octave, saying, "And it looks as though it's all over. Several police officers have left the main door of the flat, and they've allowed a team of paramedics inside…"

Ross's mobile sounded, and he grabbed it to his ear, yelling, "Why am I listening to the local radio for updates?" Then he went silent as he gripped the mobile more tightly. When the call ended, he turned to Donna and Alice.

"It's over," he said, quietly. Donna felt goose bumps crawl down her arms. Something wasn't right at all about any of this, and Ross confirmed her fears when he said, "This is worse than we thought."

Chapter 13

John Ogilvie hesitated before opening his front door. His palm was sweating despite the freezing December night air. His heart was thumping, sending shooting pains to his temples and making him feel slightly faint.

On instinct he glanced behind him. Or had there actually been a noise? When a cat leaped from the hedge that lined the pathway to his door, he heard his own voice begin to utter a cry, and stuffed his fist into his mouth to stifle it.

He pushed open the door, entered his home, and stood for a moment in his dark hallway, listening. Silence engulfed his shaken senses.

"Cerys?" he finally called, knowing now in his heart that the threat had been real. For a moment he listened to the echo of his own voice, wondering if it sounded to other people the same as it had just sounded to himself. His mind trying to protect him from the horror that he was going to have to confront, he realised with a clarity that felt like ice cold water being splashed on his face. His voice cracked and faded at his second attempt to call out her name. Now his body began to shake uncontrollably.

Almost as though fearing the floorboards might give way beneath his feet, Ogilvie began to walk slowly along the hallway.

Often, when he returned home after a shift, Cerys would be in bed, cocooning herself within her dark and troubled world. Sometimes drunk, if she'd been able to wrestle her fears and leave the house during the day, just long enough to purchase the alcohol within which she sought refuge. Those were the nights he dreaded the most. He would know as soon as he opened the door, acutely sensitive to the stench of wine fumes, and welcomed by the sight of the empty supermarket bag tossed carelessly onto the floor by the foot of the staircase, discarded having fulfilled its duty. As soon as his foot trod on the first step, the foul insults would come flying from the bedroom.

There was no carrier bag on the floor tonight. No wine fumes. No barrage of profane abuse. But neither was it the other kind of night. The ones where she would plead for his forgiveness, swear she would seek help, declare her adoration of him.

No, the air in the house felt different tonight.

Ogilvie reached into his pocket, touched his fingers to his phone, then remembered the words. He withdrew his hand as though it had been burned. His shaking began to subside as he forced his breathing to slow. Placed one foot, then his whole weight, onto the first step. Nothing, just that strange air.

Onto the second step, still no sound from upstairs, and on up to the top until he stood facing the bedroom door. He lost control of his breathing and found himself panting, a hot tear slipping from the corner of one eye. Briefly he wondered how many bedroom doors he'd stood in front of before stepping across their thresholds into varying scenes of human misery. There was always a sadness and a loneliness attached to bedroom murder scenes, he often thought. That someone should end their life because of some cold, callous act in a place that was designed to offer rest and comfort. Coming out of his brooding, he finally had to face it. He pushed open the door.

Cerys wasn't in the room. It was empty. Taking several steps into it, he replayed in his mind the words issued to him that afternoon when he'd taken the phone call during the post mortem. When he thought of them he could still picture Donna staring across at him from the viewing room. He'd been warned specifically to make sure Donna heard nothing about this. If the caller had the slightest hint of Donna's attention, he'd warned Ogilvie, Cerys wouldn't be coming home. Ever.

As if to convince himself that this was real, Ogilvie made a point of slowly scanning his eyes over every inch of the room. The action, so customary in his day to day work, brought him some sense of calm. Then he backed out, pulling the door to. He re-traced his steps back downstairs. At the foot of the stairs, he stopped, forcing himself to remember his caller's words. The back door. He had to go to the back door. He did as he'd been instructed.

There were no streetlamps out on this side of the house, the long garden stretching towards the hedgerows of the park at the edge of the reservoir. The thought of the reservoir made Ogilvie shudder. He felt bile begin to burn at his gullet, rising into his throat, and swallowed on reflex. He retrieved the set of keys and security pass from his jacket pocket, and sat them on top of the recycling bin that sat to the side of the house, hidden from public view.

He'd been told not to look around, and so he didn't. They had Cerys. He went back inside, locked the door, switched on all the house lights, and sat by the window, all as instructed, so that from the outside his every move could be clearly seen.

He sat. Waited. All the time conscious of the colour draining from his face, hearing the voice in his own head screaming, *Do something!* But he knew he had to wait.

Less than five minutes later he received a text.

"Well done," it said. "Instructions for collecting your parcel will be sent in the morning."

Chapter 14

The team room at Bell Street began to fill again with uniformed officers returning from their back-up roles in Arbroath. The clamour of their voices, thunderous footsteps, the opening and closing door, and the desk phones and mobiles that were striking back up did little to calm Donna's rage.

When Ross had told her things were worse than they'd thought, he hadn't been kidding.

Worse than a hostage situation at the beginning of a laborious murder investigation.

Worse than the hostage being held in Rory Thomson's flat.

By Jonas Evanton.

She rubbed her eyes, feeling suddenly tired. This had already been a long day, with the hostage situation punctuated by the weirdest post mortem she'd ever attended. And now that the hostage was free… Well, as Ross had said, the whole thing had become even worse.

She prowled back and forth past the evidence board, glancing up at each arrival, impatient for the return of her team. Finally, Thomas Akwasi appeared. Donna waved a greeting, a gesture close to that of swatting a fly. Thomas flung himself into a chair next to Donna.

"We just got word, boss, that Marnie Whyte's on her way to Ninewells now," he told her. Donna nodded an understanding that this was going to take some time. "The paramedics have said she's in a state of shock, and you've to ring the ward on this number in an hour." He handed a note with the number on it to Donna.

"I dread to think what ordeal he must have put her through," said Donna, pocketing the note and checking the time.

Another gaggle of officers came into the room, Stephen Morrison among them. Donna flagged him over. He came to stand towering over Akwasi, his face flushed with excitement.

"First time out with the ARU?" asked Donna.

Morrison nodded his head vigorously. "Wouldn't mind some of the action those guys get," he said.

"Go forward for firearms training, then," said Donna. "I'm sure it beats school patrol."

Morrison grinned, just as another rumble of chatter brought more officers into the room. Finally, in through the door came Fran. Donna saw her quickly take in the room and make a bee-line towards her.

"All present and correct, then," said Donna as Fran approached, catching the attention of Alice who'd been ferreting away on a nearby computer.

Drawing her team around her, Donna turned her attention to each one, allowing them to continue their buzz of excited chatter about their experiences during the hostage situation. She let the banter to go on for several minutes, their way of dealing with what had turned into an unmitigated disaster: when the hostage, Marnie Whyte, had made the final call and they'd stormed the flat, Evanton was nowhere in sight. He had staged the whole thing.

Suddenly there was a lull. Amidst the clamour and the activity of the room full of officers, Donna saw them looking at her – bullet-proof Alice, eager Fran Woods, inquisitive Stephen Morrison and steady Thomas Akwasi – waiting for her direction.

"Fran," she decided, noting the puppy-like eager-to-please expression on the DC's face. "Let's get the evidence board up to date."

The movement of her team gathering together and heading towards the evidence board seemed to instil a sense of order to the hive of activity, and gradually the officers began to settle down.

One by one their attention drifted towards and focused on Fran, who now stood with a marker pen in front of the evidence board.

"I want all of it recorded," said Donna. "Where we're at with the illegal adoptions, the hunt for Evanton, Archie McKinnes's murder…"

"McKinnes's murder?" muttered several officers, scepticism clear in their tones.

"Yes, we need to know where all of our resources are being deployed," said Donna, "and his murder is going to have Arbroath snowed under dealing with all the hundreds of suspects…"

Sniggers across the room.

"… so, his murder, and of course the details of today's debacle with the hostage situation."

Donna knew if anyone could fit that lot onto an evidence board in a way that made sense, it would be Fran Woods. She was glad of the keen DC's meticulous attention to detail. She watched as, under Fran's hand, columns appeared for each of the illegal adoptions investigation, the hunt for Evanton, Archie McKinnes's murder and the hostage situation.

"Forensics went straight in behind us," said Akwasi. "If there's any trace of Evanton having been in that flat, they'll find it."

"Good," said Donna. "We need to establish as quickly as possible whether he took her there, or whether he got someone else to do it. Get some idea of whether we can narrow our search."

The officers in the room watched in rapt silence while Fran added bullet points in each of the columns. Slowly, the enormity of the tasks they were having to deal with on limited resources became clear.

Donna looked over her shoulder and saw Ross leaning against the door frame, his arms folded, and they exchanged a look that was close to despair. For over 18 months they'd been hunting for Evanton, responsible for killing two of their own colleagues. And today they thought they'd come so close. The only way they would know if they had been would be to interview the woman he'd left terrified in the flat with instructions to phone the police with bogus updates.

Donna glanced again at the phone number of the ward that was preparing to receive Marnie Whyte. She was puzzled. Their checks so far suggested Marnie Whyte didn't seem to have any obvious connections to Evanton or his known associates, and she had certainly never been involved with the police before. If Evanton was picking on random strangers now, then he was even more dangerous than before.

"Who's looking after the McKinnes case in Arbroath?" asked Alice, breaking into her thoughts.

"Sergeant Scott Dexter as first responder," said Donna, "and DC Wilma Cornton…"

"Don't know them," muttered Alice.

"They're handling the investigation – not with much enthusiasm, I might add," said Donna. "And of course all the uniforms will be interviewing potential suspects for the rest of their careers." Her mobile rang. "Speak of the devil," she said, taking the call from Scott Dexter.

With her mind on things other than an update from Dexter, Donna half-listened in on Alice and Fran as they chatted over some of the illegal adoptions investigation, and to the snippets of discussion that broke out around the room about where Evanton could be hiding, whether he had inside help, and what he might do next. Then she did a double-take.

"Sorry, Scott," she said into the phone, "could you repeat that?"

She was aware of the voices around the room coming to a halt in abrupt unison as the tables turned. Now they were all listening in on her. They'd sensed a development.

"Well, the McKinnes murder might not take up so much of our time, after all," she announced with a grin. "CCTV has his son, Burly McKinnes legging it out of the club during half time, his fingerprints are all over the place, and two witnesses have claimed to have seen him sneaking around the clubhouse around that time. Uniform have been sent round to bring him in."

"Seems a bit convenient," muttered Akwasi.

"Burly McKinnes was never the brightest," said Alice. "Reliable witnesses?"

"He's a big guy," said Donna. "He'd be pretty hard to mistake for someone else. And it's consistent with what I learned from Agnes."

She noted the relief on Ross's face, and realised the pressure he must have been under with resources so thinly spread. At least they could count on some support from their colleagues in Arbroath, now that they would be free from what had started out as a seemingly endless murder investigation. Maybe. Donna felt a relief that seemed out of proportion to the problems they were still faced with.

"Feather in Scott Dexter's cap, then," Alice commented.

Donna saw Fran quickly update the evidence board, and the news seemed to lift the officers' spirits, despite the mess they were still in.

"I take it Aiden Moore will remain our contact for co-ordinating the hostage investigation?" Alice went on, reminding them of that very mess.

Donna nodded her head while a series of groans echoed around the room at the reminder. "I requested it specially."

A uniformed officer came into the room and sought out Donna. "We've got Burly McKinnes in interview room 2 now, Ma'am," he said.

"That was quick, and don't call me *Ma'am*," Donna told him. Then she turned to Alice and said, "Let's go and have a chat with the boy wonder, shall we?"

Alice jumped to attention, and amidst the sudden activity unleashed by the relief of having a break in the McKinnes case, she and Donna followed the officer out of the room and through the station until they reached the interview room containing Burly McKinnes. As they walked, Donna couldn't help but feel another sense of relief that she and Alice were no longer arguing.

Chapter 15

Donna thought if a brown bear was dressed in gym sweats, it would look a lot like this hulk of a man. Although she was there with Alice – and even a man the size of Burly would be a fool to try and take *her* on – Donna thought briefly about requesting another couple of officers for back up, but then decided to play things by ear. By instinct. Because her instinct was shouting at her right now, and she'd learned to trust it.

Alice turned to check the voice recorder, and looked surprised when Donna tapped her on the arm and shook her head, indicating that the interview wouldn't be taped.

"Just a quick chat," said Donna. "For now."

Burly stood glowering down at them both, his jaw slack and his bovine-like eyes half closed, his pupils floating in and out of focus. He had a defiant mood about him, Donna thought, somebody who would confess to a murder right away and then ask you what you were going to do about it.

Donna gazed back at him, and they stood in silence for several moments, studying one another. The evidence against Burly seemed watertight. He'd killed his father, alright, Donna's instinct told her, probably after witnessing his mother being beaten one too many times. She was puzzled, though: despite being a McKinnes, Burly had never been in trouble before.

Donna continued to study him. Not yet 20, he was the youngest of four boys. Donna had gone to school with the two middle ones – twins – both of whom had been in trouble ever since she could remember, and both of whom were now serving lengthy sentences. Their older brother – Archie Junior – had been killed in a motorbike accident about 15 years ago. He'd stolen the bike from a local drugs runner. All the while, the young Burly had witnessed the continual violence at home against his mother, and the police had been waiting for him to come of age. But Burly had defied their expectations and kept turning up at school, not getting into trouble.

"Let me ask you," said Donna, remembering the thoughts she'd had when she'd looked at Archie McKinnes's body at the mortuary. "How come you never got mixed up in all the stuff your brothers did?" *How did you break the mould?*

Burly's cow-like eyes glided over her. "What's it to you?" he growled.

Donna sat down. She saw the confusion cross Burly's face. He wasn't sure how to deal with the lack of hostility.

"Counselling?" she suggested.

Burly scoffed, and folded his arms across his chest in a defensive gesture.

"Don't knock it," said Donna. She brought her pack of lithium pills from her pocket and held them up, gave them a rattle. Out of the side of her eye, she caught the look of alarm on Alice's face. She winked at her colleague, *Run with this.*

Burly brought his focus onto the pills. One of his eyes narrowed, giving his face an expression of curiosity. He had no direct experience of being questioned by the police, Donna knew, but clearly this wasn't how he'd imagined it.

"These stop me being a crazy mad bitch," she told him, "but pills aren't enough. I have regular counselling, here in the police. It really helps, you know, but it took me a while to get the help. Know why?"

Burly hitched a shoulder. But he met her eye now, interested.

"I was scared," said Donna. "Scared that if my colleagues found out, they would take the piss, and that I'd get fired."

Burly shuffled on the spot, then took a seat opposite Donna. His eyes flitted from his feet, to her face, and back to his feet. He cleared his throat, and Donna saw his cheeks mottle scarlet. "Not counselling," he mumbled. "Mr Hart."

"Bleeding Hart, the art teacher?" said Donna, recalling the teacher from her own schooldays. Surely he must be retired by now? She remembered he had something of a reputation for being a soft touch. Sometimes the kids would keep him behind for ages, making up bogus stories, just to see how far they could push his patience. Then there had been the whispers – why was the man spending so much of his own time with kids? Donna had wondered this herself, at times. And now she wondered again. What was Burly telling her?

"He listened," said Burly. "He was there, and just listened. He never asked for anything back, and never judged, never said stuff about my family. He just listened whenever I wanted to talk about stuff."

"And that's why you never went off the rails?" Donna asked, surprised at what he'd just said, and feeling a little ashamed.

Burly made a non-committal grunt. "Nobody to fucking talk to at home," he said.

There was a moment of silence, and Alice whispered, "I'll go and get us coffee. What do you take?"

Burly looked confused by the question. Donna understood – he'd never drunk coffee before.

"No matter," said Alice. "I'll just be a minute."

Donna leaned towards Burly. "Thing is," she said, "I don't get it.

57

You manage to keep out of trouble all this time, despite everything that was going on around you, and now you snap? Killing your father?"

Burly's shoulders rose.

"Tape's not on," Donna reminded him, "and it's just you and me in here. Nothing you say can be used as evidence, so you can tell me whatever you like. It can only ever stay between the two of us."

Burly knew enough about admissible evidence, and knew Donna was right. His shoulders relaxed again, and he leaned forward, speaking in a hushed tone. "Girlfriend's up the duff."

"You romantic," said Donna.

Burly scowled at her. "I'm not having a kid coming into the world with him around."

"Archie?"

Burly nodded, *yes*.

"Did you talk this over with Bleeding… with Mr Hart?"

"It was his axe," said Burly.

"He gave you his axe to kill your father?"

Burly tutted, impatient. "I stole it from his shed. Saw him using it one day. He doesn't even know about the baby."

"So, you decided to break the cycle?" said Donna. "That takes a lot of guts."

"You being sarcastic?"

"No," said Donna. "I'm not. And to be honest, you've done a lot of people a favour."

Alice arrived back in the room with a tray of coffee, setting it down on the table that stood between Donna and Burly.

While Donna took some sips of her coffee, watching Burly try his, she found her mind switching to the many times she'd been called out to his parents' home, and the daring to hope that she'd seen in Agnes's eyes at the football club. Agnes had a chance, she thought, to build a new life for herself. How could she take away the one son of hers that had turned out alright? She was aware that her un-policing thoughts might start to become a problem.

"Finish your coffee," she told him, "and go home. Tell your mum everything's okay. And don't forget, you owe me one."

Burly's expression grew suspicious as he looked from Donna to Alice and back again. "Is this some sort of wind up?" His words were slightly slurred.

Donna could see Alice was about to interject, when a sudden clatter and eruption of raised voices broke the spell. The interview room door crashed open, and a wiry middle-aged man in a dark suit barged in, his face white with rage. A uniformed officer trotted into the room at his back, uttering apologetic sounds.

At the intrusion, Donna stood up. "Good evening, Mr Clarty," she said to the wiry man. Burly snorted.

"It's Clarence, and well you know it," the man spat. "And just what do you think you're playing at, interviewing my client without his lawyer present?" To Burly, he continued with a pointing finger, "Do not say anything."

"Oh, keep your knickers on," said Donna.

"Yes, *please* keep your knickers on," Alice muttered in the background. Burly snorted again.

Donna went on. "This isn't a formal interview. Burly here dropped by to have a chat with us, and it's been really cosy, hasn't it?"

Burly's head swivelled slowly until his gaze met Donna's and she saw a twitch begin at the corner of his mouth. "Aye, cosy," he said.

Dougal Clarence, criminal lawyer and public notary, stopped in his tracks. If it wasn't for his mouth opening and closing like a goldfish on cocaine, Donna would have sworn he'd actually stopped breathing.

Chapter 16

"You let him go?" Ross sounded incredulous and he looked apoplectic. He and Donna stood by the door to the team room, while Alice made her excuses and sloped off to speak to someone else.

It looked like business as usual back in the room. Most of the desks were occupied. Officers were thumbing through files, keying onto screens, talking into phones, or chatting amongst themselves, getting back on with the various investigations that were currently underway.

"Insufficient grounds to charge him," Donna replied, sending a warning look to Alice. Alice feigned *I know nothing*. Donna continued, "But he is our man. Trust me with this."

"You know Dougal Clarence is going to have our guts for garters if you've put a foot wrong," Ross warned.

"Oh, Dougie and me are like this," said Donna, holding up crossed fingers.

Alice nodded her head and tapped the side of her nose in conspiratorial agreement.

"You'd better not mess this up," Ross growled.

Before it could develop into another argument, Aiden Moore arrived at the door.

Donna was always glad to see the young PC who'd saved her life after Jonas Evanton had written her off for dead.

"How are things up in Arbroath?" she asked him.

Aiden smiled back at her as he unravelled his scarf from around his neck. His glasses were still hazy around the edges after having steamed up the moment he'd stepped inside the building.

"We're all a bit frazzled," he admitted. "Yesterday was mental, with all the football stuff, and today's been a long day. Still, at least it's calmed down now, and we'll get a bit of a breather."

Until when? Donna wondered, but didn't say out loud. It was true that the evidence against Burly McKinnes meant they didn't need to interview all those football fans, after all, and they had all been stood down from the hostage situation, but there was still Evanton's warning to think about. Something was about to happen. Donna could feel it.

The three of them found a desk to sit at.

"I've got Mo Skinner with me," Aiden said. "Where do you want to speak to her?"

At the sound of Mo's name, Alice joined them at the desk.

"Well, she's not a suspect," said Donna. "And we do owe her. She's doing us a favour, so somewhere nice."

"How about in here, so we can get on with it?" said Ross, with a warning tone in his voice.

Donna sighed. "Aiden, take Mo to the staff canteen," she said.

She saw Alice's expression of disapproval, and her heart sank at the tension still evident between them over the matter of involving Mo Skinner in the investigation. Alarmingly, she caught her mood take a dip, taken hold suddenly by a dark cloak of fear. This was no time to start losing it, she thought. She needed to speak to Libby, to be reassured that things were okay there.

"I'll join you there in a minute," she told Alice and Ross, watching them follow Aiden along the corridor and further into the building.

She made her way to the exit stairs and brought out her mobile, dialling Libby's number.

The phone rang twice before Libby picked up. "I saw the news on Twitter that you got the guy in Arbroath?"

"Well, yes and no," said Donna. "Are you okay?"

"I'm fine," said Libby, with a light and casual tone that Donna recognised as genuine. "Are you going to be late home?"

"Not too much longer," said Donna. "But do me a favour, will you?"

"Make it worth my while?" Libby chuckled.

Donna bit her lip. *This job.* "I need you to check the alarm's all properly set."

"What?"

"Just… you know, in case I am a bit late. Humour me?"

Libby paused just long enough for Donna to register her sudden fear. *This fucking job.*

When Donna got to the canteen, Ross and Alice were waiting there for her and they went in together. Mo Skinner was sitting at a table and was keying something into her phone while Aiden stifled a yawn. Mo quickly put the phone away when she saw them approach, and stood to greet them.

"Donna, Angus," she said, extending her arms towards the DI and Ross. It had been a while. The first time they'd met, during the original hunt for Jonas Evanton, Mo's husband had been in a coma – the price he'd paid for trying to block Evanton's smuggling operation.

Donna embraced Mo briefly, remembering the terse start she and the lawyer had made with one another back then, before they had realised they were both on the same side.

There was a rabble of voices while Mo and the police officers exchanged their greetings, and Donna introduced her to Alice.

A number of police officers came into the canteen and formed a queue at the counter – the late shift taking the rare opportunity for a break.

Once the five of them were settled down around the table, Mo cleared her voice.

"Aiden told me about the hostage situation," she said. "That you believe Jonas Evanton was behind it?"

"That's right," said Donna. "We were hoping you could help us try and figure out what might be going on in his head. What he might do next."

Mo looked puzzled. "Didn't you arrest him?" she asked. "I thought the woman was released?"

Ross sighed. "Evanton wasn't there. He terrified the woman into providing us with false updates to give the impression he was still in the flat with her. But when we got in, there was no trace of him. We're still waiting to speak to her to find out if he was ever there at all."

Mo's hand went to her mouth.

"What do you make of it?" Donna asked her.

Mo thought before answering. "Evanton is a man who has to be in control, and who will do anything to get out of being backed into a corner," she said finally. "So it would have been out of character for him to have backed himself into a hostage situation. I did think it sounded odd when I found out about it. Setting it up the way you've described it, though, does seem more his style.

I'd say he's trying to control you."

"Well, he's done a good job of that," said Ross. "He's had us tied in knots all day."

"And now he's just gone?" said Mo.

"That's what we're worried about," said Donna. "He obviously went to the trouble of orchestrating the hostage thing for a reason."

"It'll be all about control," said Mo. "Has he made any other contact with you?"

"None," said Ross, Donna and Alice together. They were all staring at Mo, hungry for any morsel of information that might give them the edge on Evanton.

"Then if I were you," said Mo, "I'd be expecting to hear from him soon. He'll be wanting to tell you what he wants you to do."

"Marnie Whyte," Donna said suddenly.

"The hostage," Alice explained to Mo. Then to Donna, "What about her?"

"Evanton's been speaking through her all day," said Donna.

"If he has a message for you, it's going to be relayed through her," Mo finished Donna's train of thought, catching her eye. And nodding her head, she went on, "That would be the sort of way he'd operate."

"We need to get over to Ninewells right now," said Donna.

"The nurses won't be happy with you barging in," said Alice.

"Never stopped you before," said Mo. Her comment raised a wry chuckle.

Chapter 17

Donna and Alice made their way at a snail's pace around the car park at Ninewells Hospital. Eventually Donna saw a car reversing from a space, and stopped, flipping the indicator to show she was waiting to take it.

"Come on," she grumbled, as the other driver inched his way from the space in a series of over-cautious stops and starts. She hated hospital car parks. It was as though they were specially designed to meet roughly half of the required capacity to prevent people going there.

Eventually the space was free, and Donna pulled into it.

She turned to Alice and resumed the conversation they'd been having.

"We know he's got something planned," she said to Alice. "And *you're not going to know what's hit you* sounds like something pretty big."

"I know, I know," said Alice. "But I still don't think we should have involved Mo Skinner. All we've done is put her at more risk."

"Well," said Donna, undoing her seatbelt, "he spent all that time sitting watching us. It's going to be the revenge to end all revenges, and we're going to need all the help we can get to try and second guess him."

"They'd better not cancel our leave," Alice muttered.

Donna wondered if this was why Alice had been so tetchy lately. Was the sergeant worrying that her trip with Efe might have to be cancelled? She knew how much the visit meant to her, and her heart softened.

"Not on my watch," she said, clasping Alice's shoulder as they walked across the car park.

The wind whipped at them and they hurried to the hospital's main entrance.

Donna showed her warrant card to the nurse on reception, and introduced herself and Alice.

"One of the doctors is waiting to take you," the nurse told her. "Just a moment, I'll let her know you're here."

Visitors carrying balloons, and walking wounded on cigarette missions milled around the large concourse while Donna and Alice waited. A queue formed and lengthened at the cash machine outside one of the shops. After a few minutes, a young medic arrived and introduced herself as Dr. Wyatt.

"I've been keeping an eye on Marnie," she told the police officers, "and she'll be able to have a quick word with you."

"I appreciate it," said Donna. "We really need to know what happened to her."

She noticed the doctor staring at her, though trying not to, and cursed the previous day's news report.

"She's had a terrible shock," said the doctor. "We've given her a light sedative, but I don't want her anxiety levels going up any more."

"Understood," said Donna. Her head was screaming, *Don't you understand? We need to stop this happening to anyone else!*

She and Alice followed Dr. Wyatt to the end of the concourse, left and into a lift, which deposited them on level 5, and along more corridors until they reached a busy ward. At that point, the uniformed officer standing outside one of the rooms was the giveaway that they'd reached Marnie Whyte. The officer acknowledged Donna and Alice, and stepped aside to let them into the room.

On the bed lay a young woman. Her face was chalk white and her pallor was exaggerated by the deep red curls of hair that tumbled all around it in droves. She looked to be in her early twenties, and she flinched when Donna and Alice came in. It was obvious that she'd been crying and that her slender hands, clasped together tightly on top of her chest, were trembling.

"Marnie?" Donna spoke softly. "We're police officers. We're here to ask you some details about what happened to you earlier, okay?"

Marnie's eyes stared fixedly at her and Alice, and her hands continued to tremble.

Donna walked slowly towards the bed, and sat down in the visitor's chair. Alice sat on a stool by the door.

"I'm Donna, and this is my colleague, Alice. I know you're scared, and I know it's difficult for you to talk about this, but it'll really help us to catch the man who did this to you if you can answer a few questions."

Marnie's breath shuddered in gasps and Donna could see that she was trying to get her shaking under control.

"I'll try," she whispered.

65

Donna pulled her chair in closer to the bedside, and held eye contact with Marnie. She retrieved two pictures from her pocket – a photograph of Jonas Evanton as he was before he'd altered his appearance through extensive plastic surgery, and a photo-fit of his most recent likeness as seen by Donna and Fran.

"Do either of these look like the man who threatened you?" she asked, holding the pictures in front of Marnie. Marnie gazed at them for several moments, her eyes moving from one to the other, but Donna could tell the answer was no. *Damn it*, she thought.

"Have you seen him at all before?" she asked.

"I've seen him in the papers," Marnie said, pointing to the older photograph, "but I've never met him. Isn't he that murderer?"

She drew her hand back from the picture suddenly, alarmed.

"You don't have to worry," Donna tried to reassure her. "We're asking everyone if they've seen him. Now, can you tell me exactly what happened this morning?"

"I…I already told the police when they came into the flat," said Marnie, becoming more agitated.

At that moment, Dr. Wyatt stuck her head in the door and shot Donna a warning glance.

"I'll just be one more minute," Donna told her. Then she turned back to Marnie. "It's okay," she said. "Sometimes people remember more things later on." She ran through the scant details in her mind that she'd read in Marnie's statement taken at the scene. She'd been walking up Arbroath's High Street, when a man – medium height, slim, light brown hair and an accent, maybe Eastern European – had bumped into her and threatened her with a knife. He'd told her to follow him into the flat, where he then left her with a set of instructions and no illusions about what would happen to her if she failed to fully comply.

"Actually, there was another thing," Marnie said, surprising Donna. "Did you say your name was Donna?"

Donna felt her stomach lurch, and not for the first time today the hairs on the back of her neck stood on end. Her fear, her dread, and her excitement all rolled into one as the traumatised young woman in the hospital bed sought out her bag from the bedside cabinet. She rummaged in it and brought out a folded piece of paper.

"He told me to wait until I saw you face to face," said Marnie. "He said I had to give this message to you."

Her shaking hand held out the piece of paper to Donna. Donna took it, opened it up, and saw written on it one single word: *Run*.

Chapter 18

Donna arrived home and switched off her car engine. She sat for a moment while she finished a cigarette, and stared vacantly at the front door, thinking over some of the happy and the sad times they'd lived through there. There had been plenty of both. She was glad they would soon be moving to Arbroath and closer to Danny. She mused over the changes that were ahead for them all as a family. Sally would be here in the next couple of weeks, and the baby was due not long after that. But the moment she thought about Sally, the memories of how Evanton had terrorised and almost destroyed all of them came flooding back into her mind.

Her heart sank suddenly as she watched the blinking light of the heavy duty alarm system she'd had installed back when she'd been convinced – despite everyone else's scepticism – that Evanton had been watching her. As it turned out, her hunch back then had been correct. How was she going to figure out what he was up to now, and stop him? She couldn't risk Sally arriving while he was still at large. It struck Donna now that if he knew Sally was here, she would be a target, too.

She slowed her breathing and tried to tap into the intuition that had always served her well. What was it saying? All she could hear in her head was Marnie Whyte's warning: *Run*.

She turned her attention back quickly to the house. The downstairs lights were still on. She knew Libby had finished marking the student papers last night, so that wasn't why she was waiting up. And if there was nothing serious to discuss, Libby would be tucked up in bed. But, of course, there was something serious to discuss, Donna knew. Her last words to Libby earlier that day had been to check the security system. Libby wasn't stupid.

She got out of the car, locked it, and went into the house, barely noticing any more the presence of the armed guards nearby. She could hear the TV on in the living room, and went in, fixing a smile onto her face.

Libby was sitting on the settee, nursing a cup of something hot. She was watching a re-run of the X Factor, some poor soul on the screen being pilloried for an atrocious performance. She looked up at Donna's arrival.

"The alarm's been set all evening," she said. Donna's smile faded. "What the hell's been going on?" Libby went on. "I've been worried sick ever since you phoned. Didn't you think I would need some kind of explanation?"

Donna held up her hands. "Look, it's been a long day…" *and I need a drink…*

She realised Libby was going to need one too when she told her about the day's developments.

"I'm sorry," Libby said, her voice softening as she set her coffee cup down on the floor. "I just got a fright. Tell me what's been happening."

Donna felt relief that it hadn't developed into an argument, and she threw herself onto the settee next to Libby.

"You've been hearing about the hostage situation in Arbroath throughout the day?" she began.

Libby nodded her head, *yes*. "I reckoned you'd have been kept busy with that. Were you up there?"

"No," said Donna. "I had to wait it out at Bell Street."

"They managed to handle it without you…" Libby began with a light-hearted tone that ended in unease at Donna's grim expression. "What? What is it?"

"The whole thing was staged by Jonas Evanton," Donna said. She drew herself up, looking into Libby's widened eyes. "Whatever he's been planning all this time, it's starting."

"But, on the news it said the hostage was freed," said Libby. "I don't understand."

Donna took both of her hands in hers. "Evanton had somebody else take the woman to the flat in Arbroath – it was Rory Thomson's flat…"

"Seriously?"

"And he left this message for the woman to give to me – specifically to me." Donna brought out her phone and showed Libby a photo of the message that Marnie Whyte had given her.

"Run?" Libby read it, her voice hushed and fearful.

"We think he's about to unleash his plan, whatever it is, and we've brought in Mo Skinner to help us figure out what he might be thinking."

"Mo Skinner?" said Libby. "It was her husband that was poisoned in Danny's restaurant, wasn't it?"

Donna confirmed with a nod. "Mo's agreed to help. She's the only person who knows Evanton well, and I really want this wrapped up and him behind bars before Sally moves in with Danny."

"This is the never-ending nightmare," said Libby. She looked crushed. "It's as though everyone who was involved in stopping his toxic trade two years ago is coming back together."

Donna thought about this for a moment. Libby was right. Two years ago, Mo Skinner's husband had thwarted Evanton's attempts to keep his illegal smuggling business under the radar. Bob Skinner had ended up in a coma as a result, following a poisoning at Danny's restaurant. Evanton had made sure there was enough evidence to frame Danny for the poisoning, while he moved onto blackmailing as a technique to stop an enquiry into the smuggling: he'd kidnapped Sally, the daughter of the enquiry's leading expert. Only Sally had escaped, and Donna was in no doubt now that her role in humiliating Evanton and in his capture would leave her vulnerable to what he might be about to do next.

"There's plenty of unfinished business going on," she said in response to Libby's observation. She wrapped her arms around Libby. It was going to be a restless night's sleep tonight, she thought.

Monday
Chapter 19

The start of the new working week found Donna and Alice standing just inside the main entrance to Bell Street, each one sipping from a steaming Styrofoam cup while watching the spectacle outside. A TV crew from the regional news channel had just turned up, joining several other journalists who'd set up camp sometime during the night.

"How did Libby take the news?" Alice ventured.

Donna glanced sideways at her. "Not so good."

"I suppose you're limited in how you could make the return of Jonas Evanton sound like a positive," Alice said.

"This is really affecting her," Donna sighed. "I mean, normal couples go through difficult times, don't they? But they don't have to contend with psychopaths goading you constantly, or your career cock-ups being plastered all over the news as well, do they?"

The morning's newspapers were full of it, coming hot on the heels of Lindsey Forsyth's *Weekend Special* and the public hysteria it had whipped up like a growing tornado. Social media was viralling off the spectrum. About how Jonas Evanton had held a woman hostage in an Arbroath flat yesterday. And about how, by the time the police had made entry, he'd vanished. Again.

Donna groaned. "You'd think they would get tired of us screwing up over Evanton."

"Everyone loves a screw up," said Alice, draining her coffee.

Donna smiled, thinking again about how relieved she was to have Alice back to her non-confrontational self.

They'd hurried to this spot via a rear entrance, on the instructions of the armed officers, and had managed to remain unnoticed while they watched the blossoming media presence.

A harsh light made Donna blink. The sun was yet to emerge from beneath the gloomy winter horizon. The switch-on of the TV lighting made it difficult now to see out, so Donna and Alice made their way back into the depths of the building to begin their working day.

If they didn't already know their way to the large team meeting room, they would have been drawn towards it by the racket that was coming from it now. It looked as though the whole of Bell Street was huddled in there.

Ross was there, scowling and pacing, when he caught sight of Donna and Alice. He waved them in, and a hush began to fan out across the room.

"What's the situation at the front entrance?" Ross asked.

"The media presence is pretty significant," Donna said, "and growing larger by the minute."

Ross glanced at the evidence board and continued with his scowling and pacing.

"We're going to have to give them something," he said. "This could get out of hand."

Copies of Saturday's news report were still sitting on some of the desks around the room.

"Get Burly McKinnes back in," Ross went on. "Charge him, and we can issue a statement."

Donna felt a sudden resistance deep in her gut. "I don't want him charged yet," she said. "Not until the evidence is verified."

Ross's eyes grew wide in frustration, and he threw up his hands. "I'm not asking you," he said. "I want him charged. We know he's guilty, and we have to diffuse this situation. Yesterday's hostage mess-up plays right into the public hysteria, and we're too bloody busy dealing with the McKinnes murder inquiry to give proper attention to following it up. Top brass are going to be after our scalps if we don't get some results. We need this. Get him in and charge him."

As if to underscore his words, the door burst open, and Morrison and Akwasi came in, looking shaken.

"What's happened to you two?" Alice called across the room as they approached.

"We've just been to a call-out in Lochee," Morrison said, slightly out of breath and glancing at Akwasi. "Break-in at a newsagents."

"What's the problem?" Donna asked.

"By the time we got there, a bunch of locals had formed a mob," said Akwasi. "They started off giving us lip, then they started throwing stuff at us – sticks, cans, whatever. We called the Support Unit for back-up and they got to us pretty quick – they were in the area already. As soon as they arrived, the mob dispersed and ran off. We gave chase, but they got away."

"Vigilantes?" Ross asked.

Morrison and Akwasi both nodded their heads. Ross turned again to Donna.

"Sounds like a situation that could easily have gotten out of control and placed our officers in danger," he said. "This is exactly the sort of thing I'm talking about, and it's why we need to tell the press we've made an arrest."

Donna knew he was right, and she bit her lip in frustration. They had to act now to calm things before public disorder got out of control. She was going to have to bring Burly in.

"Okay," she conceded, her voice making it clear that she was far from happy about the decision. "But get onto forensics," she said to Fran. "I want those results in today."

"You'll be lucky," Alice muttered, as Fran took herself to the nearest desk and began to make the call. At the same moment, a phone at the far end of the room rang out. The officer closest to it peeled himself from the spot he'd been rooted to. Donna couldn't make out the details of his side of the conversation above the din of activity that had struck up around the room, but the officer caught her eye and beckoned her over.

"Robbie at the mortuary for you, boss," he said, holding out the phone to her. "He sounds wired to the moon."

Donna took the call. She stood listening to Robbie's frantic words, then interrupted him.

"Slow down," she told him. "You're not making any sense."

She saw Alice watching her with an expression of half curiosity and half dread, as Robbie repeated his information.

No, she thought, as she listened, and shook her head in disbelief.

This couldn't be happening. This could *not* be happening.

All eyes were on her now as she ended the call.

"Change of plan," she told Ross.

Ross's face betrayed a moment of worry. "Change of plan, how?" he asked.

Donna tried to compute in her mind what she'd just heard from Robbie. She tried to fathom some sense from it in the hope that it would sound like something they might have dealt with before. But no matter how she weighed it up, this development was a new low in their Jonas Evanton nightmare. This was it, surely: the beginning of his plan.

"Today's just become a whole lot worse," she told her audience. "I'm not quite sure how to tell you this…"

Chapter 20

As soon as Donna relayed the news from Robbie at the mortuary, Ross began to bark orders and the officers in the team room began to spring into action. He pointed at one of the uniformed officers.

"Get on the phone to Arbroath right now," he said. "We need Aiden and DC Cornton to go back over every detail they have from the witnesses at the game, see if anything in there has any bearing on this clusterfuck."

The officer scrambled to the nearest desk and grabbed the phone.

"And while you're on," Ross yelled at his back, "get them to send Sergeant Dexter over to bring us Mo Skinner again. We're going to need her take on this, and quickly."

The officer nodded his acknowledgement while he keyed in the number.

"Alice," Ross pointed a finger at her this time, "take Thomas and get over to Ninewells. Go back over all of the details with Marnie Whyte." Alice and Akwasi nodded to one another and stood up to go. "Press her on that message for Donna to run – try and figure out what on earth it could mean, then meet Dexter and Mo

Skinner, see if she can make any sense of it."

The urgency in Ross's voice acted like a clockwork key, setting off all sorts of activity.

"Fran," he continued, "I want you to go over every detail in the forensics reports. Look for anything – anything – that might resonate with what's just happened."

Fran got to her feet, went straight to a desk and began to boot up the computer on it.

"When you've done that," Ross said to her, "you and Stephen get round door to door. Show people Evanton's photo." Morrison took the cue, and went to fetch the files that contained their target's picture.

Ross scanned the room, looking for suitable candidates for the next task. "Alice, before you speak to Mo, bring Burly McKinnes back in, but forget about charging him for now. Lean on him hard – he must know something about this…"

"I'll take care of Burly," said Donna. The tone in her voice made it clear that there would be no debate. She saw Ross sigh, a quick gesture of impatience, but time wasn't on their side.

He continued, and pointed to two uniformed officers. "You're both on CCTV duty. Look for any movement in or out of the mortuary from the time Robbie and John Ogilvie left yesterday until they got back in this morning."

Normally the task of trawling through CCTV met with some form of resistance, from howls of protest to grumbles of discontent, but Donna saw the relief on the officers' faces that they had some clear task to perform in all of this mess.

Finally, Ross turned to Donna. "You and I are going over to the mortuary." He flicked his eyes towards the armed officers. "And obviously both of you, too."

"What are we going to tell the press?" Donna asked him. "We're going to have to say something when we get out there."

"We'll have to keep it obscure," Ross said. "We're following a positive line of inquiry, or something. You'd better not say anything to them about *this*."

Donna spluttered. "Are you kidding? They're going to crucify us when they find out. It's not going to be me standing in front of them when that happens!"

Fran was quickly updating the information on the evidence board while her computer started up. The details of Archie McKinnes's murder were now centre stage, with the previous day's hostage situation and Marnie Whyte's sinister message playing supporting roles. The news now that Archie McKinnes's body had gone missing from the mortuary left nobody in the room in any doubt that the thug's death formed part of some hideous production directed by Jonas Evanton.

"We need to close this thing down right now!" Ross shouted, as he began to put on his overcoat.

He and Donna hurried out of Bell Street, careful to follow a route that meant they didn't have to pass the news reporters at the front entrance. Relieved that they'd managed to pull it off – *somebody else gets to break the good news to the press*, Donna thought – they got into Ross's car and sped off.

Ross was behind the wheel as they drove along West Marketgait, beginning the short trip to the mortuary at Dow Street. The armed officers followed behind in a separate vehicle.

"How does a body just vanish from a mortuary?" he muttered.

"Evanton was right when he told us we had no idea what was coming," Donna said. "And you know this will only be the beginning, don't you?"

Ross nodded his head. The expression on his face was grim. "We'll work out what he's up to and we will get ahead of him."

"We both know it's revenge against me that he wants," said Donna. "Just let me confront him face to face, before he puts into practice whatever else he's been planning all this time." Immediately she regretted the comment. There was paranoia followed by bravado. It was an uncomfortably familiar pattern. She knew by Ross's silence that he was trying to find a diplomatic way to ask the next question, and she decided to answer it first. "Yes, I have been taking my medication."

She saw Ross steal a quick glance at her, revealing an expression of doubt. There was another moment of silence between them.

Donna took the time to watch him closely. They had trained together all those years ago, starting out as rookie cops together. They'd encountered their first murder scene together, drunk themselves silly together afterwards, and many times since then. She had been his shoulder to cry on when his marriage collapsed. He'd been the first person she had come out to – even before she'd told Natesh. Yet she had hidden her illness from him until recently, fearing his reaction. One of her closest friends.

She bit her lip. She knew her mind was beginning to race, and she realised the signs of problems ahead, and by her usual pattern, her next step would be to think she could take on the world single-handed, ending up in all sorts of high risk behaviours. She wondered briefly if this was really why she was resisting all efforts to charge Burly McKinnes with his father's murder.

She had to trust Ross this time.

"I have been taking my medication," she said quietly. "But I think the shock of eyeballing Evanton the other week might have started a domino effect."

Despite herself, she felt a shudder when she thought about that moment she'd made eye contact with Evanton, who'd been hiding in plain sight and watching them. She thought about how she had put everything into the chase, only to lose him. And *somebody* had told the press about that. Who had done that?

Ross began to slow the car, indicated, and pulled over into a parking area off Hawkhill, bringing Donna out of her thoughts. The vehicle with the armed officers pulled in, too.

He switched off the engine, and turned to look at Donna.

"I wondered about that," he said. "And I'm glad you've told me."

Donna blew out a breath of relief. She wasn't getting the sack today.

"What do we need to do?" Ross asked her.

When Donna caught his eye, she wasn't looking at DCI Ross her boss, but at Angus Ross her friend.

"I'm going to talk it over with Libby tonight," she said.

Ross nodded. "Things are starting to get ugly now," he said. "I'm going to need you to be totally up front with me about how you're coping."

"I will be," said Donna. "And don't worry."

"Good," said Ross. "Well, while we're having a moment, I might as well be up front with you, too." Donna raised an eyebrow. "I'm also really scared about all of this."

Chapter 21

They arrived at the mortuary, where several journalists had already set up camp.

"God, they're everywhere," said Donna, just as the news reporters spotted her and Ross and the two armed officers. She wondered how on earth they'd known to come here already, then she braced herself for the attack of questions.

"What can you tell us about the latest failure to capture Jonas Evanton?"

"Are the public safe?"

"How do you respond to public feeling that the police can't be trusted?"

Donna understood how things must look, but she experienced a shiver of unease at the obvious loss of confidence in the police. This was just the sort of situation that could easily slide into public disorder and leave the gates wide open for all sorts of vigilante groups. She thought about what Morrison and Akwasi had seen. They were going to have to get the lid shut on this quickly, before it turned into chaos.

"We can't comment right now," Ross told the reporters. "But I'll make a statement and answer your questions as soon as we've dealt with our business here."

"How do you explain the disappearance of a body from the mortuary?"

"How are the police going to recover from this series of blunders?"

The barrage continued at their backs as Donna and Ross hurried inside the mortuary. Robbie was hovering by the door of his office, looking anxious as they approached.

"Come in, everyone's here in the office," Robbie's voice said. But his eyes were saying, *help, I'm a pathologist, get me out of here.*

"What do you mean, *everyone?*" Donna asked, with a knot forming in the pit of her stomach.

"The McKinnes family," Robbie said, "they're here. Er, lots of them."

At least that explained why the press were onto this particular story so quickly, Donna thought, relieved that the explanation didn't rely on the information having been leaked from inside the police.

She glanced at Ross, steeling herself now to face the onslaught of the McKinnes clan.

Sure enough, they were all there – every sibling and second cousin twice removed – all dressed in their plead-not-guilty-in-court clothes.

It began the instant the first of them, Archie's brother Dougie, spotted the arrival of the detectives.

"Fucking disgrace, you lot are," bawled Dougie, striding up to Ross and stopping nose to nose in front of him, his chin jutting like a boxer about to throw the first punch. "I'm going to sue the fucking arse off you for this."

"Pay for a nice funeral for Archie, will it?" Donna couldn't hold her tongue.

Dougie rounded on her instantly, but he was so aghast that words failed him. He stood, crimson-faced, mouth opening and closing like a convertible on a Scottish road trip.

"Look, you can stop pretending," said Donna. *In for a penny*, she thought. "We all know you hated Archie just as much as everybody else did…"

"Donna!" Ross hissed.

"Sure, it's a balls-up of monumental proportions," Donna went on as though she hadn't heard him. "I'll give you that. But don't tell me you're not rubbing your greedy bastard hands together thinking about how you can milk this for all it's worth."

"This is outrageous," blustered Dougie.

The remaining McKinnes vultures in the room formed a ring around Dougie and Donna, seeming to be unsure about whether they were defending their kinsman or watching for entertainment, but enjoying it all the same.

Donna caught a snigger escaping from one of them.

"See?" she said, pointing at the culprit, Archie's sister Mhairi. Mhairi, to her credit, did nothing to backtrack, and went on to cackle like the crow she resembled in her faux feather black coat.

"About time the old git was useful for something," Mhairi rasped from a nicotine-ravaged throat.

Another McKinnes sibling – Donna couldn't remember this one's name – took a step forward, tightening the circle to the point of suffocation. Donna's nose wrinkled.

"Did none of you bother to shower this morning?" she said. "Too much of a hurry to get here to make sure you got the most out of this?"

None of the McKinneses seemed in the least bit offended by the insults. Donna was in no doubt that their senses were being drawn to the big pound signs dangling in front of their eyes. She was equally as sure that this would be the first time they'd met together in such a number. There couldn't be a single living relative of Archie McKinnes who hadn't turned up to try and turn the situation into as much cash as possible.

Donna noticed that they all had the same bovine-like eyes as Burly, before realising with a start that the lad wasn't among the gathering. Neither was Agnes.

Robbie cleared his throat and rubbed his hands together briskly, anxious gestures.

"We need to speak to you and Ogilvie," Ross told him. "Alone."

Robbie nodded his head vigorously. "I know, yes, but..." He dropped his voice to a whisper, leaning towards Ross and away from the swarm of McKinneses. "... I can't find him."

"What?"

"I mean, he's in here," said Robbie. "He came into work this morning. It was him that called the alert, but he's been keeping out of the way ever since. Acting weird. But maybe it's the shock, you know…?"

Donna zoned out of the conversation and scanned the room, taking a head count and double checking that neither Burly nor Agnes were there. She caught a movement just outside the office door, a tuft of blond hair. She dashed towards it, and made it out into the corridor in time to see Ogilvie's back vanish around a corner.

"John!" she called. And again, "John! I need to talk to you to figure out how…"

But Ogilvie was gone. He had heard her, she was sure, and had chosen to ignore her.

Donna frowned. None of this was right. Quite apart from a body going missing from the mortuary, Ogilvie's behaviour was sending red alerts through her head. Was it possible that he knew something about how this had happened? She was about to set off after him, when Ross appeared at her side.

"You need to get up to Clatto," he said to her, referring to the city's reservoir. "Agnes McKinnes has just been pulled out of the water."

Chapter 22

Donna fastened her jacket as she ran from the mortuary. She barely registered the journalists with their sudden barrage of questions, or the armed officers, concentrating on keeping down the urge to vomit.

Press cameras flashed, capturing her almost tumbling as her boots slid on the icy pavement, but she kept on running, and threw herself into the driver's seat of Ross's car.

Taking a quick scan over its unfamiliar controls, she fired the engine, and pressed the accelerator to the floor. The car took off with a screech of wheels, and she hit the blues and twos button, filling the air with the sudden noise of the siren.

Heading towards the reservoir, she sped through the city's streets,

...back along Hawkhill Road, where she'd stopped earlier with Ross,

...taking a right onto Blackness Avenue,

...up across Scott Street, where Natesh was still camping out at his mum's until he got something sorted with Erin, *or until he moves in with us*,

...cursing as she hit road works and a tailback on City Road, and

...hitting the accelerator hard until the reservoir finally came into view,

a mantra of *Agnes, be alright, please be alright* running in a loop through her mind during the twenty minute drive.

As she approached the reservoir, she craned her neck and saw, just through the trees, a series of flashing blue lights and made her way towards them.

She left Ross's car pulled into a grassy verge near a pontoon with its *Keep off the Ice* sign, and ran towards the nearest ambulance. A huddle of people were sitting beside it. Two paramedics were hunkered down next to a slight figure who was wrapped in a silver blanket. From within the blanket, Agnes's eyes locked onto Donna's.

She quickly showed her warrant card to the paramedics and introduced herself.

"She's been insisting on only speaking to you," one of them told her, looking relieved.

"Oh, thank God she's alive," said Donna, as she knelt down beside Agnes. She placed an arm around Agnes's shoulder, and could feel the older woman's body shudder. Partly from the cold, she reckoned, and the rest from shock. But at least she was alive.

"What happened?" Donna whispered to her. She saw from the corner of her eye that the paramedics were opening up the rear of the ambulance, ready to take Agnes in. She was alive, Donna conceded, but she had almost drowned, and she wasn't long out of water that was barely at 10 degrees Celsius, and certainly in the life threatening category. Agnes's breathing was laboured and irregular, and punctuated by a series of coughing fits.

"We need to take her in," one of the paramedics urged Donna. He lowered his voice and continued, "She's aspirated quite a bit of water. We need to get her on oxygen as quickly as possible."

Donna made to move away to allow the paramedics space to get Agnes securely onto a stretcher, but Agnes suddenly grabbed at her arm.

"You said he was dead," Agnes said to her. Her voice was racked by sobs and her teeth were chattering. She began to cough again.

Donna pushed a strand of wet hair out of the way of Agnes's eyes. "He *is* dead," she said.

Agnes shook her head, fear stealing her reason.

"He's dead," said Donna.

"But he's gone," said Agnes. "How can he have gotten out? He can't be dead."

"His body's been stolen," said Donna, quite convinced that she knew by whom. "We're investigating right now, but we're fairly sure we know who's behind it. You need to trust me Agnes. He's dead. He can never hurt you again."

Agnes's eyes grew wide, the pleading in them obvious, desperate to believe Donna's words. "Why would someone want to steal a dead body?" she sobbed. "Is that what you're saying?"

Donna nodded her head, *yes*. "We think it's related to yesterday's hostage situation – you'll have heard about that in the news? But you can't tell anybody that I told you that. Do you understand?"

Tears sprouted from Agnes's eyes, and she covered her face with both shaking hands, and bawled away her terror. Donna waited until she sensed the return of calm.

"Come on," she said, easing Agnes up from the ground, "let's get you into this ambulance so we can get you a proper check-up, eh?"

At that, two of the paramedics shot forward and caught Agnes's elbows, leading her into the stretcher, keeping up a banter of cheery quips as they did so. They deftly strapped her in, made sure she was properly wrapped up, and levered her into the ambulance, where they placed an oxygen mask over her mouth.

"I'll sit with her," Donna said, and the paramedics acknowledged with words of accord. Outside the ambulance doors, Donna could see the Fire and Rescue boat being hauled back onto the shore. The other attending ambulance wheeled around and made its way back towards the city.

Donna turned to Agnes and took her hand. "So, you were going to drown yourself?"

Agnes looked miserable and nodded her head, averting her gaze.

"Don't be ashamed, Agnes," Donna said. "You've nothing to be ashamed of. But I am puzzled about one thing."

Agnes looked at her, waiting to hear what Donna had to ask.

"The call came in because you were shouting for help," Donna said. "What was it that changed your mind?"

Agnes made a self-mocking sound. Donna was aware that the paramedics and the armed officers were by the ambulance doors and were tuned in and listening now.

"I can't swim," Agnes answered miserably.

Chapter 23

Donna was drained by the time the ambulance dropped her off at Bell Street on its way back out to a call. She'd seen Agnes settled into the hospital, and phoned Burly to let him know where his mother was. Sure, he'd killed his father, she mused as she made her way inside the office complex, but there was something about Burly she liked. He was a decent kid, deep down, who'd fought against the odds and turned out not bad. Except for the murder, of course. Donna found herself back inside her turmoil over how to really distinguish right from wrong. It just wasn't always as simple as she'd like it to be, which wasn't a particularly great thought for a police officer.

As she passed by rooms full of officers and support staff, she felt an urge for nicotine, but really couldn't be bothered going back outside. It had been another difficult day, and there would be no let up. Mo Skinner was coming back in, and they were going to have to make some progress.

Donna heard it before she got through the team room door. The sound of the raucous chatter and laughter of a whole lot of police officers.

"I heard she changed her mind because she couldn't swim!"

More laughter.

She could barely believe her eyes, when she looked inside and saw an officer floundering around on the floor, flailing his arms in the air, mimicking a drowning soul.

A flash of anger propelled her into the room.

"You think it's fucking funny, do you?" she yelled at them.

The room crashed into an abrupt silence. The officer on the floor scrambled, ungainly, to his feet.

Donna stared at him, and raged on to the room in general. "A woman who's spent her entire adult life terrorised at the hands of that brute of a husband of hers. She finally gets a break, only to think he's risen from the dead. Have you any idea how terrified she is right now?"

She glared at each of them in turn.

All of them cast their eyes to the floor. The drownee impersonator had already been disowned by his colleagues.

"Well, have you?" Donna rounded on them, advancing into the room. They all shrank back towards the walls. Donna went on, "And she finally snaps. Makes the one decision she feels she can, thinks it's the only choice left open to her, and she can't even follow through on that. Can you even begin to imagine what a worthless piece of shit she thinks she is? And you lot think it's okay to take the piss?"

"Whoa there," Alice stepped out from amongst the officers and came to Donna. "Everyone in here is at breaking point. None of us has been in a situation like this before, and we've no idea what to expect next. The guys were just letting off steam. Cop humour

84

as a way to cope, you know that, chief."

"Not this time, Alice," said Donna, refusing to soften her tone. "Not this time."

She marched to the evidence board. Alice kept by her side, and gradually a low murmur of conversation began to strike up around the large office, muted in comparison to what Donna had encountered when she'd arrived. There was no sign of the officer who'd been on the floor.

Standing with her back to the room, Donna closed her eyes and took a deep breath.

"Sorry, I didn't mean to snap," she said to Alice. "It's just that Agnes McKinnes has been put down so much for so long, I'm not going to have her diminished by us, too."

"I get it," said Alice, meeting her eye. "But you're tight as a spring right now, which I understand. God knows, we all are. But you need to keep it steady." She flicked her thumb towards the melee of officers behind them. "They need someone calm in charge, now more than ever."

Donna took a deep breath. "You're right," she said. "You always bloody are." She clapped Alice's shoulder, glad to have the General by her side. She had a sudden flashback to those moments, only a few weeks ago, when they were both crouched in the bushes in rural Turkey and looking into the wrong end of a pair of assault rifles. How she thought she'd lost Alice in the gunfire that had followed. Surely what they'd been through then had been worse than this? Though, admittedly it was a close call. But they would get through it. Together, they would get through it.

Side by side they stood looking at the details on the evidence board.

"Marnie Whyte's been discharged from hospital now," Alice said. "We went to speak to her at home, but she had nothing more to add to what she already told us yesterday."

"And Mo Skinner, is she here yet?" asked Donna.

"Expecting her in any time about now," said Alice, glancing at her watch. "Scott Dexter phoned about half an hour ago to say they were on their way here."

"Good," said Donna. "If there's anyone's insight we need right now, it's hers."

Alice nodded her head in agreement, and continued her update. "It's early days with the CCTV trawl, and Fran managed to get a peek at the initial forensics reports, but there's nothing there to suggest anything other than Burly McKinnes killing his father. No hint that Evanton could be involved at all."

"That's Mo Skinner here now," a voice called from the door, making them both turn around.

"Alright, Sergeant Moone," Donna said to Alice, "let's go and see what Mo has to make of recent developments."

She and Alice and the two armed officers strode off after the officer who was waiting to take them to Mo.

Chapter 24

This time they met in Ross's office, since he was still over at the morgue. When they got there, Donna was surprised to find Mo pacing across the floor of the small office and looking anxious. Once they were all inside, Donna closed the door and she, Alice and Mo sat down in the only available seats. The armed officers took up positions that allowed them to keep an eye on both the door and the office window.

"Sergeant Dexter's filled you in?" Donna asked Mo.

Mo nodded her head. "The message via Marnie Whyte, and the body being stolen from the mortuary, yes."

Donna held up her hands in frustration. "I know there's nothing in the way of evidence to suggest Evanton had anything to do with the body, but what do you think?"

"It's certainly a bizarre and unexpected thing to happen," said Mo, "and not your run of the mill murder investigation, I'm sure."

"Last time we spoke, you said you thought he was trying to control us," said Alice.

"Well, look at the pattern," said Mo. "A bogus hostage situation that uses up all of your resources. News that Evanton has escaped again, making the police look incompetent. The message to run, which places even more strain on your resources." She indicated to the two armed officers and went on. "The body stolen from the morgue, using up your resources at the same time as making you look incompetent."

"He's taking control by making us lose control," said Donna.

"I would say so," said Mo. "And it could get a whole lot worse."

"Could it?" spluttered Alice.

"It could if one more incident happens and there's enough loss of confidence in the police for public disorder to break out," said Mo.

"You're right," said Donna. "There are already signs of that starting to happen. How the hell can we second guess him to stop another incident? What could he do next?"

Mo shook her head sadly. "There's no way to tell," she said. "But you can be sure he'll make some sort of demand on the back of it – I would say you'd be better to try and work out what he might want, and how you'll respond to that."

"Then, we need to be ready for anything to happen," said Alice.

"We do," said Donna. "But Mo's right. We need to figure out what it is he wants. He's been on the run all this time. Obviously with help on the inside, but surely he must be wanting some kind of immunity from prosecution, a safe passage to somewhere with no extradition treaty?"

"Sounds plausible," said Mo. "He won't be coping well with the idea of being hunted or cornered, so bargaining for his freedom sounds about right."

"He murdered two of our colleagues," Alice said, her voice a low growl.

"Yeah, there's no way he's going to get any of that," said Donna. "If that's his game, there's no way we can give into him."

"But then, where's it going to end?" asked Alice. "How much more can we sustain if we don't bargain with him?"

"Over my dead body," said Donna.

The room fell into silence.

Donna studied Mo closely for several seconds. Mo's eyes were cast to the ground. "Is it true to say you're the only person he ever loved?"

Mo shifted uncomfortably at Donna's question. "We were close at one point," she said eventually, keeping her gaze down. "And, as I think I told you before, we kept in touch after what happened in Bhopal." Her eyes closed momentarily. "He confided in me over the years."

"What was your relationship like with him after Bhopal?" Donna pressed, sensing something in Mo's avoidance gestures. Was she hiding something?

"He confided in me over the years."

"I thought so," said Donna, leaning back.

Mo looked up at her suddenly, an expression close to alarm.

"What are you missing out of that story?"

"What do you mean?" Mo demanded, a little too quickly.

"You used an identical phrase both times I asked the question," said Donna. "Usually that means the answer's rehearsed, so you don't let slip the truth."

Mo looked horrified.

"This is serious now, Mo," said Donna. "If Evanton keeps on going with this campaign of his, who knows how many lives will be at risk? We have to stop it right now. What have you got that can help us? I can tell there's something."

Mo sighed in resignation, and met Donna's eye. "You must promise me that this information will never get into the public domain," she said. "And Bob must never find out."

"You have my word," said Donna.

Mo's attention shifted to Alice.

"I know nothing," Alice said, placing her hands over her ears with a dramatic flourish.

There was a long silence, all eyes on Mo, before the lawyer cleared her throat and began to speak.

"Bob and I got married not long after I returned from Bhopal," she said. Her eyes closed again as she spoke, no doubt re-living some of the horror of the toxic gas disaster. "But we spent a lot of time apart in the early years. I had a couple of long term cases that I was involved in over in the States, Bob was in London a lot, getting his political career off the ground. So I guess it was more of a long distance relationship for, oh, five years or thereabouts."

Donna and Alice exchanged a glance. Enough for an understanding that they both had an inkling as to what was coming next, but didn't quite want to believe it.

"During that time," Mo went on, "I met with Jonas fairly regularly. We talked a lot about Bhopal, obviously. He was really disturbed, and I was sure it was about more that the gas accident itself. I'm convinced he was troubled by something that he himself had done during the disaster, like I've said to you before."

Donna nodded an encouragement to continue. Mo did so.

"He was needy, and I guess I used that to try and prise the information from him, but he wouldn't tell me. To be honest, though, there were times when I enjoyed his company. It could be lonely, working all the long hours so far from home."

Mo's voice had dropped to a whisper now, and Donna had to pay close attention just to catch the words.

"The second time I went out to the States," said Mo, "Jonas flew out to meet me. He stayed with me in my apartment. I won't go into the details – I'm ashamed enough – but…but a few weeks after I got back home, I discovered I was pregnant."

Donna and Alice both drew in sharp breaths. The armed guards remained impassive, continuing to watch the door and the window.

"When I was pretty sure I was beginning to show," Mo said, "I told Bob I was going out to the States again for a few months. He didn't think anything of it, it was just how our lives were at that time. Anyway, I didn't go to the States. I went down south for several months, had the baby, and… and…" At this point Mo's voice began to waver, and she wiped a tear from her eye. "And I gave her up for adoption. A baby girl."

Mo dissolved into tears. Donna drew closer to her and placed an arm around her shoulder.

"Mo," Donna whispered to her. "Does Evanton know anything about the baby?"

"No," Mo said through muffled sobs. She shook her head. "Nobody knows. Not until now, only you."

"Okay," Donna said, her tone soft. "This is really important information you've given us. I know it took a lot for you to tell us, and I'm going to ask you to trust me now."

Mo nodded her head.

"I'm going to ask my DC to try and trace your daughter," said Donna. She felt Mo stiffen, resisting the idea. "Trust me. Fran is the best person for this, and she'll be discreet. We're going to have to find your daughter – this might be our one bargaining chip with Evanton. But I need to clarify something with you."

Mo looked at Donna, her expression partly fear and partly confusion.

"When we find your daughter," said Donna, "do you want us to tell you? Or to give her your details?"

"I don't know," Mo said, after a long pause. "I'm going to need some time to think about it. I wasn't expecting to have this discussion."

"I understand," said Donna. "I'm going to go and speak to Fran now. You understand we have to move quickly on this?"

"Yes, of course," Mo sniffled. She tried to smile at Donna, and began to weep again.

Donna stood up and left the room. She made her way back to the team room, followed in silence by the two armed officers. *Mo Skinner had Evanton's child*, she thought. Her heart was beating quickly, trying to keep up with her racing thoughts. There must be a way for this to work. She found Fran at a desk, tapping away furiously at a computer keyboard, and decided she didn't have time to wait for Ross to get back from the morgue to discuss Mo's news with him – they had to act on this right away.

"A word." She nodded Fran to a corner of the room.

Having whispered the bare details to her DC and watched her nod solemnly at the need for absolute silence on the matter, Donna then found herself troubled by another thought. Mo and Evanton had history together, a complicated one. Donna couldn't be sure where Mo's loyalties might lie if push came to shove, and she wouldn't blame her either if she picked the wrong side. Mo had obviously not planned to reveal the information about her daughter today, and Donna knew more than anyone what an unexpected emotional upset could do to a person. She had to be ready with a secret weapon of her own, an *insurance policy* in the event of losing Mo, and she knew what that had to be.

Chapter 25

The Monday evening rush hour traffic had long since died down by the time Donna managed to get home.

Turning onto Claypotts Place, she felt an odd sensation on seeing the *For Sale* sign standing in front of the house.

Happy and sad.

This house had witnessed her happiest times, when she'd moved in with Libby. It had also witnessed her worst times, when Libby had kicked her out. The shame of it now, how she'd hurt Libby for the sake of a drunken quickie, burned into her chest.

She shook the thoughts away. This was going to give them a fresh start, she thought. The house move would let them finally draw a line under those awful days and enter into the next phase of their lives together. Although, she knew, her job was going to take one final toll on them before that could become a reality.

It was only Monday, she mused, and already the weekend's disasters had gotten worse now that Archie McKinnes's body was missing and Agnes had tried to drown herself. She knew that she was going to have to give her all – and more – to finally bring Jonas Evanton in. She couldn't, under any circumstances, let this go now, and she felt the stab of fear for what might lie ahead and what it might all mean for her and Libby.

She sighed in frustration, glancing over her shoulder at the car that was sitting just behind hers. Things were so bad she even had to have armed protection. Her gullet burned.

A wave of exhaustion swept over her, then she saw Libby appear at the window and wave to her. She blinked away a tear. What the hell was she going to tell Libby this time?

She gathered up her stuff, and went inside.

"Please tell me you had a better day today," said Libby, a worried frown creasing her forehead as she brought cups of tea into the living room.

"Not exactly," said Donna.

Libby turned down the volume on the TV, and waited for Donna to go on. Donna blew onto her tea.

"They pulled Agnes McKinnes out of the Clatto reservoir this afternoon," she said. Libby held onto her arm. "I drove out there, not knowing if she was dead or alive." She took a sip of tea. "She's alive, but still at risk of secondary drowning over the next couple of days, apparently."

"What happened?" Libby asked.

"Well, you know about the body being stolen from the mortuary?"

"Saw that on Twitter," Libby confirmed.

"Agnes thought it must mean he wasn't actually dead, so she tried to drown herself."

"My God." Libby's voice was a whisper now. "How do you keep going in this job?"

"I don't think I can," said Donna. "Evanton is behind this, I'm certain. And we know he has some plan of revenge he's just about to unleash, but I'm going to stop him. And once it's over, I'm handing in my badge."

"Any ideas how you're going to stop him?"

"Actually," said Donna, turning to meet Libby's eye, "tell me what you think about this. It's totally confidential, though. You can't tell anyone."

92

"I never do," said Libby. Donna knew she was right.

"We spoke to Mo Skinner again today, and you'll never believe this, but she had a baby – to Jonas Evanton – back in the '80s. Gave her up for adoption."

Libby sat up with a start. "You've got to be kidding!"

"I've asked Fran to see what she can find out by way of tracing her," said Donna. "Evanton doesn't know he has a daughter. That's got to be worth something, doesn't it?"

Libby held up her mug and they clinked in a toast. "It definitely gives you a card to play."

Donna mulled this over. It did feel like a turning point in their favour at last, she thought, and she and Libby continued to chat on into the night.

Blood runs cold
Tuesday
Chapter 26

"We're going to need a bigger evidence board," said Donna. Alice was standing by her side. Fran stood at the other end of the evidence board, watching Donna closely.

The team room was packed on this Tuesday morning, a hive of nervous activity.

"And a bigger police force," said Alice.

Extra desks had been crammed into the room, Donna noted, and at each one, a pair of uniformed officers sat diligently working their way through the sets of tasks they'd been given.

Police officers, uniformed and detectives alike, stood in all of the spaces in between the desks, some chatting and some scanning the room. Morrison and Akwasi were amongst them.

Phones rang seemingly continuously. Every centimetre of available floor space was taken.

The pressure was on today, with a press conference to be held later that morning. They were going to have to provide some plausible answers, Donna realised, if they weren't to see a repeat – or worse – of what had happened to Morrison and Akwasi the day before.

Then Ross walked into the room, looking flustered. "I don't want to see any newspapers in here today," he announced straight away.

Donna and Alice glanced at one another.

There was a sudden rustling of paper and desk drawers closing around the room.

Ross went on, "We already know we'll be getting a doing, and to be frank, we probably deserve it this time. A fucking body stolen from the mortuary! I mean, for fuck's sake!"

"We've a call out for John Ogilvie," Alice confirmed. "Feels weird to be saying that, but he wasn't returning our calls yesterday, and seemingly he's been making himself scarce at the mortuary, so we're doing it the formal way."

Donna could barely believe it had come to this – a call out for the pathologist's arrest. But she knew it was the right decision. He must have known something about this, and his behaviour yesterday certainly fit with that.

"And now for the bad news," Ross continued. There were groans around the room as the officers waited to hear what could possibly be coming next.

"ACC Loudoun will be here in fifteen minutes," he said. He spoke in a raised and rapid voice to everyone assembled, but kept his eye on Donna. "And it's not a social visit. So, what do we have for him?"

"Local thug axed through the skull," said Donna. "Queue a mile long of willing suspects, but most likely the son. Police resources needed elsewhere…"

"Right, we get the picture," said Ross. "How about any developments ACC Loudoun will be interested in?"

"There haven't been any reported sightings of Evanton overnight," said Donna. "He arranged for Marnie Whyte, the hostage, to deliver a message to me personally. Just the one word: *Run*. Confirms Evanton is involved, and that this is a personal vendetta. And because we know he's active, we also need to go with the theory he's had something to do with the body going missing."

She quickly glanced around the room and confirmed none of the other officers had anything more to add. "We'll be going back to interview Marnie Whyte later on this morning to see if we can glean any further details from her."

"Anything from your meeting with Mo Skinner yesterday?" Ross asked.

Alice cast her gaze to the floor, and Fran's cheeks flushed. Donna said, "Nothing that takes us any further forward." There was no way she was going to divulge the information about Mo's daughter in front of so many officers. Enough information was leaking out of this place. If they could use the fact that Evanton had a daughter, then she wasn't going to risk that news getting out. She would have a quiet word about it with Ross later on, in private.

"Right," said Ross, looking around the room. "Get the evidence board up to date, and tidy this place up."

There was a flurry of activity, while officers straightened up the desks and got back to the tasks they'd been doing before Ross had come in. Fran set to work on the evidence board.

There was a brief silence in the room, enough to make everyone jump when the door crashed open.

ACC Loudoun strode in, adorned in full regalia, eyes blazing. Without any preliminaries he raged, "You're the same team that let him escape the first time, the second time, and now the fucking third time!"

"To be fair, it was Belmarsh prison that let him go the first time," Donna heard Alice mutter.

ACC Loudoun didn't seem to hear, and without pausing for breath, he marched into Ross's personal space, and almost knocked the Highlander over. Thrusting his chin into Ross's face, he bellowed, "I'm having you replaced, Ross. I'm sending you up to Aberdeen to work under DCI Sherbrooke. You're booked onto the 10.33 train tomorrow morning. Make sure you're on it."

Ross blanched but said nothing.

"Do you really think this is the best time to be bringing a new DCI in here?" Donna couldn't stop the words spilling out of her mouth. Ross shot her a look that said *shut up*. It was humiliating enough to be sent to report to an officer of the same grade as himself, Donna realised, too late. A demotion in all but salary. He didn't need one of his own officers trying to stand up for him.

Loudoun rounded on Donna. The ACC was a good head taller than her, and even she felt small next to his broad, muscular frame. He seemed to fill the entire room, making the other officers shrink back to the walls.

Loudoun's face was fuschia, making his short golden hair gleam as though there should be a matching halo and wings.

"Enlighten us," he yelled into Donna's face. "Go on. Just what is it that you lot here in Bell Street have to be proud of?" He stopped abruptly, as though startled by something, and Donna suddenly became aware that she was staring intently at his hair. She saw him subconsciously pat his crowning glory with the briefest of hand gestures, and she silently chuckled at the vanity it betrayed. After the microsecond's falter, he went on yelling. "What the hell have you lot been playing at, letting Jonas Evanton run rings around you? Think yourselves lucky you still all have jobs. If we weren't so bloody short staffed…"

Donna made a display of flicking the spittle from her face, drawing a look of horror from Loudoun. Then she squared up to him.

The room was completely silent, and she wondered if any of her colleagues were still breathing.

"You've no idea what we're up against with Evanton," she said.

Loudoun looked startled, but quickly recovered himself.

"You're talking your way to a disciplinary," he growled. Donna flinched at the sour smell of his breath in her face. As she opened her mouth to answer back, she felt Alice's hand on her arm.

"Don't," whispered Alice. Donna caught her eye, and backed off.

Loudoun turned his back on them both, and addressed the room at large. "I want to see some real progress by the end of today. And Ross, 10.33 tomorrow morning, and report directly to DCI Sherbrooke as soon as you arrive in Aberdeen. Do you think you can manage that?"

Then, with no warning, he strode from the room.

Ross walked out at his back, and Donna took charge of the room. Leaving the uniformed officers to go back to their desk work, she addressed those who were left standing.

"Let's take it from the top," she said, pointing to the evidence board in front of them. Gradually the chatting ceased, except for the hum of low voices at the desks, and all eyes moved to focus on the list of details written on the evidence board.

Staring back at them was the evolution of chaos. It was bad enough when the investigation had consisted of the hunt for Jonas Evanton and tracking down the illegal adoptions. Then had come the murder of Archie McKinnes, seemingly unrelated until his body had gone missing from the mortuary yesterday. And, of course, Sunday's hostage situation – a terrified woman, Marnie Whyte, ordered to give bogus updates about being held in a flat at gunpoint by a man meeting Evanton's description. The press covering every step, and not unreasonably holding the police responsible for the growing lack of trust in public safety.

She pondered the information in front of her. She had already spoken in confidence to Fran about tracing Mo Skinner's daughter. Fran had understood the sensitivity of the matter, and now she and Donna shared a glance. That part of the jigsaw was not going up on the evidence board, they both understood.

"Our priority is to find Archie McKinnes's body," said Donna, hardly able to believe the words she was saying. "We need to restore public confidence. We also need to keep some kind of focus on the illegal adoptions. People are still coming forward. Fran, I want you to concentrate on that over the next few days."

There were more than a few raised eyebrows in the room at this order, and at Fran's instant agreement with it.

"Boss, surely we need to throw everything we've got at finding Jonas Evanton?" asked Akwasi.

"Trust me," said Donna, turning to him. "We are." She acknowledged Akwasi's nod of deference, and went on. "Now, you all have your tasks. I want everyone back here at one for a full briefing."

Ross came back into the room, stopping near the door. Donna hoped he felt more ready than she did for their next meeting with the journalists. She nodded to him. "I hope you've thought of a good line to throw at this press conference."

"Come on," he said to her, looking less terse than he had done earlier. "What's fifteen minutes of hell between friends?"

Donna and Ross left the team room and made their way to the media room for a press conference that was bound to be lively. She decided it would be best to wait until after that to talk to Ross about Mo Skinner's revelation.

Chapter 27

Fran watched Donna and Ross leave the room, and decided now would be a good time to do it. She tried to make discreet eye contact with Alice, but the sergeant was chatting to a couple of officers, pouring over some list or other that seemed to need checking.

She walked out of the team room, without attracting any attention from her colleagues, and made her way to the nearby Quiet Room, a room she had chosen on purpose because hardly anyone used it on account of its lack of internet connection or phone signal. She checked again that nobody was looking, went inside and closed the door behind her.

Donna had impressed upon her the importance of keeping this part of the investigation top secret. And she had to find some way of re-gaining the DI's confidence in her. She'd slipped up one too many times, and she knew she was lucky to still have her job. She wasn't going to botch this one up.

The only pieces of information she had was the town where Mo's daughter was born – Peterborough – and the date of birth. She sat at the bare desk that was furnished with nothing but an old landline phone that had definitely seen better days. The Quiet Room had missed out on the upgrades that the other offices in the building had seen, although nobody really knew if that had been deliberate or not. Right now, for this task, it suited Fran just fine.

She took one deep breath, and brought out her notebook where she'd jotted the contact details at Peterborough Children's Social Care, then lifted the receiver on the old phone and dialled. Surprisingly, she found herself speaking to someone who thought they could help after only one transfer, and did her best to be succinct about the information she needed.

> *Police Scotland.*
> *Trying to trace adopted baby.*
> *1980s.*
> *Yes, tricky.*
> *Murder investigation.*

(Don't mention the mess we're in).
That would be really helpful.

And now there was little else for Fran to do but to wait.

She looked around the small office, but found little of interest on its sparse walls. The odd poster with faded information about one long forgotten initiative or another.

She delved into her bag and retrieved the notes she'd begun to pull together from yesterday's door to doors in relation to the disappearance of Archie McKinnes's body from the mortuary, but found her ability to concentrate was close to zero. What she did think about, though, was the level of hostility they'd received from almost everyone they had spoken to. She hadn't been a cop for all that long, but she had never experienced an atmosphere like this, and she was no longer in any doubt about Donna and Ross's fears over public disorder.

She jumped when the desk phone rang, not expecting a response so soon, and could scarcely conceal her excitement when the woman from Peterborough spoke.

"You say it's part of a murder investigation?" the woman asked. There was a tone in her voice, which Fran couldn't quite place. Was it anxiety, she wondered?

"We're running a very complex murder investigation, yes," Fran said. "We have some vital information related to the baby's…er …birth father. And mother. Like I said, it's a complex investigation, and we have reason to believe that tracing the baby will help us with our inquiries." Fran chewed her lip, knowing that she sounded unconvincing.

The woman chuckled on the other end of the phone, a breathless chuckle that definitely came from anxiety. "The baby is now a 32-year old woman. But let me tell you what's very strange…"

Fran listened with a growing sense of unease as the caller from Peterborough continued. Donna was definitely going to be interested in this.

"Could you give me her details?" Fran asked, already knowing what the response was going to be. "It's really important…."

"I understand," said the woman, "but we can't give those details out. If you were to tell us about the birth parents…?"

"I can't do that," said Fran, feeling a burning sense of frustration creep up her neck. "This is a murder investigation…"

The woman hesitated on the line. "Look, I want to help," she said. Her voice dropped to almost a whisper. "And, as you say, it's a murder investigation, and, well…" There was another, longer pause. "It's going to take a while before the necessary paperwork goes through that would allow us to release her details, so…can I have your word that you won't let anyone know you've spoken to me?"

"I'll keep you totally out of it," said Fran. Her hand was shaking with excitement as she poised her pen over a notebook, ready to record whatever details the caller was about to divulge.

"I could lose my job," the woman whispered.

"You won't be named," said Fran. "And believe me, you could be saving a lot of lives here."

"She's called Sarah Cooper," said the woman. "That's her married name now. She married into the Gypsy Traveller community, living on a site in Wales."

"Thank you," said Fran, her heart racing impossibly fast. She took down the details of the site in Wales, reassured the woman again, and hung up.

Fran could feel her nerves tingling with excitement. She hoped the press conference would be over soon and that she could persuade Donna that a trip to Cardiff wouldn't stretch their pitiful budget too far.

Chapter 28

Donna and Ross stood at the front of the room full of journalists. The mood was hostile. Even Donna's presence didn't stifle it. And to make matters worse, the McKinnes clan – minus Agnes and Burly – were gathered like a pack of slathering hyenas right in the middle of the room. Donna wondered which journalist they'd managed to talk into bringing them here. She also marvelled that they had managed to get from the mortuary yesterday to here today without killing each other. Still, she thought with some cynicism, if they thought there was a big fat compensation payout in it for them…

Ross glanced at Donna, then stood up and cleared his throat.

"Thank you all for coming this morning," he said, and the noise in the room began to settle. "We'd like to update you on a number of strands in our current investigation, then we'll answer any questions you have for us. We're in a very difficult situation at the moment, as you'll appreciate, and it's important that we all work together."

There was a buzz of voices, the pitching of questions, but Ross talked over them.

"First of all, our main priority is the hunt for former Detective Inspector Jonas Evanton," he continued. "We can confirm that he was responsible for the hostage situation in Arbroath on Sunday. Although we believe he wasn't present with the hostage, but rather he enlisted the help of a third party who issued the hostage with instructions."

"Are you saying that Jonas Evanton is working with a gang?"

"Does he have inside help in the Police?"

"Did he murder Archie McKinnes?"

Ross turned his attention to the journalist who'd asked the last question. "No, we are following a positive line of inquiry on that. But, since you raised it, we do believe Evanton is behind the disappearance of Mr McKinnes's body."

There was a palpable collective shudder of disgust amongst the journalists.

"Isn't it fair to say the police are no longer in control of this situation?"

"Haven't you lost all credibility now?"

One of the McKinneses stepped forward, gloating in this moment. "We will be raising a law suit against Police Scotland for substantial damages…"

"How much will you be seeking?"

102

"How is the family coping with the disappearance of Archie's body?"

Ross scowled, and raised his voice, bringing the focus back on to the investigation. "We have reason to believe that Jonas Evanton remains in the area, and we are receiving assistance from sources close to him that is allowing us to close in on him."

"Who are your sources?"

Who are your *sources?* Donna caught herself wondering, as an image of Lindsey Forsyth's Weekend Special popped into her head.

"How will the police be able to restore public order?" the shouting continued.

"Is it true that a vigilante group attacked two police officers yesterday?"

"Feck, it's like herding ferrets," Donna muttered, and she caught the glance from the corner of Ross's eye. She stood up, and despite Ross's expression of growing alarm, began to speak to the journalists.

"Look," she began.

The journalists' curiosity got the better of them. DI Davenport was notoriously unpredictable, and she soon had their full attention.

"Jonas Evanton is out there."

Silence in the room.

"Don't forget how, two years ago, he was going to commit mass murder by releasing one of the most deadly toxins we know of. He killed two of our fellow officers. Men that I counted as friends. Ever since then, he's been watching us, planning his revenge in meticulous detail. Just three weeks ago I made eye contact with him. Right here in Bell Street."

Breaths being held.

"And now he's putting his plan into practice. It's started. Don't be under any illusion. We are dealing with a psychopath who will stop at nothing to get what he wants. And he has detailed inside knowledge of how we work here in the Police."

If a pin were to drop, it would sound like an explosion.

Pencils scratching furiously on notepads.

Donna went on. "I'm not being melodramatic, here, when I say we're fighting a war. The enemy is well hidden, well protected, and well resourced. But do you know what his biggest weapon is?"

All eyes on her.

She pointed a finger towards the staring reporters. "It's you guys. He's using you to create panic. He's manipulating *you*. So, I say it's time for us to work together and put an end to his plans. Jonas Evanton belongs behind bars, for all of our sakes, and we really need you to work with us. Now, can we do that?"

There was a racket of voices in response, but this time they were on Donna's side, and as the McKinneses gradually tapered out of the room, the atmosphere settled into a business-like dialogue where co-operation was the top of the agenda.

They remained in the room for another hour. Agreements were struck, and protocols drawn up for the new relationship between the police and the press. Ross couldn't stop the grin from spreading across his face as he and Donna left the press room.

"One day you will get a medal," he said. "Now I think we really do have a chance of stopping him."

Before Donna could answer, Fran came hurrying towards them. "Ma'am," she said, and glanced furtively at Ross, "I've got some information on the… er… adoptions."

"Right, you two catch up and phone me later on with a briefing," said Ross. "I've a bag to pack for my trip to Aberdeen. The *10.33 tomorrow morning*, if I'm not mistaken," faking Loudoun's voice and wiggling his eyebrows. He waved to them both as he left.

As soon as he was out of earshot, Fran hissed to Donna, "I have her contact details…"

"Already?"

"She's in this up to her neck, wait till you hear this…"

Just then, Donna's phone rang. There was no caller ID. And she just had a feeling.

"Can you give me a minute?" she dismissed Fran, noting the disappointment on the young DC's face. Donna hurried to a quiet corner and took the call, but said nothing. There was silence for a few seconds, then a man's voice, one she recognised straight away.

It made her stomach turn to ice.

"I'm going to phone you again in one hour," he said. "You're going to be sitting comfortably, all alone, and you're not going to tell anybody. Not your colleagues, and not the journalists you've just been buttering up." The call ended.

Chapter 29

Donna froze. She looked all around, and saw no sign amongst the general buzz that was doing on of anyone that could have been Evanton. How did he know about the press conference? She had only just stepped out of it. She felt claustrophobic all of a sudden, her heart racing, and more than anything she wanted to be at home.

Home, she thought with a start. That was exactly where she would go to take this phone call. Ignoring the calls for her attention, she hurried out to her car, hit the accelerator, and made the drive in a little over ten minutes, paying no heed to the stares from other drivers and the occasional peep of a horn when she cut out in front of slow moving traffic.

She arrived home in Claypotts Place, deactivated the alarm and went inside, leaving the two armed guards sitting outside. She began to pace from room to room while she waited for Evanton's call. Her phone felt dirty in her hand. Her stomach leeched acid into her throat.

When her phone sounded, much earlier than Evanton's promised hour, she wasn't going to answer. Then she saw it had no caller ID again. She answered it, wordless.

"Good decision to go home alone," said Evanton. "I decided there was no point keeping you waiting."

Donna's heart rate spiked to an alarming rate, and her eyes darted everywhere. How did he know where she was?

"What do you want?" she managed.

"What I've been wanting for the last two years," said Evanton. "Revenge."

"I figured that out all by myself," said Donna, feeling her anger begin to rise. "What's your plan?"

She heard Evanton laugh, and the sound made her stomach lurch again. Her eyes continued to dart all around. She tried hard to listen for sounds that could mean he was in here, while still being able to concentrate on what he was saying.

"Smart question," said Evanton. "Here's how it's going to work. You're going to find a burned body. In the Ethie Woods. You know where that is?"

"Yes," Donna confirmed, picturing the small woodland by the A92 out of Arbroath towards Montrose.

"You're going to have the body positively identified as me. Plant some phoney evidence, or something – you'll find a way."

Donna tried to think ahead to where this might be going. There was no way Evanton would be planning to fake his own death, simply to disappear.

"You know that's not going to work," said Donna. "Forensics won't be fooled by some planted blood sample and my word for it that I can identify the body."

"I know how slow these things can be," said Evanton. "And so do you. Let's say it buys us a couple of days."

"For what?"

"Glad you asked," said Evanton. It was killing her that he sounded as though he was enjoying this, and there wasn't a thing she could do about it. He continued. "I'm sick of hiding. Mo was right when she told you that."

How did he know Mo had spoken to them? Did he know about their daughter? Donna felt herself break out in a sweat as she remembered Fran saying something about the daughter being in this up to her neck. She wished she'd listened to what her DC was going to tell her.

"You're going to help me get to the Irish border," Evanton was saying, "and I have arrangements to be on my way from there. You do that for me, and I'll do a little favour for you."

Donna refused to say anything, forcing him to keep talking.

"I've, let's say, *persuaded* Abrim Kozel to offer himself up as the murderer. The newspapers are going to be full of it. The whole world is going to congratulate you."

"And when they identify the body for real?" Donna asked.

"Ah, you're cottoning on," Evanton said, his voice smug. "Then it'll all come crashing down around you. You'll have to face charges for falsifying evidence. I'll be free, and you'll be behind bars. You'll lose everything. Sweet. It's called revenge."

Donna was sure in that moment that she was going to throw up, but managed to keep it down.

"I knew your gut reaction would be to reject my plan," said Evanton, "so I'm going to give you a little incentive. Here's the deal: you identify the body as me, or I'm going to kill Angus Ross. You've already seen what I can do. Oh, and meantime, don't be too hasty to put in an offer on that house on Keptie Road." The call ended there.

Donna jumped from her chair and ran from room to room, checking for any sign of him. How the hell did he know everything she was doing? Who was feeding him all this information?

Chapter 30

In the cottage by Loch Kinord, Evanton sat in a room full of computers, facing one of them while talking on the phone. Alexandra peeked in at the door, listening. This looked like something from one of those old Star Trek re-runs her father liked to watch.

"I'm sick of hiding," she heard him say.

She narrowed her eyes to try and make out who he was talking to and what was going on in the screen in front of him. It looked like a tall woman sitting on a settee. Nothing dodgy as far as she could make out. The woman appeared to be fully clothed, and it looked as though he was having the phone discussion with her.

She panicked when she felt her nose tickle, but didn't have time to run before a sudden sneeze gave her away, and she found herself in Evanton's glare. Without any change in the tone of his voice, Evanton stood up from the computer desk, keeping the phone to his ear and continuing with his conversation, and slammed the door closed in Alexandra's face.

She stood outside with her heart thumping, knowing how much worse that could have ended for her. She had managed to steal another quick glance inside the room before the door almost hit her, and it looked to her as though the woman on the screen was unaware of Evanton's movement. Maybe he wasn't talking with her, after all, she thought. *Weirdo*. She made to scarper, but curiosity got the better of her and she pressed her ear to the door instead.

"You do that for me, and I'll do a little favour for you," she heard Evanton say. Her stomach suddenly churned. She listened on for as long as she dared. When she heard Evanton say, "I've, let's say, *persuaded* Abrim Kozel to offer himself up as the murderer," she knew it was time to go and find her father.

Abrim Kozel had arrived at the cottage, just as Evanton had predicted, the day after Alexandra had been brought here. As far as she could tell, Evanton's plan all along had been to press-gang her father into ordering his men to carry out various tasks. She'd watched as Kozel had made the phone calls, and she'd puzzled over why Evanton had wanted him to get his men to do things like kidnap a pathologist's wife. *Sick fuck*, she'd thought. But this was different. It sounded to her as though Evanton was planning to grass her father up. She wasn't about to let that happen.

When she found him, Kozel was standing at a window looking out onto the stream that ran past the rear of the cottage, with his arms folded. Alerted to the sound of her approach, he turned and she saw the expression of irritability on his face. Alexandra knew he'd been forced here because of her, and he seemed annoyed with her, not that she'd had much choice in being brought here, either. But she had to tell him this.

She hurried to his side. "Dad," she said, "he's going to hand you over to the police. I just heard him bargaining with them."

Chapter 31

Donna arrived back at Bell Street, still unnerved by the phone call from Jonas Evanton. The growing public panic, and the potential for more serious incidents to happen ran continuously through her mind. If she were to just do as he asked – identify the body as his – then it could all stop, and nobody else needed to get hurt. Was she willing to pay the price for that? Surely she would be cleared of wrongdoing once the truth came out? And as for the threat to Ross, was it a real one?

She made her way up to the team room and spotted Alice.

"A minute of your time," she called. Alice looked up, said something to the officer she'd been speaking to, and joined Donna outside the room.

"What's up?" Alice asked, as she walked alongside Donna.

"Jonas Evanton just phoned me."

Alice stopped in her tracks. "What did you just say?"

Donna waited while a pair of uniformed officers passed them by.

"Evanton phoned me," she repeated. "We need to go and speak to Ross."

Donna speed walked off in the direction of Ross's office, and Alice jogged to keep up with her.

When they reached Ross's office, Alice paused by the door, as though expecting Donna to knock on it, but Donna didn't stop and marched inside.

Ross looked up at the unexpected intrusion.

"Something's happened?" he asked, with a crease appearing above his brow.

Donna closed the door behind herself and Alice. She noticed his office was tidier than usual. A box sat by the side of his desk, and she realised he'd been preparing for his move to Aberdeen. She and Alice sat down opposite him.

"Evanton's just phoned me," she said.

Ross dropped the pen he'd been holding and sat bolt upright. "He phoned you? When? What did he say?"

Donna cleared her throat, feeling her temperature rise with her heart rate. "When we left the press conference, he told me to find somewhere quiet as he was going to phone back."

"And you didn't tell me then?" Ross sounded annoyed.

"It was a bit left field," said Donna. "He knew about the press conference, so I didn't really have much time to think, so I went home."

She could see that Ross was trying to keep a lid on his temper, trying to slow down his breathing and avoid criticising her decision.

"He knew about the press conference?" Alice asked. "How is that even possible? He had to have somebody here on the inside, then."

Donna saw Ross glance towards the door, checking through the frosted glass panel that the two armed officers were out there.

"What happened then?" he asked.

"Well, when I got home I took the second call," said Donna. "He knew exactly where I was, so he must be watching me himself, even if he does have somebody in here feeding him information. Nobody knew I was going home."

"He could have any number of goons keeping look-out for him," Alice said. "It could have been luck that they spotted you."

Donna knew it was something more than that. She could feel it in her gut, but decided not to say. "He told me his plan," she said.

Ross and Alice looked at one another, then back at Donna.

"He's after revenge, as we thought," Donna went on. "He's set up a murder scene, and he wants me to plant evidence there and have the body identified as himself."

Ross and Alice immediately butted in with protests about the impossibility of that. Donna held up her hand to stop them.

"That's the whole point," she said. "During the couple of days it'll take to find out I've misled the investigation, he wants me to help him get out of the country. Then, when it all goes south for me, I'll be facing charges of falsifying evidence. You have to hand it to him, it is proper revenge."

"Oh, God," Ross sank his head into his hands. "Well, you're obviously not going to go along with it, are you?"

Donna stood up and took a few steps towards the window. "There's a catch," she said.

"Here we go," Alice said through clenched teeth.

"He said if I don't do what he asks, then he's going to kill you." She looked at Ross.

Ross shifted in his chair and said nothing for a moment. He steepled his fingers beneath his chin, deep in thought. Even Alice kept quiet.

"Did he give you a timescale?" Ross asked eventually.

Donna shook her head. "He didn't, at least not that I can remember, so we need to assume it's imminent."

"I agree," said Ross. He looked again towards the armed officers.

"If I don't do what he wants, we're going to have to get protection for you right away," Donna said.

"Well, I'm on the train to Aberdeen in the morning," said Ross, "and there's no way he could know about that, so I'll be safe at least until I get up there."

"The alternative is for me to go along with his plan," said Donna, "as long as you have my back and it all gets cleared up in the end."

The three officers sat in silence again for a moment, each one deep in thought.

"The options, then," Ross said after a while. "Either you refuse to do as he says, in which case he's likely to continue with the carnage and there's the threat against me. However, we can have protection in place, and it would put Evanton on the back foot, which might unnerve him enough to start making mistakes. Or, you do as he says, identify the body as his, but we set it up as a covert operation so you don't face charges. When Evanton arranges to meet you, we set up surveillance and grab him. Downside is, we risk losing Evanton if the surveillance goes wrong. Or – even worse – we risk that he has something else planned altogether."

"That's about the long and the short of it," said Donna. "What should we do?"

There was a knock on the door and a uniformed officer came in.

"Arbroath have just called, boss," the officer said, holding out a mobile. "A body's been found in woodland up there. They want DI Davenport to go up and have a look…" Her voice trailed off when she saw Donna was actually there in the room. "Do you want to…?"

"Yes, I'll take it," said Donna, already at the officer's side and taking the phone from her.

You're going to find a burned body. In the Ethie Woods. You know where that is?

Donna held eye contact with Ross while she took the call.

"We're thinking this is all wrapped up in the stuff that's been going on," the caller from Arbroath told Donna. "And we're up to our eyeballs here – we could do with your take on it." He went on to provide Donna with the details. Sure enough, the body had been found in the Ethie Woods, and was badly burned. Forensics were already on their way to the scene.

"Let them know I'll be there in half an hour," said Donna, then she ended the call and handed the mobile back to the officer. The officer left at a gesture from Ross.

"Go along with his plan," Ross said. His voice was steady, not to be argued with. "It'll maybe stop anything else from happening for a day or two, and give us time to throw everything we have into cornering him. He's going to have to arrange to meet you face to face."

"But…" Alice began.

"I suppose Angus is right," said Donna. "This is the only chance we might ever have of getting him. And I'll be safe with armed protection. Just bloody don't let me go to jail for falsifying evidence!"

"I'll arrange for you to pick up some of Evanton's DNA samples from the evidence lockers," said Ross, "and we'll run this as an authorised covert operation." He checked his watch. "Let's get going."

"Come with me," Donna said to Alice as they all stood up.

As they walked to the car park, Donna saw Alice put her mobile into her jacket pocket, and had a sudden thought. She grabbed the jacket from Alice.

"I'll put this into the boot," she said.

112

"What is wrong with you?" demanded Alice, trying to wrestle the jacket back.

"I like my car to be tidy," said Donna, glaring at her. "Jackets in the boot."

Alice's expression of confusion gave way to one of concern. "Have you been taking your…"

"Pills? Yeah, yeah. I'm rattling with them." She jumped up and down on the spot. "Hear that?"

"Maybe I should drive," said Alice.

"What, you think I'm not fit to drive?"

Alice muttered something under her breath.

Donna threw their jackets into the boot of the car, and they waited for Ross to bring the evidence bag to them. They didn't have to wait long. Donna wondered, but didn't ask, what Ross must have told them to get it this quickly. She waved goodbye, then hit the accelerator.

She and Alice sped out of Bell Street, through Dundee and on towards Arbroath and the Ethie Woods. All during the high velocity drive, Evanton's words ran in a loop through Donna's mind, *You're going to make sure the body is positively identified as me.*

He knew about Keptie Road. How did he know?

She began to wonder about Ross's decision to go along with Evanton's plan. It had sounded alright at the time, on balance, giving them a chance to set up surveillance and finally trap him. But now she wasn't so sure. Weighing against that was the risk she might be putting Ross's life at risk by refusing to go along with Evanton's instructions. No, she determined, Ross was right. He knew what he was talking about, and she would do as her DCI had ordered. She should play along.

Chapter 32

The wood burner in the cottage by Loch Kinord gave the room a sleepy glow, but the real fire was in Abrim Kozel's eyes. He shoved

Evanton against the wall.

"You're going to hand me over to the police, eh?" he growled. "Is that why you brought me here?"

Evanton made a point of straightening his tie and patting down his expensive shirt while he righted himself.

"I wouldn't try that again if I were you," he told Kozel, his expression betraying a smouldering fury. "And if you pay attention, you'll see exactly how this is going to go."

Kozel backed off; Evanton had a gun tucked into his belt.

"Alexandra heard you," Kozel said. "You're going to frame me for a murder and hand me over as part of a deal?"

"Alexandra's a kid," said Evanton. Out of the corner of his eye he saw her approach the room and stand in the doorway, with her arms folded and an expression of teenage defiance on her face. "She doesn't know what she heard."

"What did she hear, then?" Kozel demanded.

Evanton crossed the room and sat down in one of the armchairs. He folded his hands behind his head, enjoying the knowledge that Kozel was afraid of him. But he caught the look that the gangster shared with his daughter. A muscle twitched at his temple, and it struck him that no matter how he came out of all of this, Kozel would still have something far more valuable than he would ever have. What he might once have had if things had turned out differently between himself and Mo.

He'd been thinking about her a lot over the last couple of days, since he'd seen her turn up at Bell Street on Sunday.

"Evanton is a man who has to be in control," she had told them then. Nobody knew him the way she did.

He hadn't expected her to return to the Police HQ the next day, and cursed that he'd only become aware of that visit when he'd spotted her leaving. It had disturbed him to see she seemed to be crying. What could have upset her? Was it something to do with him?

He had to breathe slowly to push away the sudden anger that flared in his chest. He hadn't got what he'd wanted with Mo, but he was certainly going to get what he wanted from Donna Davenport.

"You got your man to dump the body?" he asked Kozel.

Kozel affirmed with a nod. "Followed all of your instructions."

"Good," said Evanton. "Well, this is what's going to happen next. The police are going to attend the scene as soon as your *dog walker* makes the call. I've instructed Donna Davenport to identify the body as me."

Kozel looked puzzled. "How can she get away with that?"

"Oh, she won't even try," said Evanton. "At least, that's what I'm betting on."

"I don't understand," said Kozel.

"I've given her an ultimatum," Evanton said, "and it sounds pretty convincing, if I say so myself. I've told her I'll kill her DCI – oh, and he happens to be one of her closest friends – if she doesn't do it."

"You're a sick bastard," said Kozel.

"Sicker than that," said Evanton, leaning forward. "I know she won't be able to bring herself to do it, and she'll take a gamble that I won't be able to kill Angus Ross."

"What's the point in all of this, then?" Alexandra butted in.

Evanton shot her a glare. "Shut up," he told her. Then he smirked. "But since you ask, here it is. She'll defy me because she doesn't believe Angus Ross is going to die. But when I do kill him, I'm then going to threaten her little woman, Libby Quinn, and you can bet your ass she'll do whatever I want her to do then. She'll be too terrified to defy me a second time."

Kozel moved towards the window and lit a cigarette. "I still don't understand," he said, as Alexandra scuttled towards him. "Why bring me into this?"

Evanton shrugged, a relaxed gesture. "There is the small chance that she will do as I've asked this time," he said, "and I like to make sure I have every eventuality covered. If she goes along with it, she'll end up being charged with falsifying evidence, and you'll be able to claim compensation for wrongful arrest. Call it a little payback for your inconvenience. It's a win-win situation, really."

He was feeling pleased with himself, until he saw Kozel placing a protective arm around Alexandra. The gangster clearly thought he was dealing with some kind of psycho, but he was wrong. Evanton tried to name the emotion he was battling with every time he watched the dynamic between Kozel and his daughter. What was it? Jealousy? Longing? Loss and grief? Perhaps all of these things, he thought, standing up and heading out of the room. But it didn't matter. What mattered was that he was about to take away from Donna Davenport everything – every*one* – that mattered to her.

Chapter 33

The Ethie Woods lay off the east side of the A92, just two miles out of Arbroath heading towards Montrose. It would normally be pitch dark out here at this time, being well away from the town's streetlights, and with only a couple of houses tucked away on the other side of the road and set well apart. There were few signs of activity to give away the existence of the nearby tiny hamlet of Marywell, or of the farms in the surrounding area.

Despite the road being single carriageway, it was the main route for long distance truckers going between Aberdeen and all routes south. It didn't take much for the route to become snarled, and by the time Donna and Alice approached, a line of police and other vehicles were snaked along the coned-off northbound road. Their blue lights, flashing silently, obscured any view there might have been of the night sky. The thrum of idling emergency vehicles provided a steady soundtrack to the trucks that were following the white-capped traffic cop's directions, passing north and south, one at a time.

Donna glared at a lorry driver who leaned out of his cabin window to gawp at the scene on the other side, and flicked her head, indicating for him to get a move on.

The traffic cop halted the flow of trucks to let Donna and Alice cross the road to the woods.

PC McClure was standing there, wearing a heavy overcoat and enormous gloves, like goalie gloves. Donna found herself wondering if he'd nicked them from the McKinnes murder scene, but pushed the thought away again just as quickly. He was stamping his feet, and breath clouds blew from his mouth. As soon as he saw Donna and Alice, he used his teeth to remove one of the gloves, and fished his notebook from a pocket to record the fact of their entering the crime scene. Behind him was the head of a rough track that quickly disappeared from view as it plunged into the darkness of the woods. To his left and right, yellow police tape trailed across the trees that lined the roadside.

"Follow the crowd, Detective Inspector," he said, indicating a spot further into the woods, where the vague outlines of human shapes created the illusion of movement amongst the dark, bare trees.

A cloying, sickly sweet smell seemed to cling to the trees as Donna and Alice picked their way along the dirt track, crunching their way through dried leaves and bracken, careful to step over the gnarled roots that veined the way.

On reflex, Donna brought tissues from her pocket and covered her mouth and nose, as she would do at a post mortem. She noticed Alice doing the same. The smell, now like burning rubbish, found its way through the tissue, and it was all Donna could do to stop herself from gagging as the noxious air reached for her taste buds.

Just as the stench threatened to overpower, she and Alice found themselves at the backs of a team of blue-clad forensics personnel. One of them turned round, alerted to the arrival of the two officers. Donna saw that he recognised her from the murder scene at the football club. He nodded to her, trying to form a smile, but the grim line his mouth made only served as a warning of the horrific scene she was about to look at. He allowed her to peer past him and lean in for a look.

"Oh, dear God," she heard Alice at her shoulder.

A dark shape lay on the ground, which looked to be flattened –

charred – for quite a circumference around it. On the far side of the body, several forensics personnel were crouching around what looked to be a set of bags and boxes. They must be setting up their tent and lighting, Donna guessed. They would probably be here well into the witching hours, recording every detail for later analysis.

Evanton's words, *You're going to find a burned body. In the Ethie Woods* swam back into her mind.

She scanned the personnel and found the pathologist. This was one she hadn't worked with before, although she recognised him.

"What's the state of play here?" she asked him.

"You can come over for a look," the pathologist beckoned.

Donna, still with her nose covered by the tissues, stepped forward onto the aluminium plates that had been set down, and joined the pathologist beside the body.

As her eyes adjusted to the gloom, and she began to be able to pick out its details, she gasped in surprise.

Despite the extensive burning of the body, there was no mistaking its identity. Donna heard the pathologist rattle off a list of details, but she didn't take them in, as the surprise became mixed in her head with Evanton's instructions, *You're going to have the body positively identified as me.* Her head began to pound.

All she had to do was tell the pathologist this was Jonas Evanton, and the carnage would stop. Was there really any alternative?

"I know who this is," she told the pathologist.

Evanton had promised to end the chaos. End the growing terror. Ross had been right, hadn't he? She only had to do this one thing, identify the body as Jonas Evanton. They would set up surveillance, she would be the decoy, and they would have him. And it could all end, once and for all.

Donna took a deep breath, feeling the weight of responsibility. She had the means to end all of this. To prevent further tragedy. Wasn't that her duty as a police officer?

"I know who this is," she repeated to the pathologist.

A surveillance operation being able to outwit Jonas Evanton? She didn't think so.

She took another deep breath and said, "This is Archie McKinnes."

Chapter 34

"I told you to go along with his instructions!"

Ross's face was purple, and his voice carried along the corridor, making officers pop their heads around doorways to listen to the shouting match.

"I've already called Loudoun and got the surveillance operation okayed," Ross raged on. "Now I've got to go back and tell him we've changed our bloody minds, and now we need more armed protection? For fuck's sake, Donna, what were you thinking?"

Alice was backed into the doorway, silently mouthing, *Oh God oh God oh God*.

Donna felt her own anger rising. Ross hadn't been the one left for dead by Evanton back then, and he hadn't been the one to have listened to Evanton's cock-sure voice on the phone this afternoon.

"A surveillance operation has no chance of capturing Evanton," she shouted back at Ross. "He's been running rings around us for the last two years. Do you seriously think he hasn't planned for that?"

"It was our only chance to find out where he actually was," said Ross through clenched teeth. "And to get some kind of break from all of this madness…"

He stopped abruptly and stared at Donna. She knew right away what he was thinking.

"I have not lost the plot," she said. "I made a perfectly rational decision."

"You were acting a bit weird on the way there," Alice chipped in, catching Ross's eye.

"Nobody asked you," Donna shot at her, and regretted the comment as soon as she saw the wounded expression on Alice's face. She turned back to Ross.

"It would have been a trap," she said, "following his instructions."

"Well, now we'll never know," Ross snapped.

"Do you want me to get a protection detail organised?" Alice asked.

"Yes, get in touch with Aberdeen," Ross said, glaring at Donna. "I'll be fine until I get up there, but it won't be long before Evanton realises that's where I am, and we need to be ready in case he is serious about carrying out his threat."

"And we'll be telling the press we've recovered Archie McKinnes's body?" Alice asked.

Ross rubbed his hands across his face, a gesture Donna recognised as trying to calm himself down. He nodded his head in response to Alice.

"At least that's one thing," he said. "Something to tell them that doesn't make us look like complete idiots."

"It will help," said Alice, ever the peace-keeper.

"You'd better be right about this," Ross said to Donna.

He knew about the house, Donna kept thinking. She knew she was right about it.

"Right," said Ross, sounding calmer now, "get Burly McKinnes in here and charged. Make sure there's security around Archie McKinnes's body until we can release it to the family. We'll lean hard on John Ogilvie when we get him in, and we'll have a clearer idea of how Evanton made it happen. Then we can let the press know that at least the whole McKinnes fiasco is dealt with." He gave Donna a withering look.

"You know deep down this was the right decision," Donna said. She could tell from the look in Ross's eye that he was coming round to that conclusion. "How could we mount any kind of surveillance operation when we don't even know how he's been managing to watch our every move, or who's been feeding him information from the inside?" *And who's been talking to the press?*

"I know, I know," said Ross with an exasperated sigh. "But what the hell has he got in store for us now? That's what I'm worried about. What's his next move?"

120

Chapter 35

Gary Tweedie hurried into Dundee train station and made his way directly to the staff offices. He checked in the mirror that his hair was tidy and his navy tie straight. At least he'd had time to see Leanne off to school this morning, and had had a couple of hours to himself before the shift, so he felt fairly refreshed. But with the roads being bad at this time of year, the trains were busier than usual and the rosters were hectic. He wanted plenty of time to get to grips with his routes for the day and the inevitable notices about delays.

He scanned his docket and thought, *Not bad*. He was scheduled to take over from Ian when the 13:00 to Aberdeen came in, then he would be taking the 14:39 from Aberdeen to Glasgow. He'd have two hours' break in Glasgow, then get back to Dundee for about quarter to nine. That was a civilised enough hour to collect Leanne from her aunt's, he reckoned, where hopefully she would have done some studying for the prelims. *Imagine having exams right after the Christmas holidays*, he thought, as he signed off his paperwork for the shift.

He honestly didn't know what he would do without his ex sister-in-law. Despite his messy split with Amy, there had never been any hard feelings between him and Grace, and she'd been a godsend, being there to watch Leanne during his odd shift pattern. Although, without blowing his own trumpet, he felt he was doing a pretty decent job of being a single parent, now three months into the role. Leanne seemed content, anyway. It was just a pity things weren't going so smoothly on the ex-spouse front.

He checked the time again, and decided to have a cuppa before making his way to the platform ready to take over from Ian. Slotting the plastic cup under the nozzle and selecting black coffee from the machine, he was surprised when his phone began to ring.

It was from an unknown caller.

He hesitated, with his heart sinking, wondering if it was just a nuisance call, or whether it might be Amy, with a new number again. Generally they only communicated via Grace if they really had to, but now and then she did call him directly just to have a go at him. So he answered, hesitant but curious as to what he might have done this time.

"Dad?"

The voice on the phone was tear-ridden, full of fear.

Gary gripped his mobile, feeling the twin sensations of panic and confusion. His 15 year old daughter should be in school right now, so how could she be phoning him? If something was wrong, why wasn't it the school phoning? But something was wrong. He knew fear in his daughter's voice when he heard it. The palm of his hand suddenly sweated, and he thought he might drop the phone.

"What's happened? Where are you?" He hoped he sounded reassuring, but wouldn't have put money on it.

Gary's stomach churned and his chest tightened, vice-like, when the next voice on the phone wasn't his daughter's, but a man's voice.

"Gary," the man said, "you play nice, and little Leanne here will come home safely. Tomorrow."

"What? Who is this?" Gary tried to sound strong and threatening, but succeeded only in sounding as terrified as he actually felt. He had broken into a sudden sweat, his heart pounding wildly. The staff offices constricted around him, the walls closing in and threatening to crush him. He thought he was going to urinate right there, unable to control the urge.

"She's in safe hands for now," said the voice on the phone. "Now, I'm going to give you a set of instructions. I'm only going to tell you once, so you're going to have to pay attention…"

"You've got my daughter!" Gary yelled, unaware of the arrival of two concerned colleagues who'd heard his raised voice. "Who the hell are you? What's going on?"

"Last chance," said the voice. It had turned into a growl. "Follow the instructions I'm about to give you, or you'll never see Leanne again. Not alive, anyway."

"Everything alright there, Gary?" one of the newly arrived colleagues asked.

Gary gulped, and thought quickly. He had just been told that Leanne's safety depended on him following a set of instructions. "Fine, fine," he blustered. "It's just Amy kicking off again. Give us a minute, will you?"

The two drivers glanced at one another, shrugged, and went about their business. They were used to hearing about the hassle Gary got from his ex.

Gary tucked himself into the staff toilet. "I'm listening," he told the man on the phone. "What do you want from me?"

"Wise decision," the man said. "Now, here's what you have to do…"

Chapter 36

What a hellish day it had been, Donna thought as she arrived home. Her car chirped as it locked, and she keyed in the house alarm to let herself in. Surely it wasn't worth all of this, she felt. What she wouldn't give for her and Libby to have a normal life. To be able to go out whenever they pleased and not have to look over their shoulders for a revenge-obsessed psychopath. Or to have armed guards trailing around behind them.

"Ross is being sent up to Aberdeen," she told Libby as soon as she came inside. "And I've fallen out with Alice. And Evanton phoned me and told me to mislead a murder investigation. He's threatened to kill Ross, but I couldn't do it…."

"Whoa, hold on there," said Libby, her eyes as wide as saucers. "What did you just say?"

Donna stopped in her tracks and tried to imagine what it must have sounded like to Libby. The TV was on with the volume low, but Christmas carols were drifting from it. The house was warm against the freezing elements outside. She ached for normality, and reached for Libby. The two stood in silence, holding one another for several moments before Donna could speak again.

"It's been a really bad day at the office," she said. "Can you tell me nice things?"

Libby led her into the living room and sat her in an armchair. She poured a shot of something clear, and handed it to her. Donna gulped it down in one, letting its fiery sting travel into her stomach and haze her head. Then she felt Libby's hands on her shoulders and relaxed into them, groaning in the sheer indulgence of the gentle massage.

"I've got a free hour at eleven tomorrow morning," Libby's voice drifted into her contented thoughts. "We could meet and phone the solicitor, if you want."

"You know," said Donna, "there's nothing I would rather do more." And that was the truth. Moving house would be a new start for them, in more ways than one, and she was keen to get their offer into the solicitor as soon as possible.

She forced all other thoughts from her mind, and concentrated only on the new house, picturing how they would furnish and decorate each room, and enjoying the feeling of Libby's hands on her skin.

"Donna?" Libby's voice interrupted her thoughts.

"Uh huh?"

"Let's get you up to bed."

"It's bit early...unless..." She looked hopefully at Libby.

"You were snoring," said Libby, hands on her hips in mock reproach. "Go on. I'll tidy up down here, and if you're still awake when I join you, well...who knows?"

Donna was suddenly wide awake.

Wednesday
Chapter 37

Donna hurried along the corridor towards Ross's room, worrying that she might have missed him, and was relieved to meet him coming towards her. He had his overcoat on and was carrying a large briefcase in one hand, while pulling a suitcase along behind him with the other.

"I need a word with you before you go," said Donna.

She saw Ross glance at his watch.

"I don't have a lot of time to catch this train," he said. "If I'm not on it, Loudoun will have us all for breakfast."

"Something I need to bring you up to speed on," said Donna. "It's confidential."

"Come on, then," said Ross. He nodded towards the Quiet Room, which lay unoccupied and was on his way out. "We can have a word in here, but it'll need to be quick."

"It will be quick," said Donna, falling into step with him. "But this is important."

Ross glanced at her, and she wasn't sure if he looked sceptical or hopeful. Either way, he looked tired, and she knew the move up to Aberdeen was something he could do without. Hell, they could all do without it.

"Have they got security sorted out for you?" she asked as they walked.

Ross nodded his head. "I'll be met at the train station by a couple of armed officers just like your two."

Donna felt relieved. At least nothing could happen to him, and they could concentrate on getting the media hype calmed down while they waited for Evanton's next move. She closed the office door, and Ross put his briefcase on the floor before perching himself on the edge of the desk.

"So, what is it?"

"I didn't have a chance to tell you yesterday, what with everything," said Donna. "It went clean out of my head, but when

Mo Skinner was in on Monday, she told us something I think we could use."

Ross kept quiet, but nodded his head for Donna to go on.

"She told us she had a daughter, back in the '80s."

She saw Ross's eyebrows rise, and the quick calculation going on in his head.

"She gave the girl up for adoption," Donna went on. "It was Evanton's child. He never knew anything about her."

"Mo told you that, for real?" said Ross. "I wasn't expecting you to say anything like that. Why isn't it up on the evidence board?"

"Mo told us in strict confidence," said Donna. "And if it's something we can surprise Evanton with, then we can't risk the information getting out." Ross conceded with a nod, and Donna went on. "I've got Fran checking it out on the quiet, just to be sure."

"And Mo definitely said Evanton doesn't know about the daughter?"

"Positive," said Donna. She leaned towards Ross. "We know Evanton has a soft spot for Mo, so if he has a daughter to her that he didn't know about, then I've a feeling this could be the thing to up-end him and give us the advantage. We just need to find her – and quickly." *Before he does*, she found herself thinking, and wondering if they might already be too late.

Ross stood up. "Look, I need to run for this train," he said. "But good work. It does sound promising. And it's not as if we have anything else going for us in this case. Keep me in the loop, okay?"

Suddenly he patted his pockets and looked exasperated. "I've left my mobile back in my office. Could you...?"

Donna smiled. "Sure. Go and get loaded up. I'll bring it out to your car."

They left the Quiet Room, Ross heading in one direction and Donna in the other.

Conscious of the time, she hurried to Ross's office.

When she got there, she reached across his desk, largely empty now, and without really knowing why, straightened the few papers that still sat on it. She touched a finger lightly to his landline phone.

She glanced at the two armed officers who'd shadowed her there, and was grateful for the way their gazes were discreetly aimed elsewhere.

Suddenly a lump came to her throat, and she realised how much of an anchor Ross had been for her ever since she'd come back to Bell Street. Then she swallowed and gave herself a mental shake. He was only going to be an hour up the road.

After a brief brush of her hand over the back of his well-worn leather swivel chair, she briskly opened the drawer where she knew he kept his mobile, and retrieved it. She turned and marched back out of the office, intending to take the shortcut out to the car park.

Before she took another step, however, a uniformed officer came hurrying towards her, his face red from the strain of carrying a heavy box.

"'Scuse me, Ma'am," he grunted, as he pushed by into the office, and with a vocal exertion, hefted the box onto Ross's desk.

"What's that?" Donna asked.

"DCI Marsh is stepping in for DCI Ross, Ma'am," said the officer.

"Marsh?" said Donna. The name was vaguely familiar... then her heart sank. "DCI Marsh from Perth?"

"Yes, Ma'am," said the officer.

"It's Donna, that's my name, not *Ma'am*." She was aware of the irritation in her voice. It wasn't the PC's fault, but the news of Marsh's arrival had rattled her. And the speed of it. Ross wasn't even off the premises yet.

The officer stuttered something incoherent and looked to his armed colleagues for help. He got no reaction from them.

"Sorry," he muttered.

"No, it's me who should apologise," said Donna. "It's not your fault. I hadn't realised it was Marsh who'd be coming in. He's such a complete arse."

She waved the officer on, seeing that he would rather be anywhere than in the middle of a spat in the higher ranks. He scuttled off.

Donna looked back into Ross's office, her nose wrinkling at the sight of the box now sitting on top of his desk.

"What's wrong with Marsh?" asked one of the armed officers.

Donna was momentarily caught off guard at this first verbal communication. Then she thought back to the heated arguments she'd had with the Perth DCI on the few occasions she had met him.

"He's a Tory," she said.

The armed officers tipped one another a knowing nod.

"It's all we fecking need in a sensitive situation…" Donna began, before she heard a door swing open along the corridor and heard the footsteps approach. The footsteps accompanied by That Voice.

"…just get the little bastard behind bars," it was saying at top volume, "and that'll calm the proles. At least it'll look as though we're doing something to get on top of this mess."

The slender form of DCI Harry Marsh took shape in front of the oily voice. He stopped dead at the sight of Donna and the two armed guards in front of Ross's door.

"Welcoming committee?" he quipped.

"Get *who* behind bars?" Donna demanded.

"Wrong side of the bed this morning?" said Marsh. He shouldered past Donna and went into Ross's office, then turned back to face her. "Get me a coffee, there's a love."

Donna turned to address the armed officers and thumbed towards Marsh. "And there you see a prize tit and how it behaves."

With that, she set off on her way again, followed by the bemused armed officers.

"Milk and two!" Marsh called after her.

"Yeah, yeah," Donna called back. She gritted her teeth, and gripped Ross's mobile tighter than she needed to.

Chapter 38

Gary Tweedie arrived at Dundee Station to take over the driver's seat on the Aberdeen train. He walked down the stairs slowly as he made his way towards the staff rooms, looking carefully at everyone as he went.

The rush hour commute had come and gone more than an hour ago, but the station was still busy. Passengers were arriving from Arbroath and Perth to get a spot of Christmas shopping in before the festive mayhem set in for real.

There was a long queue at the cigarette counter, and a shorter one at the cash machine, but nobody paid him any attention, and he felt close to tears at the thought of what he'd been asked to do. Been ordered to do.

He had a killer of a headache. He hadn't slept at all during the night, spending the torturously long hours pacing from one end of his flat to the other, desperate to think of some way to find Leanne. Several times he'd almost phoned the police, but his fear of what Leanne's captors might do to her if they found out made him stop each time.

His little girl, the one person in the whole world he should protect, had been taken, and he had no idea why he'd been targeted like this. He wasn't involved in anything dodgy, didn't owe any debts. It didn't make sense why this had happened to him in particular. But the one thing he did know was that he had to do exactly as he'd been instructed. And although what he'd been told to do turned his stomach inside out, he had to make sure he did everything possible to get Leanne home safely.

As he entered the staff room, loosening his tie, he saw his supervisor do a double take. He was aware of the sweat dripping from his forehead, and his shirt was already damp and crumpled. He felt drawn and pale, felt sick, and slightly dizzy. If he'd been in the gaffer's shoes right now, he would have done a double take, too, and would certainly be questioning the driver's fitness for work today.

A moment of panic took him, when he thought there might be a chance he would be removed from the roster. He had to be on that train, there were no two ways about it, and he caught himself wondering what lengths he would go to if the gaffer told him to go back home.

He gulped, and tried to give the appearance that he was calm. "Alright, Gary?"

Gary nodded, and the movement caused a ripple of nausea in his gut.

The gaffer turned his full attention onto him, with a frown on his face, and nodded to the side room. "Drugs and alcohol test," he said.

Gary hadn't been drinking. He hadn't dared do a thing that might jeopardise his shift. He continued to constantly tell himself he had to follow the instructions he'd been given. Leanne's life depended on it. Still, he hadn't reckoned on being tested today, and realised with alarm that the delay it implied could mean he would miss his scheduled shift.

His breathing became even more rapid and shallow. What was he going to do? He glanced at the time. There was an hour before his train was due in, but if they had to call in a sample collector from the lab, he could be sitting in here for much longer than that.

He breathed a sigh of relief when the gaffer confirmed there was a workplace sample collector on site today. He watched, feeling wretched, as his supervisor arranged the necessary paperwork and retrieved the breathalyser while the call went out for the sample collector.

Gary wasn't sure he actually had the necessary breath for the breathalyser, and in fact it took two attempts before he was able to provide a successful sample. As he knew it would, the test came back negative, and the gaffer grunted as he took the equipment back. Then the sample collector arrived, completed the paperwork and sent Gary into the toilets with a urine bottle. By the time Gary came back out, the sample collector had completed all of his admin and didn't seem to have any wish to hang around.

"Think it's been one of those 24 hour bugs," Gary said, trying to sound convincing. "Paracetamol's kicking in now, and I think it's beginning to shift."

"Everything alright at home?" asked the gaffer, clearly uncomfortable at asking a personal question.

Gary drew him a look of annoyance in return, hoping his casual act would convince the gaffer to let him get on. Eventually he did seem convinced, and with a sigh, he told Gary to get his kit ready and head off towards the platform.

With all checks in order, Gary tried his best to focus on each of the tasks in turn, in an attempt to keep his mind numb. But he still found himself shaking with fear.

Follow the instructions I'm about to give you, or you'll never see Leanne again. Not alive, anyway, the words from the previous day's phone call haunted him over and over.

He had to delay the train at Dundee for several minutes, then he had to carry out his instructions once it left Arbroath station.

He checked the time again. The train was due in at the platform in five more minutes. A sizeable number of people were already standing there waiting for it. He glanced along to his left, where he saw several people part in order to let a man in a wheelchair through. An older man, it seemed to be, with a hat and scarf, and wrapped in a large blanket. The man seemed to be dosing, while two others brought the wheelchair close to the platform's edge, and stood waiting with the rest of the passengers. Gary checked the time once more, and adjusted his tie again.

He continued to re-live the words of the phone call, and forced his breathing to slow down. Finally, he saw the train emerge from the tunnel and trundle into the station.

Chapter 39

Donna felt a little empty as she returned to the team room, having seen Ross on his way.

Everywhere she went these days there was a constant clamour of officers and journalists at her back, wanting her opinion on this or her instruction on that. And here in the team room there was plenty to be getting on with, now that the sprawling details on the evidence board were beginning to resemble a map of the London Underground. But there was still an empty space, left behind by her long-time friend Angus Ross. Even though he would only be an hour's drive away or at the end of a phone call, Donna knew the job just wasn't going to be the same without him there. It didn't help that there had been growing tension between her and Alice lately.

She kept her back to the activity going on around the room, while she contemplated how the rest of today might go. There was to be a closed press conference at 4.30, where the police and the journalists would exchange information as per the deal she and Ross had brokered with them the previous day. One of the items she had to bring to them was Burly being charged with his father's murder – having him offered up as a sacrifice to the god of smooth relations with the media.

But she was still uneasy about charging Burly, and then her eye caught the details on the evidence board again about Agnes's near drowning. As things stood, she thought, Agnes McKinnes was finally free of her brute of a husband. She had a chance, at last, to settle into a peaceful home life with the one son of hers that had turned out alright, and to be a grandmother to his unborn child. The one chance, at long last, to have a life containing joy and without fear. If Burly got put away for murder, Donna realised, Agnes would lose it all. Her son, her grandchild, all of it. And for what, she wondered? Again that blurred line between right and wrong found her questioning this job.

Damn it! she resolved. Whatever she had to do, she was not going to let Burly go down for murder, especially when he had done them all a favour. In that moment she knew she'd been right when she had told Libby she would hand in her warrant card as soon as this was all over. She could no longer play a part in enforcing laws that couldn't reflect the complexities of the diverse realities that shaped people's motives and decisions.

Would it be enough, though, she fretted, to bring only the resolution of the body theft to the press conference? Could she gamble that they would have little interest in knowing who actually killed Archie McKinnes, as long as they knew it had had nothing to do with Jonas Evanton?

She was shaken out of her thoughts when she heard Fran clear her throat.

Fran whispered into Donna's ear, "I need to fill you in on Mo Skinner's daughter. I know where she is."

"Oh yes," said Donna, also keeping her voice low. "I'm sorry, things got messy yesterday, I forgot to catch up with you. Let's get Alice and find somewhere more private to speak."

She called to Alice, and Fran led them both to the Quiet Room, where they listened while Fran told them about her phone call to Peterborough.

"And this Travellers' site is near Cardiff?" Donna asked once she'd finished.

"That's right," said Fran. "The woman in Peterborough was certain Sarah Cooper is still there, because – wait for this – she also phoned a couple of days ago asking about her birth parents!"

"That's a bit too much of a coincidence," said Donna. "I want you to go down to Cardiff. Check when there's a…"

"There's an overnight train tonight," said Fran.

"I should have known you already checked," smiled Donna.

"Gets into Cardiff just after ten tomorrow morning," said Fran.

"Good," said Donna. "Go and get yourself organised for the trip." She turned to Alice. "And I want you to call South Wales Police and sort out a liaison officer, someone who can meet Fran off the train."

Fran looked pleased, while Alice still looked pissed off about yesterday.

"I don't like this coincidence," the sergeant said. "What if she's involved, after all, and we're sending Fran into a risky situation?"

"Then get her a good liaison officer," Donna said.

She glanced at her watch. She had to meet Libby and Natesh in town for a quick brunch, to make their final decision about the offer they were going to put in on the house on Keptie Road.

"I'm going out in half an hour, so let's have it sorted by then. Chop chop."

Alice glared at Donna, then she and Fran melted away. Donna made her way back to the team room, thinking over the potential advantage this line of inquiry might give them.

Alice and Fran weren't gone long, and ten minutes before Donna was due to leave, they both appeared back in the team room. Donna sat down with them at one of the desks.

"Your liaison at Cardiff is a DS Tom Jones…" Alice began.

Fran snorted a laugh. "Tom Jones!"

Donna failed to hide a smirk. "Keep the reason for your visit as vague as you can. We've no idea how far Evanton's reach is. So, even if you feel like throwing your knickers at DS Jones, don't."

Fran laughed. "Can I leave my hat on?"

"This isn't funny," said Alice. "I'm not happy about any of it." Her lips were pursed, her arms folded.

"Not happy?" said Donna, the laugh carrying her voice across the room as it gained several decibels. "Just wait till you see who we've got as acting DCI. Remember that wee prick, Harry Marsh…?"

A change in the air made her stop talking and turn around.

There, standing in the doorway and staring blazing daggers into the back of her head, was the man himself.

"Oh, crap," Donna muttered.

DCI Marsh scanned the rest of the room, pinning all of the officers to the spot with his stare. "Yes, I'm in charge now," he directed towards Donna with his oily voice, "so let's not waste any time."

He strode up to the evidence board. "Tell me what all this is about…" waving at it… "and tell me you're getting somewhere fast."

Chapter 40

Donna drove slowly past the Waterstones book shop on Commercial Street, looking out for a parking space. She could hardly believe her luck when she spotted a car pulling out of a bay just past the bus stop.

When she got out to stick 50p in the meter – she'd be lucky if she would actually have an hour to spare – she caught the annoyed look on the driver's face in the car that had been behind her. *Oops!* She'd forgotten about the armed guards.

She watched, impressed, as they ignored the No Entry sign and drove into Exchange Street to grab a cheeky parking spot just outside Rancho Pancho on the corner, all seemingly without taking their eyes off her.

She left her parking ticket on top of the dash, locked the car, and walked back along towards the Waterstones. She stuffed her hands into her pockets, and felt the grit on the pavement crunch beneath her boots as she went, all the time cringing at her latest encounter with DCI Marsh. Shoppers hurried along the street, wrapped up against the cold.

She paused to let two women out of the book shop, then went inside. As always, the table displays with new books themed by genre were tempting, and she wanted nothing more right now than to stop and pick them up one by one, and to leaf through their brand new pages. But she didn't have time.

She bounded up the stairs to where the cafe was, leaving the armed guards awkwardly trying to blend in with the shoppers around the bookshelves. She quickly scanned the seating area that ran around the rim of the floor space, and spotted Natesh already at a table near the food counter. She could tell by his posture that he was on his phone, probably playing Planets Under Attack, his favourite game. Despite his concentration, though, he looked up and saw her approach.

"What's that?" she asked, pointing at the plate sitting in front of him.

"Cheese and onion panini," he said, holding it up to show her the half-eaten snack. "Couldn't wait, I'm starving." He took a bite, as though to prove the point.

Donna took the seat facing him.

He leaned forward and, muffled through the panini, Donna was sure he said, "Were you up at that body that was burned?"

"Yep," she confirmed. "Never a dull moment."

"Gotcha!"

Libby grabbed her around the waist from behind, making Donna turn in delighted surprise.

135

"Ow, you're freezing," said Donna.

"The cuppa you're about to get me will soon heat me up," Libby smiled. Then to Natesh, she said, "What's that you've got?"

"Ngangingi," he said with his mouth full again.

"I'll have one of those, too," said Libby, sitting down next to Donna.

While they waited for their food, and with Natesh happily munching his way through his, they took another look at the brochure for the house on Keptie Road. They chatted happily, looking at the details of the rooms and discussing how they might furnish and decorate each one.

"Are we doing this, then?" beamed Natesh, wiping his hands on a napkin.

Libby and Donna glanced at one another, and laughed. Natesh joined in. They chatted for a few moments more, then Donna and Libby agreed on the offer they would put in for the house. Natesh went to collect their food while Libby rang the solicitor's number.

"Natesh does realise that he's not buying this house with us, doesn't he?" Libby whispered in Donna's ear while she was placed on hold.

"I'm not one hundred per cent sure about that, now you mention it," laughed Donna.

By the time Natesh returned to the table, Libby had spoken with the solicitor, and their offer was in.

"All we have to do now is sit back and wait," said Libby.

Donna knew that Libby's heart was set on this house. Getting a knock back would be devastating, but much as she wanted to wait there with them for the solicitor's response, she had to go.

She gulped down her coffee, and stood. "Sorry," she said, "you're going to have to wait it out without me. Duty calls, and all…"

Her mobile rang, and at the same time she heard a burst of police sirens outside, seeming to come from all directions. She answered the call, a sense of foreboding in her gut. Alice's voice was rushed when she came on the line.

"Where are you?" the sergeant demanded.

"Commercial Street," said Donna. "What's happened?"

"There's been a shooting," Alice sounded breathless. "Just outside the Caird Hall. All units are on their way."

"I'm two minutes away," said Donna. "I'll be right there."

She saw the worried look on Libby's face.

"I need both of you to stay right here," Donna told her and Natesh. "Do not move. There's been an incident, I need to attend. I'll call as soon as I can." And she dashed for the stairs.

On the ground level, she beckoned to the two armed officers and called to the bookseller who was behind the till. "You need to lock the door and bring the shutters down."

The bookseller looked startled, and then shocked, when Donna held up her warrant card.

"There's been a shooting nearby. Everyone will have to stay in here on lockdown until further orders. Do you understand?"

The bookseller followed Donna's instructions, and locked the door immediately behind her.

As soon as she was outdoors, Donna became aware she'd left her jacket inside. There was no time to go back in for it.

She shouted into the shop next door, telling them to get their shutters down, and dashed across the street to the hairdresser's to tell them the same thing. Then she raced towards St. Paul's on the corner and turned left onto High Street, where she almost lost her footing on the cobbled stone pedestrian zone.

She realised, with a sinking heart, that she simply didn't have time to warn all of the shop workers about the danger they were in. She had to get to the scene. The best she could do, as she ran along the streets, was to hold her warrant card out, yelling warnings at the top of her voice for doors to be locked.

The first of the police vans came screaming past, and the growing cacophony of sirens filling the air from all around left nobody with any desire to argue back with her. In her wake, Dundee quickly became a city of people cowering behind lock and key.

Before she knew it, she was coming to the large elegant piazza that was City Square, where the Caird Hall sat. A row of benches faced it, where on warmer days people would take the weight off their feet. The Square itself looked out along Reform Street towards the city's High School at the end, and was flanked on both sides by shopping centres – the Keiller Centre off from its right arm, and the Overgate from its left.

Shoppers spilled from the Overgate shopping centre directly ahead of Donna, having not yet been alerted to the danger and wondering what all the fuss was about. Within seconds, the large crowd came bustling onto City Square. Beyond them, Donna could see more police vans arriving, and hoped the officers would be quick to contain the throng before mayhem broke out.

The growing crowd of people was right in front of her now, and the Caird Hall itself was to her left. Immediately to her right was the Desperate Dan statue, and at its feet lay the crumpled form of what looked most like a woman, although it was hard to tell since the body was being shielded by two armed police officers.

It was chaos ahead, and a ghost town behind her.

The deafening shriek of countless sirens as emergency vehicles ploughed onto the High Street and began to surround the scene at the statue.

Screams audible from the nearest shops on Reform Street.

Officers now shouting at the crowd, erecting a barrier to restrict entry to the scene.

Alice had said this was a shooting.

Donna glanced upwards, and stared at the upper levels of the surrounding buildings, and shuddered to think the shooter might be watching them from behind one of those windows right now, waiting to take his next shot.

Chapter 41

The ten thirty-three train pulled out of Dundee station a few minutes late. As it gently and quietly moved off, passengers were still scouring the carriages for empty seats. Frustrated mutterings punctuated the air as the *Reserved* tickets warded them off.

Sitting in a window seat, with its ticket reserved all the way to Aberdeen, sat DCI Angus Ross. His eyes were closed already, his head resting on his arms on the folded down table. The seat next to him had no ticket on it, and a woman carrying several large bags flopped into it, loudly exclaiming how much her feet were killing her. She quickly apologised for bumping into him, then tutted when he didn't bother to acknowledge her.

"Ladies and gentlemen, welcome aboard the ten thirty-three train to Aberdeen," Gary Tweedie's voice came over the tannoy.

"Bit late to be telling you if you're on the wrong train," the woman muttered to the slumbering man beside her. He didn't respond. She sighed and glanced at the man sitting adjacent to her across the aisle. He didn't acknowledge her either, engrossed in his laptop.

The woman drew her mobile from her pocket and joined the others in the carriage by shifting her attention onto her digital world.

None of the passengers had any idea that the train delay was on purpose, that the driver was following instructions from some thug who was holding his daughter captive.

Gary clocked the two men who had been with the wheelchair user on the platform earlier. They stood watching the train as it moved off. The wheelchair was still there, but empty now, and Gary had a sickening feeling that it had something to do with what he was being made to carry out today.

Through the window behind him, he could see the ticket collector start to make his way towards the carriages. This was a man Gary had known only a short time, but knew him to be a decent guy. He thought about all the passengers he'd seen coming onto the train at Dundee, and the ones who had been on it since Edinburgh. He was suddenly gripped by fear, terror struck at the carnage ahead for this packed passenger train. And there was nothing he could do to warn anyone or to stop it.

Chapter 42

An eerie hush drifted slowly like a dark cloak over City Square.

The sound of sirens could still be heard in the distance and approaching from all directions, but High Street to one side and Reform Street ahead were deserted now. News that this had been a shooting had flown fast.

Several shopping bags littered the ground, dropped in the panic to escape the sniper's view.

The thrum of emergency vehicles as far as the eye could see, blue lights flashing but without the sirens.

Officers hurriedly taped off the square with yellow police tape under the protection of ARU colleagues, their eyes darting upwards, scanning for signs of the shooter in the buildings around them.

The crowd that had come from the Overgate centre had mostly dissipated now, but the few observers who remained at the police barrier looked on in silence. Most of them were holding onto the person standing next to them or were huddled in small groups. Some of them were holding up phones, videoing the scene, and most of the rest were either texting or speaking on their mobiles.

Donna called to the officers at the barrier. "Keep moving it back, away from here," she told them. Armed Response Unit officers had spread themselves around the buildings deemed most likely to have accommodated the shooter, and Donna could make out some sort of logical sweep of the area taking place, but she worried that the barrier was still too close, keeping these people within shooting range and right in danger's way. Her own armed guards were keeping very close to her, and she noted how they scanned constantly for any sign of a threat towards her.

Every minute, emergency vehicles were arriving at the perimeter the ARU officers had set around the scene, and the police presence began to swell. It wasn't long before Donna felt confident enough to leave the other officers to protect the remaining members of the public, and she turned her thoughts to the shooting victim.

She walked toward the Desperate Dan statue, and made a path

through the police and paramedic personnel who were gathered around the motionless body. Several of them glanced at her warrant card, and she could see adrenaline-fuelled reflexes masking their fear. When she got to the front, her eye was instantly drawn to the victim.

A woman.

The body lay crumpled, felled by the clean shot to her chest, and there was no question that she was dead. The paramedic who'd been kneeling over her stood up at Donna's arrival, and shook her head, looking pale and crestfallen.

Donna's breath caught in her throat.

She recognised the coils of red hair that splayed out from the murdered woman. The same red coils of hair she'd seen on the pillow at Ninewells hospital on Sunday evening when she and Alice had gone to visit Marnie Whyte.

Donna quickly took the paramedic's place and knelt at Marnie's side, taking hold of the hand that had held out the note containing Evanton's message for her to *Run*.

She was only vaguely aware of another team spilling from a van that parked very close, and that began to unload the screens that would provide privacy for Marnie Whyte in death and a safe space for the forensics personnel to work in.

Donna looked up and recognised one or two faces from Archie McKinnes's murder scene on Saturday.

She took a deep breath, stood back up to let the forensics team in, and began to issue further orders to secure the wider surrounding area and to oversee the orderly and systematic search of all buildings that could have a view of the murder scene.

Then she phoned Alice, noticing a string of missed calls.

"Thank God you're okay, chief," said Alice.

"Well, reserve your judgement on that," said Donna. "The victim is Marnie Whyte." She heard Alice swear, and went on. "So, now we know this whole thing is linked – Archie McKinnes's body, the hostage situation, and now this."

There was a brief silence from Alice, then, "What are we going to do?"

Donna had never heard anxiety in Alice's voice before. The gung ho ex-Army sergeant was known for throwing herself into the crossfire, literally. The multiple scars that tracked her face told of her enthusiasm for being in the thick of it. The fear in her voice now made the hairs on Donna's arms stand on end.

What are *we going to do?* she asked herself, looking around the scene.

Extra boots had already been drafted in to help deal with recent events. More armed officers had been called into this scene from surrounding forces. They were all stretched beyond their limits, and everyone was exhausted. Yet they were no nearer to any clue as to the whereabouts of Jonas Evanton. A growing dread began to fill Donna's gut.

She was still holding the phone to her ear, when she heard a commotion coming from the direction of the Overgate. She turned to look, in time to see one of the uniformed police officers at the barrier stumble and fall, clutching at his face.

There was a sudden flurry as emergency personnel around the scene began to find cover, fearing their colleague had been shot at.

Then she saw a stone come flying towards the police from within the bystanders.

Donna realised in that instant that the crowd there had suddenly grown, and the mood had turned against the police.

She yelled into her phone, "We need riot gear down here right now."

"Riot gear?" Alice sounded incredulous.

"Mob of vigilantes just turned up," Donna shouted quickly, "and we've an officer injured. It's getting ugly. We need a riot squad here immediately."

She could scarcely believe what she was seeing. All of the police and paramedic resources they could muster were here trying to secure a murder scene while protecting the public from any further danger, and now they were being pelted with stones by a snarling mob that was growing by the minute.

What the hell are we going to do?

Chapter 43

The train pulled into Arbroath station. Gary wiped a tissue across his face as he watched several passengers get out onto the platform. He wanted to shout at all of the remaining passengers to get out, too, but he had to hold it together, even though he knew what was going to happen next and that this train wasn't going to reach the next station. He couldn't risk drawing attention to this journey, and had to make sure he followed his instructions to the letter. Leanne's life depended on it.

He glanced back at the platform and saw a couple of people getting onto the train, then he pushed away any thoughts about what might happen to them, and checked the time. The man holding Leanne had been very specific about the need to delay the departure from Arbroath by three minutes.

The station guard had already signalled that the train was good to go, but Gary had to remain where he was for another minute and a half. He saw the puzzled look from the guard, and gave a casual wave out the cabin window, hoping that would deflect any further attention.

A minute and a half could seem like the blink of an eye, and usually did on the mornings when he was trying to get Leanne out to school on time. But to Gary right now it felt like an eternity of agony.

Finally, he could pull the train away from the station, even though every synapse in his brain was willing him to keep it right where it was. But he followed the instructions, barely noticing the huge billboards that lined the platform on the way out.

Coming under a bridge, he brought the train's speed from 20 to 30 mph as it approached the signal. To his right he was passing by some business units, trees to his left. He could hardly bring himself to look at the signal. If it was red, as his caller had said it would be, then this would be the moment that would mark the point of no return, and the whole horrible thing must actually be real.

He forced himself to look ahead and up to the signal.

Red.

Leanne's frightened voice played back in his mind. And again, those terrifying words, *Follow the instructions I'm about to give you, or you'll never see Leanne again. Not alive, anyway.*

He brought the train speed up to 45 and passed the signal, as instructed.

Now his eyes were bulging and his head was pounding.

There were fields on both sides of the track now as the train approached the first curve. Normally this curve would be taken at 50 mph, but they were at 60. Enough to make the ride noticeably a little more bumpy than usual. Or perhaps that was his heart beating wildly in panic at what he knew was coming.

Another curve to the left, and the speed at 65.

More fields to the right with large domed cold frames protecting the ground from the frost. The speed at 70 and another curve, now to the right. Gary swore he could feel the train's centre of gravity destabilise as he approached the first bridge. It was an arched stone structure, and as the train sped through it at 80 mph, he realised how little room for error there was between its narrow walls. His mouth was dry and he felt tears burn his eyes.

At 85 and then 90 mph, the train sped on through open country, coming to another curve and a second stone bridge. Gary didn't have to count any more. It would happen at the third one.

Pushing the train to its 100 mph limit, and now on the final long curve of this particular journey, Gary saw the third stone bridge ahead.

As he stared at it, he found himself thinking about some of the happier moments he'd shared with Leanne. He had been a good dad. Leanne had done well, and had settled much better at school since she'd come to live with him, away from the destructive influence of her mother. Surely his sister-in-law Grace, who'd been such a help, would take Leanne in? Tearfully, he wondered if she would miss him.

Then he saw the set of blocks bolted onto the track, as he'd been told. Enough at this speed to send the train into the side of the stone walls of the narrow bridge.

Sabotage on the line would prove to be part of the cause of this derailment, he knew, but his jumping a red signal and speeding over the limit would be enough to put him behind bars, if the crash itself didn't put him six feet under.

He had an absurd thought. He wanted to survive, so that at least he would have the opportunity to explain himself at his trial. And Leanne would know he'd done it to protect her.

The wheels crushed over the first of the blocks, then caught on the second and third of them, throwing the weight of the carriages violently off balance.

In the split second before the end passenger carriage hit the stone wall, Gary heard screams, instantly drowned out by tearing metal and the screech of wheels crossing the lip of the rails.

Then he was thrown forward towards the cabin windscreen as the carriage that had hit the bridge dragged the front carriages to a sudden stop, and everything went black and silent.

Chapter 44

Donna felt herself grow dizzy, and her body gave way to wracks of shivering – and not just from the cold. With all of the activity of the forensics tent going up and the battle going on with the vigilante mob at the barrier, she was barely aware of a squad car pulling up in the square. She watched anxiously as some ARU officers continued their painstaking search of the buildings surrounding City Square, while others took care of controlling who could come into the immediate scene, and she wondered where the hell the riot squad had gotten to.

Then she became alert to the sound of a squad car door shutting, and she saw DCI Marsh alight from it, followed by Alice, Akwasi and Morrison.

On instinct, she grabbed her phone to her ear again, having pressed Ross's number.

His last words to her, *I've a train to catch. The 10.33, if I'm not mistaken*, ran in a constant loop through her head.

Voicemail.

She felt her heart jackhammer. She really could be doing with Ross by her side in this situation, not stuck on a train half way to Aberdeen.

She eyed DCI Marsh, barely able to disguise her contempt.

She tried Ross's number again.

Voicemail again.

I've a train to catch. The 10.33, if I'm not mistaken. Ross's voice wouldn't let go.

"You'll catch your death out here," said Marsh, suddenly at her side. He was peeling off his overcoat and then holding it towards her.

She glared at him.

"Look," he went on. "I'm not the enemy here. It's two degrees above zero, there's a gunman on the loose, and I really need you not to faint from hypothermia right now. Truce?" He held out the overcoat again.

"Okay, truce," said Donna, taking the jacket and wrapping it around her shoulders. "As long as you piss off back to Perth when this is done."

"Fine by me," he said.

Donna was unable to help the glimmer of a smile that betrayed her sudden relief at being joined by some of her team. Fighting with Marsh was something she could do without, and she noted his expression of scepticism that it had been that easy.

"I don't see that DC of yours anywhere," he said.

Donna was taken off guard for a moment. Marsh was more observant that she'd given him credit for. But she didn't trust him enough to tell him why she'd sent Fran home. She needed Fran to be fresh for her overnight journey to Cardiff, and under no circumstances was prepared to call her into this scene.

"She's following up a line of inquiry elsewhere," she told Marsh.

"She should be here," Marsh challenged.

Donna glanced at the time, exasperated that they were still

waiting on riot squad, and needing to get Marsh off the topic of Fran's whereabouts.

"I know the victim," she told him. "It's Marnie Whyte, the woman who was set up as the hostage on Sunday."

"Really?" said Marsh. He looked shocked. "This has to be Evanton's doing, then?"

Donna nodded, *yes*.

"Unbelievable," he said. "Where does this end? How the hell can we deal with all of this?"

"I've a bad feeling about it," said Donna.

"You don't say?" Marsh retorted. His mobile rang, and he held Donna's eye while he took the call. Receiving the information, he nodded to her and held up his arm to indicate the riot squad were arriving at the scene. Donna looked over towards the crowd at the barrier, and was relieved to see the line of riot shields going up at last.

Then another van pulled up behind them on the deserted High Street. Two men and a woman jumped out, holding cameras and recording equipment.

"Oh God," Marsh and Donna said in unison.

"I'd better go and speak to them," Marsh said. "You stay here, and get everyone in as soon as ARU give us the go ahead."

He cast a weary glance around the area, then headed off to meet the journalists.

Donna quickly gave orders for Alice to liaise with the Armed Response Unit, for Morrison and Akwasi to check with their uniformed colleagues that the surrounding shops, pubs and restaurants were secure, then made her way to the ambulance where the officer who'd been hit by the stone was being treated.

The officer sat on the floor of the ambulance, with his feet dangling out. He was holding a bandage to his eye, while protesting with the paramedics that he was fine and wanted to get back to duty.

"I'm going to need an officer over at Ninewells in case we have casualties to bring in," Donna told him. "Are you up to that?"

"Yes, Ma'am," said the officer. The sly grin on his face showed that he knew what she was doing.

Finally, Donna looked around and saw order begin to take shape. Marsh was talking to the journalists along on High Street.

Forensics had begun their work, and behind them Reform Street was empty of civilians, now cordoned off at both ends.

The crowd at the barrier were being inched backwards and away from the scene by the riot squad, although they continued to shout abuse at the police.

A safe and orderly search for the gunman was underway.

Her thoughts turned to Libby and Natesh in the Waterstones bookshop. They would know, via social media, what was going on out here and that there had been a shooting. They would certainly be worried about her, but at least she knew they were both safe. She could give Libby a quick call while they awaited authorisation to get onto the scene, and then get on with directing this operation.

A crack ripped through the air.

A man's voice yelled in agony.

Screams from the vigilante crowd.

People scattering in all directions.

And PC Thomas Akwasi lying in a pool of blood in the middle of City Square.

Chapter 45

An unearthly quiet took hold of the Angus countryside, just north of Arbroath.

Moments of disbelief and shock.

Then two men racing, yelling, from the farm next to the railway. They scrambled down the embankment, and stopped, bewildered at the sight of the train wreckage. It was a sight too big to take in, and the enormity of the situation paralysed both men until they began to hear screaming from inside the mangled and toppled carriages. They ran as fast as they could to the nearest one.

A thrum of helicopter blades grew louder, a Marine unit out on exercise circling back towards the unexpected scene.

More residents spilled from nearby houses, and ran to the crash site.

As they arrived, they saw a man in uniform stagger from one of the carriages. The driver? Ticket officer? He stumbled and fell onto the grass verge, and the two men from the farm went to him.

He was searching his pockets.

"I need a phone," he said, breathless.

"Are you alright? What happened?"

The man had a cut on one cheek and looked dazed. Close up, the farm workers could see from his uniform that he was the ticket collector.

"I need to tell the signaller to stop other trains on the line," he told the farm workers. "I can't find the driver. The front carriage...I don't even know where that is..."

The train had consisted of four carriages. The rear carriage now lay on its side a little beyond the bridge. The one in front of it lay at an angle and off the rails. Its front looked crushed, and had impacted the carriage in front of it, which looked to be in a worse state, with obvious breaches in the mangled metalwork. When the front carriage had hit the wall of the bridge, the impact of the rest of the train behind it had sent it up the embankment and its own gravity had brought it plunging back onto the tracks so that it now lay alongside the second carriage but facing in the opposite direction.

The Marine helicopter set down in a field on the other side of the road.

"I'll phone 999," said one of the farm workers as more people arrived beside them. "Who should I ask for?"

"Fire and Rescue," said the ticket officer. "Tell them the train's derailed...I can't tell if we collided with something...but they need to contact the signaller. We can't do anything until we get signal protection."

"We need to get people out of there," someone said, while the farm worker called 999.

"It's not safe," said the ticket officer. "For all we know, another train's heading our way, and could plough into everyone if we evacuate…"

"But if there's a train coming, we can't leave them sitting there!"

"We have to wait."

As they watched, they saw movement inside the rear carriage, but hardly any sound came from it.

The call from the signaller came in just around the same time as the first of the Fire and Rescue appliances and police cars arrived, along with soldiers from the helicopter. One of the fire officers took charge straight away, and reassured the ticket collector that there was no risk now from other trains.

It took some time for the ambulances to begin arriving at the scene, by which time, a small number of people had got themselves out of the train wreckage and were wandering aimlessly along the side of the carriages.

"Aren't you going to help them?" one of the farm workers demanded angrily.

"Look son," said the fire officer in charge, "they're walking wounded. Our priority is to find out if we have passengers in there with more serious, life threatening injuries. Just let us get on with the rescue operation, and stand back."

More ambulances arrived, and remained lined along the road above the railway bridge. Paramedics ran to the scene and took direction from the fire officer. One of them was sent to talk to the farm workers and the others from the area who were waiting there to help.

"There's a golf club near here?" the paramedic asked.

"Just over there," one of the residents pointed.

"That's where we're going to set up the medical assessment centre," said the paramedic. "Anyone who's not in immediate danger will be taken there, and I'll need as many volunteers as possible to help set it up and to help deal with any relatives who could start turning up."

Glad to be able to do something to help, the farm workers and the others followed the paramedic back up to the golf club to get things organised there.

The fire officer led a team of thirty or so personnel towards the tracks to assess the rescue operation. More walking wounded were emerging, but for the most part, the carriages were ominously still and quiet. And then it began.

"I can't breathe! I can't breathe!" came a shriek from one broken window.

"My mother can't move!"

"My leg! My leg!"

"Fucking get us out of here!"

The fire officer turned and faced the emergency personnel. "This is going to take a long time. Are we ready?"

Chapter 46

Donna raced to Akwasi's side, yelling out his name, and ignoring the attempts of an armed officer to stop her. She noticed Morrison and Alice running towards him, too, along with several other officers and paramedics.

Akwasi let out a muted scream through clenched teeth, and Donna saw quickly that the blood was coming from a wound at his shoulder, or perhaps his neck.

The paramedics rushed in, cut off his overcoat and worked feverishly to locate the wound, check his breathing, stem the bleeding, take his blood pressure and check for other injuries, and wrap him up again against the biting cold. When it looked as though the immediate trauma was seen to, Donna moved back in.

"Gunshot wound to the shoulder," one of the paramedics told her. "He's lost a lot of blood very quickly, so we'll need to get him to hospital right away."

"Go with him," Donna heard Marsh say to her, surprised that he was standing next to her.

She placed a hand on Akwasi's forehead. His eyes were closed now, succumbed to the hefty dose of painkiller he'd been given, but he was still groaning.

"You're going to be okay, Thomas," she whispered into his ear. Then to Alice, who was now hunkering down at Akwasi's other side, she said, "Call his wife."

"Already done," said Alice. "I told her to make her way directly to Ninewells."

Another commotion from further back towards the Caird Hall caught Donna's attention, and she became acutely aware that she and Alice were now very exposed in the spot where the gunman had just shot their fellow officer. Then she saw one of her armed guards having an exchange on his radio. She stood up.

"What's going on?" she asked, noticing that the vigilante mob at the barrier had now vanished.

"We've got the shooter," said the guard. "One of the ARU lads spotted him when he fired, and they've just confirmed the arrest."

"Was he alone?" Donna asked.

"No details, Ma'am," said the armed officer. "But it looks like ARU are being stood down now."

Sure enough, three of the armed response officers now appeared from within the building that contained a travel agency on the corner of City Square, and their helmets were removed. Donna watched them make their way back towards their vehicle, while another set of black-clad officers emerged with a man in cuffs.

Donna breathed out a sigh of relief. She was in no doubt the shooter was some expendable stooge of Evanton's, but at least they were all safe here now, and could get on with processing the crime scene. The area would be closed off for at least a full day, and she felt sorry for the businesses who would be forced to remain closed at this vital time in the trading year. But if they didn't stop Evanton fast, that would be the very least of their worries, she knew.

She quickly tried Ross's number again, and swore when the voicemail came back on. Then she felt suddenly uneasy. Why would he still be unreachable? And why would Evanton have bothered to orchestrate Marnie Whyte's execution and the attempted murder of Thomas Akwasi, when he'd specifically made the threat against Ross? Something else was going on, she felt sure. And whatever it was, it wasn't receiving half the response it should be, because all of the area's emergency responders were right here at the Caird Hall.

She was brought back out of her thoughts by the paramedic calling to her to join Akwasi in the ambulance. DCI Marsh waved her on, and she left the crime scene for him to manage as she jumped into the ambulance and strapped herself into the seat beside Akwasi's stretcher. Sitting in the back of ambulances was becoming an unwelcome habit, she thought.

Akwasi's injured shoulder was on the side nearest to her, so she held on tight to a railing to make sure she didn't fall against it during the ten minute sprint across the city to the accident and emergency department. Once there, she ran alongside the trolley as the paramedics rushed Akwasi inside, where medics were already waiting to receive him. They whisked him straight into a room, while he remained unconscious to everything that was going on around him, and Donna was asked to wait in another room nearby.

She sat down on one of the institution-chic chairs and had a look at her phone. There was a voicemail from Libby. Libby never called her on her work phone, so she knew that word about a police officer having been shot must have done the rounds, and that Libby would be worried sick. The signal was very weak, so she stood just outside the door, where it was better, and quickly dialled.

Libby picked up at the first ring. "Are you alright? Where are you?" Her words sounded frantic with worry.

"It's okay," Donna said. "I'm at Ninewells…"

"You're in hospital?" Libby half screamed.

"Yes, but no," Donna told her. "Not me. Thomas Akwasi's been injured. I came in with him in the ambulance. I'm going to wait here until his wife arrives. Where are you?"

"Me and Natesh are still in the Waterstones," said Libby. "They've only just opened the doors, but we saw all the stuff on Twitter. Was it Thomas that was shot?"

"A shoulder injury," said Donna. "It looks fairly serious, but I reckon it'll be a while before we're told anything."

"When can you get home?" Libby asked.

Donna stood up and began to pace back and forth as she spoke. "I'm not sure," she said. "But with all that's happened, it could be a late one again." She was about to apologise for leaving Libby for yet another extended shift.

"Do you need me to bring you anything into your office?" Libby said, before she had the chance.

Donna thought for a moment. "I need for you to get in a taxi," she said, "go straight home, and get the security on. I don't think we're done with incidents yet today." She left it at that. There was no way she was going to break the news over the phone that the shooting victim had been Marnie Whyte. Libby sounded freaked enough.

After the call, Donna sat for a while longer, every so often peeking out of the door and trying to catch something of what might be going on next door with Akwasi. All she could see in there were lots of people in scrubs.

Back in the waiting room, the door burst open, and a woman hurried in. Donna recognised her from the photograph that sat on Akwasi's desk.

"Monifa?" Donna asked, standing to greet her.

The woman looked on the verge of hysteria.

"Why can't I see him?" she demanded.

"He's been quite badly injured," Donna told her, "but he's in good hands. Here, sit down with me and we can chat until they're ready to give us some news."

Looking uncertain, Monifa did as Donna asked, and sat down.

"I'm Donna, I work with Thomas."

"I knew something like this would happen," cried Monifa. "I told him, if you join the police, you're going to get killed…" And she burst into tears.

"He's not going to die," said Donna, hoping she sounded more convinced than she felt. He had lost an awful lot of blood. "Look, why don't I go and get us a cuppa?"

Monifa nodded her head, and blew her nose into a tissue. "Thank you."

Donna emerged from the room and pushed through a set of double doors, finding herself in the A&E assessment area. All of the cubicles were occupied, and human sounds of all sorts emanated from within their curtained frames. A nurses station stood in the centre of the area, and two porters arrived through another set of doors with a trolley, presumably to take someone off for an x-ray or to a ward.

Suddenly her phone began to sound as it found a signal, and she saw a litany of missed calls and text messages.

Her heartbeat sped up.

The last half a dozen or so calls were from Marsh. She saw many more from Alice. She hit the return call button for Marsh.

"Donna, I need you back over at…" his voice faded out as the signal wavered.

Donna moved quickly to another spot, but the signal was still bad. It sounded as though Marsh was on the move, but before she could have a proper listen to what he was trying to say, the doors to her left crashed open and a team of medics and nurses rushed out towards the A&E ambulance bay. At the same time, running towards them were paramedics with somebody on a trolley. They were followed closely behind by another set of paramedics with a second trolley.

Donna froze. She shouted into her phone, "Harry, what's going on?"

"Train….derailed….Arbroath," were the only words she could make out.

Chapter 47

It was odd to be home unexpectedly in the daylight, Donna thought, as she pulled onto the drive in Claypotts Place. The sleet was fast turning into snow, and she gazed for a while at the attempts of the struggling pot plants next to the front door to hang onto grim life. Someone else would be re-planting here in the Spring, she thought, and tried to imagine what this house would be like with somebody else living in it. She was trying to fill her imagination with anything, really, that didn't involve frantic worry about Angus Ross. But it was too late. Before she knew it, her head was whirling with the details they had just been given by DCI Marsh.

He had gathered her and her remaining team, along with most of the early shift, and relayed the news that a train had derailed between Arbroath and Montrose. It was a busy passenger train with four carriages, with expected casualties in each one. The huge search and rescue operation was still underway, and Marsh had emphasised the painstakingly long time that it could take to get each individual out of a wreckage like that. He'd had the Chief Fire Officer on the phone leaving him under no illusions about it, while reassuring him that they had adequate personnel on the ground, with military support from the Marine base in Arbroath.

Marsh had sent Donna and her colleagues home – *Get some kip, it'll be your last until we get on top of this mess* – while the back shift were called in early to replace them. A complicated workforce operation was underway to try and make sure they would have enough cover to deal with everything that was being flung at them now.

Donna felt a pang of guilt, wondering if she could have prevented all of this if only she had followed Evanton's instructions about the body in the Ethie Woods. But the guilt was swept away by a flash of anger. None of this was her doing. The blame for all of this was on Evanton's head, and no matter what it took, she was going to find him and make him pay.

Marsh was staying on without a break, and was on his way up to the crash site. He had told them he would let them know as soon as there was any news, particularly about Angus Ross's whereabouts. Donna's stomach had turned to water when Marsh had confirmed the derailed train was in fact the one Ross had been booked onto.

A soft *tap tap* on the car window brought Donna out of her nightmarish reverie. There was Libby, shivering in the cold, and with a puzzled look on her face.

"Are you alright?" she asked, opening the driver door and leading Donna out by the elbow.

Donna felt her mind numb over, and suddenly found it difficult to speak. An irresistible fatigue washed over her, and her limbs felt like ton weights. With a monumental effort, she followed Libby into the house and allowed herself to be seated with her feet up on the settee.

Libby knelt beside her, took hold of her hands, and studied her eyes closely.

"We're way out of our depth," Donna said, shaking her head sadly. "Thomas Akwasi got shot today. We don't know if he'll make it, and if he does, what sort of injury he might have to live with. He's got a baby."

Libby closed her arms around Donna. "Is that why you got sent home early?"

"No," said Donna, her voice flat. "It gets worse. The victim who got shot to begin with was the woman that was held at the flat in Arbroath. The one who gave me that message from Evanton to run."

She felt Libby stiffen. "Do you think he had her shot because you didn't cave in to his threat?"

"His threat was to kill Angus Ross," said Donna. "And Ross got on the train to Aberdeen earlier, the one that derailed while we were at the murder scene, and now we can't get hold of him nobody knows where he is and I've been trying to get him for hours he's not picking up his phone or returning calls it's just going straight onto voicemail…"

"Slow down, shush," Libby soothed, rubbing her shoulders in an attempt to calm her. But Donna's breathing had grown rapid, and the vortex of thoughts and fears and pieces of the multitude of investigations now underway tore its way around inside her head, turning everything into a blur.

She was unaware that she was springing to her feet and beginning to shout.

"I'm going to find him! I just need to get in front of the TV cameras and he'll see me. I'll make him meet me face to face…"

"Donna, you're scaring me," said Libby, also standing up.

"I can end it!"

"Where are your pills?"

Donna made a dash for the door, but Libby got there first and blocked it.

"Stop," she told Donna. "You need to rest. It sounds like you're going to have some very long shifts coming up. You need to rest, or you'll burn out."

Donna paused, and felt Libby's words rescue her stricken mind. She nodded her head, exhausted, and returned to the settee, where she lay down and closed her eyes.

Run wild
Thursday
Chapter 48

A buzzing noise seeped into Donna's consciousness. She lifted her hand and swatted at the imaginary wasp. Libby lay in the depths of sleep beside her. In her bleary state, she wondered how she'd gotten from the settee to the bed. She didn't remember.

The buzzing caught her attention again.

She opened her eyes, and realised it was her phone. She felt Libby shift around onto one side and heard her mutter words in her sleep as she did so. Donna lifted the phone from the bedside drawer, and slipped into the bathroom to answer it.

"Donna," DCI Marsh's voice sounded sombre, "I'm afraid I have some terribly bad news to tell you."

Donna was suddenly fully awake.

"I…I don't quite know how to say this," Marsh's voice wavered. "I understand you and Angus Ross were close friends…I'm so sorry, but DCI Ross has been identified as a fatality on board the derailed train. He's dead."

Donna sank to the floor of the bathroom. Her head swam, filled with slow turning concrete, while Marsh's voice trailed on somewhere in the background, saying something about informing the rest of the team in the morning. She wasn't aware of putting her phone onto the floor without switching it back off.

It couldn't be true, she decided eventually, and the thought began to clear her head a little. They must have made a mistake. There was no way Ross could be dead. Still only three in the morning, she rang his mobile again. Attempted call number thirty-six. And again it went to voicemail.

There had to be an explanation. She just had to figure it out. Was it Evanton playing with her head?

A run, she thought. Going for a run would help calm her mind so that she could work this out.

She began to scramble around in the dark for her running gear. Reflective gear was what she needed. Yes, she decided suddenly, she should replace her running shoes, tops and joggies with new, reflective gear. Keep safe in the dark. She quickly logged into Amazon and her fingers began to tap on the items while she continued to search in the dark room for the real ones. Better order several sets, she thought, as the new items appeared on her screen.

She paused before hitting the button that would make the purchase.

Had a thought. Did she want to be drawing attention to herself in the dark? Perhaps some new dark running gear would be better. Or, why not a treadmill so that she could stay indoors and run? *Genius!* Item after item came up on her screen, all offering a hundred reasons to spend the money.

She caught sight of the tub of lithium pills sitting on her bedside cabinet. Partly from some subconscious understanding, and partly from the fear sparked by a sudden lucid moment, she scooped two of the pills into her mouth, then went downstairs to the kitchen for a glass of water.

She spent the next forty-five minutes pacing and sweating, anxiously fighting off a bombardment of unwanted thoughts, while at the same time a plan began to form in her mind when she remembered her own words from earlier, *I just need to get in front of the TV cameras and he'll see me.*

Evanton had known about the house on Keptie Road. And about the deal with the journalists as soon as it had happened. He had also known what Mo had said about him. He'd been watching, alright, she knew now. And it was his constant watching that Donna was going to use to trap him. Her gut told her this was the way to get him, while her mind tried hard to figure out exactly what she might have to do to pull it off.

Finally, her head began to calm and, her body exhausted, she let herself fall onto the living room rug, where she lay and sobbed.

It was still dark, but Donna felt sure she'd slept in, when Libby's concerned face appeared in front of her.

"What happened last night?" Libby asked. "Running clothes scattered all over the place, lithium pills empty, and there's a confirmation email from Amazon for a £5,000 treadmill. So don't try and tell me nothing happened."

Donna sat up slowly on the rug. Amazon? Treadmill? What was Libby talking about? She tried to open her mouth to protest, but nothing came out. She caught something in Libby's eyes. What was it? Fear, perhaps. Despair. Her heart began to quicken.

Libby had mentioned the lithium pills... and slowly the events of the early hours swam back into her consciousness, and she realised that Libby must be fearing another breakdown. She wasn't far wrong, Donna thought, and knew Libby's fear came from not knowing how they were going to get through this one.

Then she suddenly remembered the reason for her late night blow-out: Harry Marsh's phone call.

She recalled his words – the words that couldn't be true. She fumbled for her phone. There would be missed calls on it from Ross, she knew there would be. He couldn't be...

But before she realised what was happening, her own mouth said the words to Libby. "Angus Ross is dead."

Libby's hand went to her mouth, and her eyes began to fill.

Donna felt momentarily confused. Why was Libby reacting as if this was the truth?

"The train that derailed yesterday," Donna found herself going on. "Ross was on it."

It felt as though she was watching the ghost of herself saying these things. She tried to make it stop, but it wouldn't.

"I can't believe that," said Libby, sitting down next to her, and bringing her into her arms.

"Neither can I," said Donna. "Ross is one of the good guys. He can't be..."

All of a sudden, Ross's smiling face came into her mind, as clearly as though he was standing there in the room with her. She saw the sparkle in his eye and the raised brow that meant he was about to say something that was guaranteed to make her smile back. "Ross was one of the good guys." Her heart was being torn from her chest, and she wanted to scream.

Then she began to remember fragments of the plan she'd begun to form during her restless night.

Chapter 49

Bell Street was a sombre place that morning. Plenty of activity was going on, more than usual even, but the discussions were muted and functional.

Donna slipped into the Quiet Room and phoned Fran, using the landline. She wondered briefly whether to bring Fran in on her plan, but decided it was too soon. There were details she still had to check before she would know if it was even viable. Besides, the young DC had enough to contend with at the moment, and Donna wanted to make sure Fran kept her focus on finding Sarah Cooper.

"We're going over to the camp right now," Fran reported, when she answered Donna's call.

"Good," said Donna, "but there's something important I have to tell you, and I need you to follow my instructions no matter what. Are you clear?"

"Alright," said Fran, sounding uncertain.

"There's been a security breach here, and we can't risk any details of your assignment getting out," said Donna. "So you need to remove the battery from your mobile phone as soon as we're done, and only contact me via a secure landline. Have you got that?"

After the call, Donna made her way back to the team room and hoped Fran would keep to her word this time.

DCI Marsh met her with a hand clasp at the door. "I've called for an urgent briefing to let everyone know," he whispered to her. "But there's more information to add, and I wanted to tell you first. Cause of death was a knife wound to the abdomen. Ross was dead before he ever got on that train."

Donna stared blankly at the acting DCI as it occurred to her that ACC Loudoun was the only person who knew the exact train Ross would be on. Could he be the mole? Just as quickly, she dismissed the idea. Loudoun didn't know about the things that Evanton had known – that she'd gone home to take his call, or about the offer on Keptie Road.

The more she thought about it, the more convinced she became that she was on the right tracks with her plan to trap Evanton. She could feel it.

"Donna?"

She flinched, brought back to the here and now, at Marsh's voice. "I would have suggested you take some time off after a shock like this, but to be honest we need you here, now more than ever before."

Marsh was checking his watch, and called out, "Okay everyone, I need your attention."

Donna watched as the officers in the room began to assemble, facing Marsh. There were shared glances amongst many of them, she noted, a sign that they had already heard rumours about DCI Ross but didn't want to hear them confirmed.

As more officers filed in, it was standing room only, and Donna sought out her own team. She spotted Alice consoling Morrison with a pat on his arm, and realised with alarm that they were now all she had. Akwasi was in hospital, Fran was in Wales, and Ross was...

She refused to let her eyes well up, and made her way to the front of the room to stand with Alice and Morrison.

Harry Marsh looked around as though to check everyone was there, and cleared his throat. Donna could see the strain in his features, and remembering his gesture of giving her his overcoat outside the Caird Hall, began to wonder if he might not be that bad, after all. She took a good look at him, and could imagine how he might have had to adopt the arrogant facade to survive in the police with his posh public schoolboy accent and his slight frame. Or was she simply scraping the barrel for allies? She wasn't sure, and she didn't have the energy right now to figure it out.

"As you all know," Marsh began, "a passenger train derailed yesterday morning between Arbroath and Montrose. It was a particularly tricky rescue operation that went on into the evening, and we've now had confirmed 32 casualties, with eight of those in a serious condition."

He paused and cleared his throat again, and Donna could definitely hear a waver in his voice as he went on, "I'm most terribly sorry to have to report to you that there was also one fatality, identified late last night as DCI Angus Ross."

There was a collective intake of breath around the room, and words of disbelief mingled with sobs of shock. Donna noticed tears glistening on Stephen Morrison's cheeks.

"The pathologist has told us the cause of death was a knife wound to the abdomen, not related to the train crash itself," Marsh said. "So this is now a murder investigation."

Zombie-like, Donna looked from one person to another around the room. She saw the red-rimmed eyes. Felt the despair and the fear. There had been no mole, she determined. She was right about her plan.

"The train driver is in a critical condition, but stable," Marsh was going on. "He's in the Western General Hospital in Edinburgh, where some of the wounded passengers were also taken, as Ninewells had to close its doors to admissions early on. We've got others at Aberdeen Royal Infirmary and a serious spinal injury at the Queen Elizabeth in Glasgow. We've got officers in attendance at Edinburgh waiting to speak to the driver as soon as possible. Our working theory is he was ordered by Evanton – directly or indirectly – to derail the train. We'll find out, no matter what it takes."

Donna let Marsh's words trail on in the background, and she leaned into Alice and Morrison, indicating to them to listen.

"I don't want Fran to know anything about this until she gets back," she told them.

"Understood," said Alice.

"Where is she?" Morrison asked.

"She's following up a sensitive lead," Donna replied. "I need her full attention on that – it could be our only way of luring Evanton in."

"Won't she see the news on social media?" Morrison remarked.

"I've taken care of that," said Donna, wondering about his uncharacteristic challenge. She swiftly put it down to the horrific situation they were all in. How would any of them know how to react?

Marsh was still going over the various details, assigning officers to tasks like re-interviewing the Dundee shooter…

"We got nowhere with him yesterday…"

…bringing in John Ogilvie…

"As long as nothing else happens today, get him in here…"

…and a hundred other lines of enquiry that needed following up or re-checking.

A clamour built up around the room as officers set about their various duties.

"I do understand," Marsh shouted above the din, "that you've had a terrible shock. The best thing we can do right now is to pull out all the stops to find Jonas Evanton before he gets the chance to cause any more tragedy."

Further tasks were issued, and the activity and noise levels in the room grew with the renewed vigour amongst the officers to capture Evanton.

"One final thing," Marsh bellowed. "Obviously the media interest in all of this is massive, and once they find out about DCI Ross it'll be off the scale. We'll be holding a press conference later on today, but until then I want you to remain tight-lipped. We need some time to assess the impact of any information we put out there – this city is a powder keg right now, so we don't need any inflammatory messages going out. And that's an order."

He stared into Donna's eyes. She could see him searching for a response. All she had in her were the details of her plan, growing louder and louder. She had to do it, and now. She was going to play Evanton at his own game, and she would fight to win. She stepped to the front of the room and picked out a couple of uniformed officers.

"You," she pointed at them. "Bring in Burly McKinnes. It's time to start clearing up."

Alice threw her a confused scowl. Marsh nodded his approval.

"Go and fetch him now," said Donna, seeing the hesitation on their faces as they stood, uncertain. She went on. "Alice, you and I will question him. I'm looking to have him charged with his father's murder, and we'll let the press know this afternoon."

"What's got into you...?" Alice began.

"Do you not understand an order when you hear one, sergeant?" Donna snapped.

Alice looked taken aback momentarily, then her expression softened. "Look, I know you've had a shock, chief..."

"Damned right I've had a shock," Donna said. "We all have. And it ends now. We're going to begin by closing down the McKinnes murder investigation, just like Angus Ross wanted us to do in the first place. Then we're going to bring in John Ogilvie and lean on him hard until he tells us – because he knows, alright – how the body went missing."

Conversations stopped abruptly.

Every eye in the room was fixed on Donna.

The air was charged electric.

"You two, did I not just tell you to get out of here and bring in BurlyMcKinnes?" she bellowed.

Both PCs scarpered to the door without further hesitation.

"Well, what are you all standing around gawping for?" Donna shouted across the room. "There are plenty fucking lines of inquiry to be getting on with."

There was a sudden springing to action again around the room.

"Well, I see you've got everything under control here," said Marsh, looking as though he wanted to be anywhere else. He made his way out the door, adding, "Come and brief me once you've charged McKinnes."

Chapter 50

Fran was still unnerved by Donna's warning about the phones, and as instructed, she'd removed the battery from her own mobile. All contact, like the DI's call from the unknown number, was to be by landline only. It felt a bit like having lost a limb, not having access to her mobile – it must be what policing was like in the old days, she thought – but at least she would be back home tomorrow.

She could tell something else had happened, though. Nobody had answered or returned her calls from the previous day, and Donna had been very evasive when she'd asked. Well, whatever it was, Fran thought, looking out of DS Tom Jones's car window at the disappearing cityscape, she had a job to be getting on with.

"Traffic's always like that," chirped DS Jones.

His accent made Fran smile. It had taken an age to drive through Cardiff. While the congestion was about the worst she'd seen anywhere, the city itself seemed very attractive, and she found herself hoping that Jones would offer her a tour once her task was done.

They seemed to be heading towards the coast and into more greenery.

"Won't take us long now," said Jones.

They drove on past a large retail park, and Jones suddenly pointed across Fran to something out of her side.

"Pinewood Studios, that is, over there," he announced.

Fran looked, and sure enough there was a building with confirmation on its signage that it was indeed Pinewood Studios.

"I didn't know that was in Cardiff," she said.

Jones chuckled. "It's one of the studios. Not the James Bond one, but series four of Sherlock did get filmed here, you know."

They came towards some storage depots and a car wreckage yard, before turning along towards what looked like a residential area.

"That's us," said Jones, pulling into a small housing scheme.

Fran looked around, surprised. "This is Shirenewton?"

Jones looked at her, as though wondering why she seemed surprised.

Fran looked around, and realised that the houses were actually static homes, and here and there amongst them were vans and the odd mobile home.

"What were you expecting, tents around a campfire?" Jones laughed.

Fran's cheeks flushed. She sort of had been.

She got out of the car and made her way along the path that led into the scheme. She passed by what looked like an office, and was surprised to see a sign declaring it to be Cardiff Housing. Bemused, she watched as two women came out of the office complaining loudly to one another about the exorbitant water rates they were being charged compared to the city's settled residents.

"Bloody daylight robbery, it is!" one of them concluded.

The women glanced at Fran suspiciously and walked on.

Having been surprised that this wasn't the way she'd imagined a Traveller site to look, she was feeling rather alone right now. She glanced back over her shoulder. Tom Jones was sitting in his unmarked car at the edge of the site as she'd asked.

The site was fairly quiet. She felt foolish about her expectation to find bare-footed children in rags running around trying to steal from her pockets. She realised the reason there were no kids here was they were probably at school. But, to her surprise, there weren't a lot of adults around either.

She was about to go into the housing office, when she spotted two older men deep in conversation about something that was under the raised bonnet of the car they were standing in front of. She reckoned they might be more likely to know Sarah Cooper, if she even lived here, so she braced herself, wary of a hostile reaction as soon as she identified herself.

The two men looked up and watched as she approached them, stopping their conversation in mid flow.

Fran wondered if she should actually conceal her identity, and quickly scanned her brain for a plausible reason why she – *not* being a police officer – would be looking for Sarah Cooper.

"You're not one of the local plods," one of the men commented straight away.

Damn it, she thought, frustrated and on edge.

"How can we help you?" the other man asked her.

Fran blinked. "Um, do you live here?" she asked, and immediately wanted to hit herself over the head.

The two men looked at one another and burst out laughing.

"For a little while, yes," said one of them. "I'm Peter Clark." He held out his hand, and it took a moment for Fran to jolt out of her thoughts and return the handshake.

"DC Fran Woods," she said. "I'm here from Dundee, trying to trace a Sarah Cooper. Do you know her?" She held out her warrant card, which the men glanced at briefly.

"The police wanting to talk to Sarah?" one of the men asked, his eyebrow betraying his surprise. "You'll have a bit of a wait," he went on. "Unless you want to go to the college?"

"Is she a student?" asked Fran, bringing out her notebook to take the details.

"Lecturer," said both men together.

Fran felt the flush of shame spread across her face once again, wondering if she could just be a fraction more patronising.

"How far is it to the college?" she managed to muster herself.

"Take you about twenty minutes in the car," said one of the men, nodding towards Tom Jones's car. Again Fran felt ridiculous, muttered a few words of thanks, and scurried back to the car.

"Find out what you were after?" Tom Jones asked in his sing-song voice.

Fran forgot all about her useless mobile, and the shame of her naivety having been so obvious, when she got back into the car beside him. Unlike his singing counterpart, this Tom Jones was fresh out of police college, and just Fran's type.

She smiled at him as she asked him to take her to the college, then reminded herself about the trouble she'd gotten into the last time she'd allowed a guy to take her eye off the ball. There was no way she was going to be distracted this time, she determined. But she still stole another glance at him.

Chapter 51

While the two PCs were away to arrest Burly McKinnes, Donna decided this was her chance to test her theory, and she knew exactly who to talk to about it. She threw her jacket onto the nearest desk, and winced as her mobile, which was in the pocket, *thunked* against its surface. If her hunch was right, then she had to leave it here. And, she thought bitterly, she had to get out of this team room, away from the oppressive sadness of it.

Evanton had known their every move, she pondered, as she walked towards the stairs. He'd known details that nobody else could have known, and as soon as they'd happened. ACC Loudoun had made the arrangement for Ross to be on that train. While he could have been the mole on that occasion and could have passed the details to Evanton, there was no way Loudoun could have got hold of the other information. He definitely wasn't the mole, Donna knew in her gut, and nobody else was, either. Ross had been right about that, and her new theory explained it all.

"...*he's definitely watching me,*" she remembered saying. The question was: how? And now she was about to discover if she had worked it out.

She picked up her pace, then ran up two flights and along a corridor until she arrived at the office she was looking for. The poster on the door said,

In a maths emergency call:

$$\left(\frac{18}{\pi}\right)^2 \int\limits_0^1 \frac{\ln\left(1 + \sqrt[37]{x}\right)}{x}\, dx$$

She walked into the room without knocking. Four large desks sat together in the centre of it. Two of them were occupied, but the officers there didn't look up from their screens. Then Donna saw Bruno, an officer she had worked with before, coming in through a door at the far side of the office.

"DI Davenport," he addressed her. "What brings you up here?"

"I need to run something past you," said Donna.

"Sure," said Bruno. "Come on through."

He led her back through the door he'd just appeared from, and into his office. There were no windows in this part of the building, and although it was a pleasant enough space, it was stuffy.

Donna impressed upon him the secret nature of her enquiry as he settled himself down at his desk. She waited while he poured coffee, then began as soon as she had his full attention.

"Can somebody watch and listen to you via your mobile phone, without you knowing anything about it?" she asked.

Bruno's expression grew serious, and he leaned closer to Donna, adding to the covert nature of their discussion.

"They certainly can," he said. "Just ask Prince Harry. Remember the News International phone hacking scandal? And technology's moved on a hell of a lot since then. What makes you ask?"

Donna felt goose bumps crawl along her forearms.

"You'll know the basics of our investigation into the whereabouts of Jonas Evanton?" she asked. Bruno nodded that he did. "Well, the recent hostage situation, the body theft, the shootings at the Caird Hall, and the train crash – " she couldn't bring herself to mention Ross's murder – "are all linked, and we believe Evanton has been orchestrating a campaign to bring us to our knees."

Bruno began to tap a pen on his desk, as he continued to watch Donna intently.

She went on. "He's been a step ahead of us at every point, and he's known information – things he could only know if he was actually watching us. Particularly me. And some of it is stuff he couldn't really know by physically following me around, at least not without being seen."

"So, you're wondering if he's watching you remotely?" said Bruno. "Using your phone as, like, a reality TV show?"

"Exactly," said Donna. "And he could be doing that?"

"Yes, he could," said Bruno. "Especially if he's not too fussed about breaking the law." He chuckled. "There are actually several different methods he could be using. Can I see your phone?" He held out his hand.

"I left it downstairs," said Donna. "Just in case I was right. I don't want him to know I'm onto him."

"Good move," said Bruno. "Well, there are methods that rely on spy software being installed onto your phone. It's really easy to come by, but the user needs to have physical access to your phone, although only very briefly. Is there a chance he – or somebody working with him – could have handled your phone for a few minutes?"

Donna thought. Of course it was possible. She didn't always carry her phone on her. But would Evanton really get someone to tail her for that moment, on the off-chance, that she might lay it down?

"It's possible," she said, "but I'd say pretty unlikely."

"Well, in that case," said Bruno, "there's another method, one that doesn't require physical access to your phone. It uses what we call a StingRay device. Basically, it mimics a mobile phone mast, and tricks your phone signal into connecting with it, then your phone is hacked. US intelligence services use it as a surveillance method, although they spend a lot of time in court arguing that they don't…"
Donna suddenly had a picture in her head of Mo Skinner discussing her court cases with Evanton during one of her trips to the States, while Bruno continued. "If it's a StingRay, you've no way of knowing your phone's been hacked, unlike the spy software, which you would be able to find if you knew where to look."

Donna began to feel sick at the thought of Evanton using her phone to watch and listen to everything she did and said.

"There's more bad news to be aware of if it's a StingRay," said Bruno. "If that's what he's using to watch you, he'll be able to watch everyone else who's near you, on their phones, too, and it would also take us much longer to remove the threat."

The nausea began to turn to excitement. What Bruno had told her sounded plausible. Very plausible indeed, and it definitely fit with the last few days' experiences. If Evanton was spying on her – on all of them – using a StingRay device, then she knew now exactly how she was going to fight back.

"I'd like your take on what I'm planning to do now," she told him.

As she outlined her thinking, she could tell by Bruno's expression and his nods of approval that she was on the right tracks. This was going to work, she felt. At last, there was hope of trapping Jonas Evanton. Just as long as she could keep a clear head.

Donna thanked him, and then left to carry out her next task. This she had to do without anyone from her team seeing her, so she took a circuitous route through the building so as to avoid passing the team room on her way out.

She went to the Bell Street exit, again realising that she was going out into the freezing December air without a jacket, and ran at full speed out of the police complex, left along Marketgait and past the Shell garage until she came to the shop she was looking for, unassuming with its shabby exterior.

The shopkeeper barely registered her when she made her request, simply confirming in a bored voice, "Five of them?"

Donna felt dismayed that the lack of fuss probably meant this sort of thing went on regularly here, so close to police HQ. But at least it meant nobody was going to be talking about her activities. Taking her package, she made a mental note to have this shop checked out at some point. But not right now.

Shivering in the cold, she hugged the package close to her body and hurried back to Bell Street.

Chapter 52

When Donna got back to Bell Street, she saw that the car park was full. She had a feeling the press room was going to be packed out, and no wonder.

Alice was pacing up and down the team room when Donna got there, impatience leeching from every pore.

"There you are," Alice exclaimed. "Where have you been? That's Burly McKinnes in now."

The sergeant didn't look best pleased as Donna grabbed her things from the desk where she'd left them, and strode off towards

173

the interview room without answering. Alice marched after her.

They went directly to the interview room where Burly McKinnes would be waiting for them, along with – Donna hoped – his lawyer.

"Go easy on him," Alice said, as they approached the room.

"He's guilty," Donna said flatly. "We need to show the press we're on top of this. We need an arrest today."

"You're acting weird," Alice muttered.

"Things have changed," Donna retorted.

The door to the interview room opened just as they reached it, and the uniformed officer who was there nodded Donna and Alice inside.

Burly was there, sat at the table in his gym sweats that still looked soaked, as though he'd been lifted straight from a workout.

Dougal Clarence was there, too, and he sprang to his feet, fire spitting from every pore as soon as he saw the officers. Burly's expression, however, changed to one of relief when he saw that it was Donna, and he sat back in his chair, relaxing his shoulders.

"Don't get too comfy," Donna told him. "I'm charging you with the murder of Archie McKinnes."

"What?"

"This isn't procedure," Alice whispered in Donna's ear, before Dougal Clarence exploded.

"This is outrageous!" he bellowed. "You know fine well you can't just come in here and do this."

Donna strode into his personal space and thrust her chin into his face. "Oh, really?" she sneered at him. "What are you going to do about it, then?"

"I demand to speak to your superior," Clarence stood his ground, eyeball to eyeball. "I have never heard the likes of this in all of my career."

"Huh," Donna scoffed. "Let's take it outside the room, shall we?"

"What the fuck?" Alice mouthed desperately.

"Yes," Donna said, turning to include Alice, "let's just step outside the room and have a little word with Mr. Clarty…" Dougal Clarence bristled… "You don't mind, do you, Burly? I mean, with all the evidence against you, he's going to be pretty useless to you now."

Burly McKinnes looked panic stricken.

"This is unbelievable!" Clarence protested as Donna roughed him from the room. The uniformed officer's eyes were wide in astonishment at the scene he was witnessing, but he closed the door after Donna, Alice and Clarence, and he stayed in the room with Burly.

"You have so lost it this time," Alice hissed, before shrinking back at the strange look in Donna's eyes.

The desk sergeant remained silent as he watched the scene before him – a DI issuing the verbal equivalent of a summary execution of the young lad in the interview room, not to mention the demolition of his lawyer. Donna glared at him, willing him – daring him – to challenge the way she was dealing with the lawyer. She knew her behaviour was verging on police brutality, and at one point, when she shoved Clarence hard back against a wall, even she thought she might have gone too far.

Alice looked like she was going to explode as she watched the shaken Clarence retreat back into the interview room to confirm that his client had indeed been charged with murder. She shared a brief look of disgust with the desk sergeant as she took a deep breath and followed Donna back out and in the direction of the press room.

Donna was already on the phone to Morrison, checking everything was set up for the press conference.

"It's standing room only," Donna told Alice when she finished the call, "which is exactly what we need. It's about time everybody started talking about how we're clearing this mess up."

"Until you get the murder charge thrown back in your face," said Alice. "And an assault charge on Dougal Clarence. There's no way you're going to get away with that farce, and what do you think the press coverage is going to be like then?"

"Oh, give it a break," Donna sighed. Alice's jaw fell open. "You can go back to the team room. I'll handle the press conference on my own."

"Like hell I will," said Alice. "I'm not letting you loose with them, the mood you're in."

"For God's sake, Alice," Donna snapped. "Can you follow an order for just once in your life?"

"That was an order, was it?" Alice shouted back at her. "Well, fuck you, DI Dickhead. We're all gutted at losing Ross, you know."

"You think this is just about Ross?"

The two officers came to a stop outside the press room. Donna continued the shouting. "Have you any idea how much worse this can get? Have you?"

"Well, it's not going to get any better, the way you're going about things," Alice yelled back.

The rumble of chatter that had been going on inside the room grew quiet, and Donna became aware of the shuffling of feet and a collective breath-held silence moving towards the door from the inside.

"This investigation is at a critical stage," Donna said, "and I'm not going to risk it being jeopardised by your constant questioning of my decisions."

"What?" Alice challenged loudly. "Are you having me up on a charge, then?"

The press room door began to open, and as soon as there was enough space, out came a camera lens and there was a burst of flash, and the next day's front covers were taken care of, courtesy of the angry face-off between Donna and Alice.

Donna glared in at the journalists, reached out a long arm, and grabbed the nearest camera lens.

"Watch it! What do you think you're doing?" the photographer shouted at Donna. More flashes caught the scene.

"Get back inside," Alice pleaded with the journalists.

There was a scuffle as the reporters closest to the door tried to move back into the room, while those furthest away pushed forward.

A number of uniformed officers, alerted to the commotion, ran towards the press room.

"Get this lot back inside and settled down," Donna told them. "We've charged Burly McKinnes with murder, and I want it

176

covered."

"You've got someone for the McKinnes murder?" one of the reporters asked. It brought with it a fresh barrage of questions and jostling.

"Yes," said Donna. "So, if you want the details, get back inside and I'll tell you everything."

"You haven't run any of this past DCI Marsh," Alice said loudly, at her back. Donna turned and glared at her in response, then elbowed her way into the press room.

Chapter 53

Tom Jones chatted all the way back into the city centre as he drove Fran towards the college.

"It's not far from the train station," he pointed out as they drove past. And he wasn't wrong. Within minutes, they had worked their way to the front of the traffic queue, and arrived outside a large shiny glass affair. Jones turned a sharp right, and manoeuvred into one of the staff parking bays.

"Am I waiting here for you?" he asked.

"Could you, please?" Fran asked. "I'm not really sure how long I'll be, though."

"Not a problem," said Jones, pulling a newspaper from the glove compartment. "I came prepared."

Fran laughed, then got out and found her way to the college main entrance.

Inside, she found herself in a large atrium from where she could look up and see several levels of glass-panelled teaching rooms, and right up through a massive skylight. There was a snazzy snack bar on the ground level nearby, and lots of seating. The place was all glass and primary-coloured blocks. It reminded Fran a little bit of an oversized nursery school.

It was a busy place, with hoards of students rushing about from one end of the building to the other, up and down stairwells, and in and out of rooms.

Fran made her way to the main reception, where she asked for Sarah Cooper. The woman at the reception desk looked faintly alarmed to be shown Fran's warrant card, and promptly made a phone call to ask the lecturer to join them.

"You can use that interview room across there," the receptionist said, pointing to a door next to a drinks vending machine. "I'll ask Mrs Cooper to meet you in there, that alright?"

"Perfect, thank you," said Fran. She made her way to the small room, pausing only to consider whether to get a drink from the machine and deciding not to, and sat down, wondering how this might go.

It took about twenty minutes, but just as Fran was beginning to get annoyed at the wait, there was a soft rap on the door and a blonde-haired woman who looked to be in her mid-thirties came in. Fran had to stop herself from gasping out loud. There was no mistaking whose daughter this was. Sarah Cooper was the image of Mo Skinner. And, from the photos she'd seen of Jonas Evanton before his plastic surgery to disguise himself, she could see that Sarah had his distinctive piercing blue eyes. She suddenly felt queasy.

"Are you okay?" Sarah Cooper hurried forward, holding out her hand as if to prevent Fran from falling off her seat.

Fran recovered herself and introduced herself to Sarah.

"Has something happened?" Sarah asked, then her worried expression changed to one of surprise. "Oh my God, you're a Scottish copper, are you here about the adoptions?"

Fran took out her notebook in an attempt to give herself a moment. The adoptions? It sounded as though Sarah Cooper knew more about her investigations than she'd thought. She wasn't sure how to play this. She wished she could get Donna on the phone for advice right now. But she was on her own. She took a deep breath, and began.

"I'm hoping to ask you a few questions," she told Sarah. "And actually to ask for your help."

"My help?" Sarah asked. She laughed softly. "It's not often we get the police asking for our help, if I'm honest. What on earth could I help you with?"

Sarah's innocent expression was disarming. But if Fran had learned one thing from bitter experience, it was never to be deceived by a person's outward appearance.

"I spoke recently with Peterborough Social Services," she began. She noticed right away how Sarah's face blanched. She had certainly hit some kind of nerve. "Can you tell me why you were in touch with them?"

Sarah shifted in her seat, obviously uncomfortable.

"I was brought up by adoptive parents," she began. "I never met my birth parents, and the only thing I knew was that my mother came from somewhere near Dundee in Scotland."

Fran watched as Sarah's expression grew serious and faraway.

"Then a couple of months ago," Sarah went on, "I heard something on the news about illegal adoptions connected with organised crime gangs based in Dundee. Are you here about that?"

She looked into Fran's eyes, and Fran saw the pleading in them. Sarah Cooper was hurting, and desperate to know about her own adoption, she realised.

"Not about the illegal adoptions, no," said Fran gently. "But please, go on. I'll tell you why I'm here once you've finished what you were saying."

Sarah looked confused, but went on. "I know it seems far fetched," she said. "To think my adoption over thirty years ago could have something to do with the illegal thing going on today. But I was desperate to know, and it seemed very odd that my birth mother came from the same place, so I contacted Peterborough to find out what I could." She threw Fran a quizzical expression. "Does that sound silly?"

"Of course not," said Fran. She felt a huge relief. It seemed that Sarah had genuinely been spooked when she'd seen the news coverage of the illegal adoptions, and given her circumstances, it was no wonder. It meant, Fran realised, that Sarah hadn't been in contact with Jonas Evanton, after all. "And I can tell you that your adoption is in no way related to the investigation we've been conducting. However, I am here about a different investigation, and it involves both of your birth parents."

Sarah Cooper drew in a sharp breath, and stared at Fran.

"This might be difficult for you to hear," Fran said. "Would you like to call someone to be here with you while I explain?"

Sarah looked horrified, but shook her head. "No. Just tell me what's going on."

Fran put her notebook down, trying to remove any unnecessary barriers between her and Sarah, then she continued. "Your birth mother is helping us with a very serious matter," she said. "We're dealing with a number of serious crimes that are targeting the police around Dundee. The man who's behind them has already murdered two of our fellow officers. This man, I'm sorry to have to tell you, is your birth father."

Sarah let out a sound like a sob, but held her composure and continued to stare at Fran.

"We need to find a way of luring him out of hiding," Fran said. "And your mother told us about the daughter she had to give up for adoption. She never told your father about you, so he has no idea he has a daughter. We think, if we told him about you, that it might make him start talking to us. Or at least shock him enough that he makes a mistake and give us a chance of catching him."

There was an agonising silence. Fran tried to imagine what it could possibly feel like to have been told the things she'd just told Sarah. But time wasn't on her side.

"Look, Sarah, I'm so sorry to have landed all of this on you so suddenly," she said. "But will you help us?"

Chapter 54

"Well, that was a prize disaster," Donna said as she and Alice returned to the team room after the press conference.

"Are you surprised?" said Alice. "You handed them cops fighting

180

with each other – DI Donna Davenport losing the rag – and you really think they'd rather cover the fact that Burly McKinnes has been charged with murdering a local thug?"

"Just keep out of my sight for a while, will you, Alice?" Donna said, as she strode to the front of the room. Alice stood staring after her, a carousel of bewilderment, anger and hurt coursing around her face.

Stephen Morrison was sitting at the desk nearest to the evidence board, in the spot usually occupied by Fran. Donna wondered briefly how the DC was getting on in Wales, and whether they would be able to make use of the fact that Jonas Evanton had a daughter. Would he care? She remembered Fran's finding that the daughter had recently been in contact with Peterborough Children's Social Care to enquire about her birth parents, an uncomfortable coincidence. Possibly, as Fran certainly seemed to believe, an indication that she already had some involvement, and may already have been in contact with Evanton. Donna felt a slight chill at the thought, suddenly wondering if Fran might actually be at some risk, as Alice had already hinted.

"What are you staring at?" she snapped at Morrison, coming out of her thoughts. Morrison jumped in his seat, and looked around the room at his colleagues, who were also staring at Donna.

"Is everything alright, boss?" he asked. His eyes were still red.

"No, everything is bloody not alright," said Donna. "Take a look at that evidence board!"

All eyes turned to the board. Burly McKinnes had been charged with his father's murder. Archie's body had been found, dumped and burnt in the Ethie Woods. The Dundee shooter was in custody, although refusing to speak. DCI Marsh had already provided some details of the train derailment. Donna read them over, but the words jarred when she saw Ross's name up there.

"Jonas Evanton got a body stolen from the mortuary, and had it burned to a crisp and dumped in the woods," she said.

She banged her fist on the nearest desk.

"He got a sniper into Dundee city centre and executed a witness we were supposed to be protecting, and shot one of our own officers," she went on, heaving a pile of folders off of the desk. They made a noise like an avalanche as they plunged across the floor. The circle of officers closest to her took steps backwards away from her.

"He murdered Angus Ross and put his body on a train, that he then arranged to have fucking derailed!"

She grabbed the phone that still sat on the desk, yanked it from its socket and threw it against the wall. The loud clatter made all of the officers in the room jump.

"Angus Ross!" she shouted. "Angus Ross!"

She screamed.

Howled with rage.

Threw fistfuls of paper from another desk onto the floor, smashed a mug against the wall, then upended the desk itself.

Several officers ran forward and grabbed at Donna, but she flailed and struck out at them, sending one of them reeling, blood on his lip, and it took several more to finally wrestle her to the ground.

Two ambulances and a paramedic car sat outside the front entrance to Bell Street, with their blue lights flashing glare into the dark December night sky. Thirty journalists stood assembled to one side of the vehicle huddle, and in the car park beyond, punters from the pubs across the road were gathering in the freezing cold to see what was going on, drawn by the screaming sirens going into the police HQ. One or two of them attempted to pile forward into the group of reporters to ask what was going on, only to be marched back by a row of uniformed officers that were being formed into a human barrier.

The paramedics had been inside now for around forty minutes.

The reporters began to fan out around the emergency vehicles, and TV crews began to hastily erect their equipment.

Alice came to the closed front doors and peered outside, the blue flashing lights and the television lighting making it difficult to decipher what was going on out there.

182

Here inside the office complex, a near silence had fallen like a dusting of snow over everything after Donna's screams and yells had subsided to sobs and then to a glazed stupor as the paramedics brought her frenzy to an end.

Donna now lay strapped into a stretcher and wrapped in blankets, with Libby walking alongside and holding her hand while the paramedics prepared to bring her outside.

Squinting out there, Alice recognised the reporter who stood shivering beside the nearest ambulance and who was clutching an over-sized microphone, her familiar woollen hat and scarf no match for the plummeting temperature outside. This one had been there to broadcast the bird's-eye view of Jonas Evanton's capture and arrest two years ago. She had headlined the serial killer theory during the recent Moira Cowan murder investigation, and had crossed many lines with Donna along the way. Lindsey Forsyth. Alice eyed her as she glanced along the route towards the ambulance, then took in a sharp breath when she spotted PC Stephen Morrison emerge from behind the ambulance and hand a drink to Forsyth.

Suddenly the silence was shattered, and Alice felt as though she was being pitched into fast forward as the paramedics burst through the doors and marched towards the ambulance, with Donna in the stretcher in the middle of them. Alice hurried out, keeping right behind Libby.

As the stretcher reached the ambulance, Alice was surprised to see an expression of shock on Lindsey Forsyth's face. Just when Donna came into position for the perfect shot, Lindsey waved her cameraman away, and shook her head, *no*. She met Alice's eye, and Alice mouthed a silent thank you, wondering what role Morrison had played with the journalist. While the news would cover the details of Donna's removal from duty, at least she was being spared the humiliation of having to star as herself on screen.

Chapter 55

Alexandra Kozel stared out of the cottage window, while her fingers casually picked off the skin of a tangerine. A large stag had stopped in her line of vision, giving her a fright as it appeared out of the darkness, and it stood stock-still, as though listening to ripples in the air. It cocked its head, then suddenly sprinted off into the nearby woodland.

The teenager sighed. It had been exciting at first, being part of something mysterious and dangerous. Now it was just boring. This was the sixth day without her phone. Books, Freeview TV, and even stags in the field weren't cutting it any more.

Her father walked into the room.

"I want to go home," Alexandra told him.

"Don't use that tone with me," Abrim Kozel answered. "You can go home when the business here is finished."

"I thought you were the boss," she said, "but it looks more like he's calling all the shots."

"What do you understand?" Kozel shrugged. "It's a complicated business. Not for kids."

"Why can't you just get us out of here?" she demanded.

"We can leave once the business is finished, I told you," he said. She could tell he was getting impatient with her. "If we go before that, he'll come after you and hurt you, okay?"

They were suddenly alert to the noise of something crashing against walls in one of the rooms at the far end of the cottage, and the sound of Evanton's voice blazing in rage.

Alexandra felt her face blanch and her chest constrict. On reflex she scuttled to her father's side and cowered close to him.

"Someone's found us," she whispered.

They both stood, as still as the stag had done, and listened. There was the sound of another crash. And a yell.

"Wait here," said Kozel, taking several cautious steps towards the door.

"You can't leave me here alone," Alexandra pleaded. "What if it's the police?"

"I'm only going to the door here to have a look," Kozel said.

Alexandra saw him pick up an old walking cane from its place beside the door, holding it in front of his chest like a weapon. "And move away from the window."

Alexandra was only too aware of what he was implying, and she ducked behind the armchair she'd been sitting in, noticing a piece of tangerine peel that she'd dropped there.

She watched as her father used one hand to carefully open the door. He held the walking cane ready, and edged his head into a position where he could see out of the room and along the hallway.

Another crash made her jump, and she saw that it made her father jump, too. Then came the raging voice again. Now that the door was open, it became clear that it was Evanton who was doing all the shouting. There was no sound of anyone shouting back at him.

Alexandra realised at the same moment that she saw her father understand, there were no police. Nobody had found them, after all. This was Evanton having a tantrum. She stood up from her place and joined her father by the door.

Kozel threw her a puzzled glance, lowered the walking cane, and strode off in the direction of the disturbance.

Alexandra crept through the door, all the better to listen in on what was going on now.

"Bitch!" Evanton was screaming.

Alexandra felt alarmed.

"Bitch!"

She heard her father urge Evanton for an explanation.

Alexandra listened on, straining to make out the words, and realised with relief that Evanton hadn't been referring to her. He was going on about being screwed over by some Donna, and how he was going to make this Donna pay.

Cut and run
The lost days
Chapter 56

Donna woke up in a room that looked strange but felt familiar. An odd sensation in her head had her mind both at once racing and fighting through sludge. She was lying on a single bed. Crisp white sheets. Those were the giveaway. She looked to the side and saw the standard utilitarian bedside cabinet. Looked out of the window behind her. It was pitch dark outside, and all she could make out were streetlights dotted in rows in the distance.

Her eyes felt gritty, and it took a monumental effort to keep them open. When she leaned onto one elbow to get a better look at her surrounds, her head swam and she felt nauseous.

The door to her room was closed, but she knew it wouldn't be locked. It was the outer door of the ward, instead, that would be locked. This was the second time in two years she'd been admitted to the secure psychiatric unit, and she knew she hadn't played any part in making the decision to come here, so she knew she must have been sectioned.

Taking her time, she sat up and lowered her feet from the side of the bed until they reached the cold tiled floor. She wondered briefly about the biological matter that must have been cleaned off these tiles over the years, and began to feel sick again.

She needed to speak to Libby. Moving slowly, she reached into the top drawer of the cabinet, wondering if her phone was there. It wasn't. She muttered a curse under her breath.

A knock on her door didn't bring much reaction. It was too much of an effort to look round.

"Oh, you're up," observed the nurse who now joined her. "How are you feeling?"

Donna began to respond, but her throat was dry, and only an incoherent croak got out.

"Don't worry," said the nurse. "You've been pretty unwell. Do you know where you are?"

Donna nodded, *yes*, then felt a thump of pain in her temple.

"It's most of the same team you saw here last time," the nurse went on. "Would you like us to ring Libby for you? She's been phoning every hour to find out how you're doing."

Donna nodded again, keeping her eyes closed to keep the pain at bay. "What time is it?" she managed to whisper.

"It's 6.30, Friday morning," said the nurse. "You came in late yesterday afternoon and have been sleeping ever since."

Donna, with the nurse's help, got back under the bed sheets and lay down again.

"Just some routine bloods to do," said the nurse, far too cheery for that time in the morning. "Then I'll phone Libby for you. The doctor will be round in a couple of hours to have a look over your meds and we'll have a better idea after that how long we'll be keeping you in for assessment."

Donna nodded that she understood, and held out her arm as instructed, for the nurse to take her blood samples.

"There you go," said the nurse when she was done. "Breakfast will be here shortly. In the meantime, is there anything I can do to help you feel more comfortable?"

"I need my phone," said Donna, feeling her head begin to clear suddenly. "There's stuff I need to order online before it's too late."

"I'm sorry," said the nurse, with genuine regret in her voice. "We've had to remove your phone. I'm afraid you were...em... using it in a way that was harmful to you, but the doctor will talk all of that over with you when you're feeling a bit better."

"No, no," said Donna. "I need it, I really do, just to place one order, is my card here, my credit card? I'll only take a minute..."

"Shush," soothed the nurse, bringing a cup of water to Donna's lips. "Here, you're due your next dose, take this for me."

Donna gulped down the pill and water. It didn't take long before she started to feel drowsy again.

"I'll go and phone Libby for you now," said the nurse, patting Donna's arm before heading back out of the room.

Donna managed to half open one eye to watch her go.

At the same time, and only a ten minute drive into the city, Fran was dragging herself off the train at Dundee, swearing she would never travel overnight again.

Stupid o'clock in the morning, she emerged onto Riverside Drive following the ten hour train journey from Cardiff to be met by a heavy flurry of snow and a single taxi sitting – driverless – in the taxi rank.

Never again, she repeated to herself. But at least the trip had been worthwhile, she consoled herself. Donna and Ross would be pleased with what she'd found. She wondered if there had been any developments here while she'd been away, feeling slightly unnerved at the radio silence her team had kept up these last couple of days.

She caught sight of the taxi driver sauntering back with a cup of something steaming, and called to him. She would go home and try to get a couple of hours' sleep, then get herself back to Bell Street to share her news.

Chapter 57

Alice passed by the vending machine on her way to the team room. Normally on a Friday morning either she or Donna or Ross would stop by here to fetch some goodies for them to snack on while they caught up in their weekly huddle. She couldn't remember ever feeling such pain as she felt right now. She forced herself on.

When she entered the team room, she stopped in her tracks. Amidst the hub of activity going on around most of the desks, she immediately spotted DCI Marsh standing with his arm around Fran's shoulders. She couldn't see Fran's face, but it was obvious the DC had just been informed about Ross's murder, Akwasi's gunshot injury, and Donna's admission to the psychiatric ward. It struck her just then what a quagmire they really were in. No wonder Fran was in a state.

Alice made her way directly to them, and heard Marsh insisting

188

that Fran take the day off. Fran was shaking her head vigorously.

"I want to stay and help," she was telling Marsh through great, heroic gasps. "We've got to end all of this. I can't believe Angus Ross is… is…" The rest of her words were lost in a flood of tears.

"You really ought to take some time," Alice said gently.

"How can I?" Fran said. She was beginning to sound angry. "No. I'm staying." She took several deep breaths, and drew her hand across her eyes. "I'm staying, and I'm fit for duty. What would you like me to focus on first?"

Marsh met Alice's eye and shrugged his shoulder.

"Well, I can't pretend we don't need you here," he told Fran. "Let's get the team together and go over where we're at. There has to be an angle we haven't covered yet."

"I'm just going to have a seat while everyone gets here," said Fran, now sounding stunned.

Alice watched her go to a quieter corner of the room. She didn't seem to have her phone on her, and she seemed to be casting her eye around the paperwork on the desk she was sitting at as though looking for something to do, but it wouldn't be long before she came across the coverage and footage of Donna being stretchered away from the front steps of Bell Street the previous afternoon. Although the journalists had held off from filming it, there had been plenty of punters watching and capturing the whole sorry episode on their phones. The morning papers, radio and TV news – even the national news – were covering it. The chat on social media was about little else.

Before long, officers began to trickle into the room, called for the morning's briefing. Alice thought quickly. She wanted to speak to Fran in private before everyone got here.

"Can you come with me for a moment?" she called.

Fran stood up, robot-like, and followed her out of the team room, and they made their way to the nearby Quiet Room.

"We've never been in a situation like this before," Alice told her. "I've got some really important information to tell you – to tell the whole team, actually. But I'm hoping you might have something for us from your visit?"

Alice was relieved to see a spark of hope ignite Fran's face.

"I actually spoke to Sarah Cooper," Fran said, her voice low. "It turns out the reason she got in touch with social services recently was because she saw the news about the illegal adoptions, and she panicked in case her own adoption was somehow part of the whole thing."

"So, she hasn't been in touch with Evanton?" Alice asked.

"She didn't know a thing about him," Fran confirmed. "In fact, she was shocked when I told her why I was there."

"Poor woman," Alice muttered.

"However," Fran went on, "she has agreed to come up to Dundee to help us. I asked her to stand by for me to get in touch once I found out the plan. Donna said there was a problem with the phones, so I couldn't contact anyone...Is that still the case?"

"It is," said Alice. "That's why I brought you in here to discuss this – we can't, under any circumstances, let information about Sarah's existence reach Jonas Evanton. Not until we're ready to use it. I'm going to give more details at the team briefing about the security issue. So for now it's important that we don't say a word to anyone yet about your visit, okay?"

Fran looked worried. "But shouldn't we tell Marsh?"

"We will," said Alice. "When the time's right. But we need to speak to Mo first. I'll arrange that. Leave it with me."

"Okay," said Fran, still looking unsure.

"Let's get to this team briefing," said Alice. "But remember, do not say anything about Sarah Cooper."

They slipped into the team room in time to hear Marsh informing everyone that a government Cobra meeting was to be convened first thing on Monday morning to discuss Police Scotland's request to the Home Office for military assistance with the mess they were in and the implications of the loss of public confidence.

"Surely they have to get us help in now from the Army or MI5 or something to track him down?" one of the officers in the room said.

"We can but hope," said Marsh, sounding anything but hopeful.

Alice stepped forward. "There's an update I need to let you all know about," she addressed the room. Marsh nodded for her to go on. "There's been a security breach, and Donna confirmed yesterday that Jonas Evanton has managed to hack our phones, and has been using this to watch our every move and listen to our conversations."

There were sounds of outrage and disbelief from the officers around the room.

Alice continued. "IT Security are working on a solution, and Bruno will be along shortly to explain more. The bad news…" groans of protest from around the room… "is that Donna told me she had come up with a plan to try and trap Evanton using the fact that he would be watching us. But now, of course, Donna's in hospital, and I'm afraid she didn't go into the details of her plan with me."

"Oh, for Christ's sake!" Marsh exploded. "So, he's been watching everything we say and do, and there's nothing we can do about it? Where the hell does that leave us?"

Alice's mobile rang then, and she answered it quickly. Marsh looked annoyed at the interruption, until she said, "That was Libby Quinn. Donna's awake now."

Chapter 58

Donna woke up again, alerted by the sound of chairs scraping across the floor and making her head hurt even more. When her eyes focused she saw Libby sitting looking at her.

"Am I going home?" she asked. She was aware that her words were slurred. Her tongue felt as if it was stuck to the roof of her mouth.

Libby leaned in and took her hand. "You're going to be here for a few weeks. Like before, remember? You're going to get the help you need to get better. For good this time. Deal?"

Donna sighed and nodded in compliance. "What about the

investigation?" she managed.

"Don't you worry about that," said Libby. "I phoned Alice, and she told me to tell you everything's under control."

Even in her drug-induced stupor, Donna could tell when Libby was lying.

She knew she'd left her colleagues at Bell Street to deal with the biggest challenge they had ever faced. They needed her now more than they'd ever needed her. She had worked out how Evanton was watching them, and had begun to put a plan together for trapping him. And now here she was locked up in a secure psychiatric unit. She knew they would be hurting and bewildered right now, and that Libby would be, too.

"I'm so sorry," Donna began, and her voice faded to a whisper. Libby held her close.

"You've nothing to be sorry about," said Libby.

She chatted quietly to Donna, gently reassuring her, and Donna gradually began to revive and sat herself up.

"I've brought you some clean clothes," Libby told her. She held up a sports bag. "Do you want a hand to get a shower and freshen up?"

Donna let herself be led to the shower, and with Libby's help, got washed and dressed. Then, feeling a little more human again, she sat down in the other visitor's chair next to Libby.

"The offer on the house has been accepted," Libby said.

He knew about Keptie Road, Donna shuddered, feeling her heart rate quicken.

Oblivious, Libby went on, "Danny's over the moon. So is Natesh."

Donna forced herself to chuckle, but she could see from the concern in Libby's expression that she hadn't pulled it off. It was breaking her heart that Libby was going through this at a time when she should be excited about their impending house move and the imminent arrival of Danny and Sally's baby.

"When does Sally get here?" Donna asked, trying to keep the topic light.

"Sometime tomorrow, actually," Libby said. "Danny's over the moon about that, too."

They chatted on about family matters, and all the while, Donna couldn't help but fret about the one shot she'd had at getting to Evanton, and whether she'd blown it.

Chapter 59

It was difficult to say what time of the day or night it was now. Donna fought to clear her head, but her eyes felt glued into her skull and her brain felt as though it was made of cement. Sitting up made her feel queasy.

Once more she studied her surrounds and remembered all over again that she was here in the secure ward.

As she stared at the featureless walls, she began to recall something from earlier. Had it been from that day? Or was the memory even real, she wondered? She remembered looking up at the sound of her door opening, and being slightly surprised that the person coming into her room wasn't a nurse. It wasn't Libby, either – it had been after her visit, now that she thought about it – and certainly wasn't Natesh.

She remembered having to blink several times to clear her vision, and the fact that it took a while before she had eventually recognised her visitor, although she remembered thinking at the time there was something different about her.

She had watched, silent, while Agnes McKinnes had taken a seat next to the bed.

What was it that was different about her, Donna remembered thinking at the time? Then she had realised: Agnes somehow looked taller.

Donna remembered being puzzled at thinking the woman's neck looked longer than usual. Why had that been? Thinking back, Donna now realised it was because Agnes hadn't been hunching her shoulders like she always did. She'd been relaxed.

Making another attempt to sit up, Donna became intrigued with the memory and wanted to recall more of its details. She still couldn't figure out whether it had been earlier that day that Agnes had visited. Parts of days and nights amalgamated into one cloud of gloop in her head.

What she did remember was simply staring at Agnes for a long time, unable to form words. But she must have done, because she suddenly remembered the sound of Agnes laughing in response to something she'd said.

What was it, she battled now to remember?

She closed her eyes, concentrating. In her mind's eye, she remembered Agnes taking her hand and saying something about returning the favour.

What favour, Donna wondered?

"You were good to me plenty of times," Agnes's words came back to her. "Now it's time for me to return the favour."

Ah, that was it, Donna smiled to herself. She remembered now.

And she also remembered being surprised at Agnes going on, "I'm 46 now," while looking every day of sixty. Saying something about wanting to set up a support group for women battling depression, low self esteem, that kind of thing. Donna had suggested calling the group *Mad Cows*, and that was when Agnes had laughed. A squealing sort of laugh, like a little girl, and Donna had been struck by the fact that after all these years of knowing Agnes, it had been the first time she'd ever heard her laugh.

Donna was roused by a knock on her door while she was deep in thought about Agnes's visit, then smiled when Paul popped his head into the room. His white nurse's uniform almost glowed in the dimness.

"I heard you were back in," he said.

"Couldn't keep away," Donna said, the words slightly slurred.

"Well, I'm just about to head home," he said. "But I wanted to pop my head in and say hello. I'll maybe drop by tonight when I'm back on?"

"That would be good," Donna said, remembering with fondness her late night chats with Paul from the last time she was in here.

"I'll bring the coffee and you can fill me in on some of your gruesome stories," Paul winked. "Makes the night shift fly in."

Donna watched him leave. It genuinely would be good to have a chat with Paul, she thought. But, more importantly for now, it meant her plan just might work. As long as Alice managed to get here soon.

Chapter 60

"Well, luck seems to be on our side for once," said DCI Marsh. He looked astonished at the news that Dougal Clarence hadn't objected to Burly McKinnes being charged with murder. "I know it's not much, in the scale of things, but at least it's one less headache to be dealing with."

Alice, along with Morrison and several other officers were standing in front of the evidence board, and Fran was back in charge of updating it. All the details were there, and growing: Marnie Whyte forced into the bogus hostage situation; the message she had passed on that they were not going to know what was about to hit them – and wasn't that the truth, Alice thought – as well as the message for Donna to run; the theft of Archie McKinnes's body; the evidence against Burly; Evanton's phone call to Donna and his demand that she identify the body in the woods as his; its positive ID as Archie McKinnes; the threat made on Ross's life; the shootings at the Caird Hall, killing Marnie Whyte and injuring Thomas Akwasi; the derailed train; and the murder of Angus Ross. Not to mention the disturbing rise in vigilante incidents around the city and the number of police officers coming under attack in the wake of the growing media call for something to be done about the ineptitude of Police Scotland.

By the time the current details were added, Fran's hand was shaking. Everyone in the room looked exhausted. It was a full week now since Archie McKinnes had been murdered, and they'd been run ragged from one crisis escalating to another non-stop since then. It was obvious they were in no fit state to keep on going as they were for much longer.

Marsh sighed, turning away from the board, and went on, "I got an update from Ninewells this morning, and Thomas Akwasi is doing better. He's out of immediate danger now, and is expected to make a decent recovery, though time will tell if and when he'll be able to return to duty. I understand he's to have more surgery early next week."

"I'll go and visit him this evening," Fran said.

"So, our top priority is to locate Jonas Evanton," Marsh continued, after a nod of approval at Fran. "Even though we now know he can listen in on what we're saying, we still need to get on with what we can. What do we actually have?"

"If he was planning on meeting Donna," Alice said, "then he must still be in the area, or at least not too far away. She said he was looking for time to get to the Irish border."

"Do we know if he was in the flat in Arbroath with Marnie Whyte?" Morrison asked.

"Nope, forensics not back on that yet," said another officer.

"What?" Marsh said. "That was nearly a week ago! This is an unprecedented level of urgent, they know that! Get them chased up right now."

The officer dived at the nearest desk and quickly made the phone call, muttering under his breath, *we'll be lucky, on a Saturday.*

"Has there been any further contact from Evanton, beyond his phone call to Donna?" Marsh asked.

There was silence in the room in response to his question.

"I'll take that as a *no*," Marsh went on. "What about the train driver?"

"Still critical in the Western General in Edinburgh," someone replied from across the room. "We've not been able to speak to him yet."

Marsh grunted. "And his daughter?"

"We're still waiting on the go-ahead to speak to the youngster," another officer responded.

"Damn it!" Marsh was growing red in the face and he thumped the nearest desk in frustration. "Then get John Ogilvie back in here. I've had his statement checked over, and I'm pretty sure there's more he can tell us. He's been far too tight lipped. We need to lean on him harder."

"If what we've heard about the train driver's daughter is correct, and he was blackmailed," Alice said, "then it could be that Ogilvie was, too."

"That's what I've been thinking," said Marsh. "If Evanton blackmailed the pathologist and the train driver, then it's possible both men saw or spoke to the same people. Between them, they might be able to give us enough details to give us something to go on. But we'll need to get to Ogilvie now, and with protection, in case Evanton is listening in and decides to silence him first."

A number of officers hurried from the room to get the call out for John Ogilvie. Meanwhile the rest of them remained standing in front of the evidence board, turning over every angle of the investigation, with growing dismay that there seemed to be no other obvious suitable way forward.

"Get moving, then," Marsh barked. "I want John Ogilvie in here right away."

Alice caught a glance from Fran, and realised it was time to go and speak to Mo Skinner and let her know they'd found Sarah Cooper. If bringing John Ogilvie back in was the best they had at this stage, when anything could happen, then it seemed likely they were going to have to go ahead and use Sarah as their secret weapon to lure Evanton out of hiding.

Chapter 61

Libby sat on the settee in the living room. Even though it was a Saturday, another set of student assessments lay scattered across the coffee table, waiting to be marked. But she couldn't look at any of them. Tears streamed down her face. How was she going to find

197

her way through Donna's illness this time? Always being the one to say the right things, being the strong one, being the shoulder to lean on, the rock. She just didn't think she had the stamina to do it any more. Not without help, but who on earth could she talk to?

The door bell went, and she froze. Going over the actions in her mind, she rehearsed the steps of setting the alarm, and knew for a fact that she had set it that morning. Knowing this, she relaxed a little. Still, she wasn't expecting any visitors, and anything out of the ordinary at the moment was not a good thing.

She checked the app on her phone, and almost laughed out loud in relief. On her screen she saw that it was Natesh standing on her doorstep, shivering in the cold and sleet. He was holding what looked to be two pizza boxes.

He hurried inside as soon as she opened the door, then he paused in the hallway, looking apologetic.

"It's not a bad time, is it?"

"It's a terrible time," said Libby. "But I'm actually really glad to see you. Go through, and I'll get the kettle on." She eyed the pizza boxes.

"Oh these," Natesh said handing them over. "Don't get too excited – I made them myself. Egg and spinach pizza."

"Egg on a pizza?" Libby was unable to hide the disgust from her voice, even though she was grateful for his gesture.

Taking the boxes from him, she watched Natesh rub the cold from his arms as he made his way into the living room, and she quickly went to the kitchen to set out their meal. Doing so, she realised that she hadn't eaten today, and she recalled the times when Donna had defended her friend's haplessness by saying how thoughtful and kind he was. Libby knew for a fact that Donna attributed her own survival to him, after he'd been the one to insist she go for medical help when her symptoms of bipolar disorder had first begun to manifest. And, Libby noted, he had just appeared at the door like a guardian angel the moment she'd begun to despair.

Natesh was sitting in his usual armchair by the time she came back through, but he wasn't looking relaxed.

"It's a bad one this time with Donna, isn't it?" he said right away. His eyebrows were knotted together with worry.

Libby nodded her head, and it took all of her willpower to stop the tears coming again.

"It's different," she told him. "I really didn't see this one coming. Normally…"

"I know," Natesh cut in. "Normally you see it coming and have lots of arguments about it because she doesn't believe you."

"Do you argue with her?" Libby was surprised.

"Only when she thinks I'm over-reacting," said Natesh, taking his coffee from the tray that Libby had set down beside him. She watched as he blew on it and took a sip, and almost laughed when she saw him try to conceal the fact that he'd still burnt his lip on it. Yes, she thought, she could see why he and Donna were inseparable, and she could see that he was hurting almost as much as she was.

"That's kind of hard to imagine," said Libby. "She adores you, you know." She felt her voice begin to waver, so stopped talking and diverted her gaze to the other side of the room. Absent-mindedly she picked up a slice of pizza and began to nibble on it. Natesh took a piece, too.

"This must be awful for you," Natesh said. "I'm lost without her too, you know? She's there, but not there, know what I mean?"

Libby eyed him, wondering how much she could bring herself to confide in him. He was Donna's best friend. Obviously she could trust him. But she'd never actually sat and had a proper talk with him. It felt a bit weird. Or, she wondered, was it that she just wasn't used to talking about her own feelings with anyone?

"Yeuch," she suddenly spluttered. "I'm really sorry, Natesh, but this pizza…"

Natesh covered his mouth to stop spraying his mouthful across the room as he laughed. "I know," he said, "it's horrible, isn't it?"

Chapter 62

Donna sat on the side of her bed. A couple of days of dodging the medication, and her head was feeling a little more steady. It was dark outside again, but she had no real way of knowing if it was four in the afternoon or four in the morning. Just like her previous stay here, time was all upside down in this place.

As the drowse of deep sleep cleared from her mind, she began to recall Alice's visit before she'd dropped off.

She had been delighted to see the General – Alice had told her it was Saturday, and had assured her that nobody was aware of the visit.

They had discussed Fran's trip to Wales, and Alice had brought her up to date with the latest on Sarah Cooper.

Alice had agreed to instruct Fran to bring Sarah to Dundee, but under the radar. Donna remained adamant that where Sarah was concerned, their biggest advantage would be the element of surprise, so they had agreed on how they were going to handle it. While she would have had no hesitation in trusting Angus Ross to go along with her plan – how her heart lurched and ached at the thought of him – she wasn't so sure about Marsh. She certainly wasn't about to take the chance of Marsh blabbing to all and sundry that Evanton had a daughter, and so she wanted Alice to handle it on her own.

It made her tired to think about the things they'd discussed. Having the conversation with Alice, having to make plans that made sense, took up much of the little energy she had right now.

Then a thought struck her, and she reached under her pillow. Her fingers found the hard casing of what definitely felt like a mobile phone, and she almost let out a whoop of delight. Alice had brought it. As if to confirm she wasn't imagining things, she brought it out and studied the red mobile.

The plan was on.

And the next part of it would depend on Paul.

Donna double checked that the phone was on silent, and

squinted at the time on the tiny screen. Almost two in the morning, it was. She scrolled to the contacts list, and saw that, as she'd instructed, all it contained were the details for the four other red mobiles.

Perfect, she thought, at the same time realising they were now into the early hours of Sunday morning, and a full week on from the hostage situation.

She smiled when she heard the soft rap on the door.

"Come in, Paul," she called.

A night shift coffee and chat with Paul on his break wasn't so bad, she thought, although she did feel a little subversive about using him in the way she was about to.

Chapter 63

Alice groaned when she saw the headline. Fran had placed the newspaper on the desk in front of the sergeant.

"Not content with the weekend special last week, and the scoops we've been giving them every day since then," Alice muttered, "now they're running *another* full length special feature on how incompetent we are!" She held her head in her hands.

DCI Marsh chose this moment to saunter past Alice's desk.

"Having a browse at the Sunday papers?" he said.

"Take a look for yourself," said Alice, holding it up.

"Oh, not again."

"I thought we'd struck a deal with the press," Alice said, anger beginning to leak into her voice.

"Hmm, well, I did get a call about that," said Marsh. "Seemingly now that Ross and Donna are out of the picture, all bets are off."

"Charming," said Alice. "Kicking us when we're down."

"Can't really blame them, can you?" said Marsh. "So, let's get our plan of action up and running, and then maybe tomorrow they'll have something more positive to report on."

"Plan of action?" Alice's eyebrow arched.

"Yes," said Marsh. "The one you're about to tell me, after your visit to Donna. My office. Now." He pointed at Alice and Fran.

Alice shifted uncomfortably.

"Well?" said Marsh, heading towards the door.

"Dodgy tummy," said Alice, jumping to her feet and hurrying past. "I'll join you there after I've... you know..." And she sped from the room, leaving Marsh looking suspicious.

Alice made her way to the Ladies. There, she quickly checked that all of the cubicles were empty, and locked herself inside the first one. Her heart racing, she carefully lifted the loosened panel from below the waste pipe, and retrieved a red mobile phone. She became aware that she was holding her breath when she clicked open the message that was waiting on it from Donna. There were two attachments. She checked them. They weren't the best quality photos, and she hoped to God they would be good enough for Bruno to work on.

Then she took a moment to gather her thoughts. This was getting complicated, keeping the details of Donna's plan between just the two of them, keeping the existence of Sarah Cooper between her, Donna and Fran, and keeping Marsh out of it all. On top of that was the added complication of having to carry on with business in the team, with everybody knowing that Evanton was listening in. But she had to get on with it.

Checking again that the coast was clear, she ran along the corridor and up the stairs, going straight to Bruno's office.

They didn't have to exchange words as Alice handed over the phone. Bruno simply nodded an acknowledgement and muttered, "Tomorrow at five."

Alice made her way as quickly as she could back to Ross's... to Marsh's office, where she arrived out of breath to join the DCI and Fran.

"I'm fine," she said in response to Marsh's raised eyebrow.

She found herself glancing around the room, feeling Ross's presence in every cubic centimetre of it. Her eyes suddenly began to well, seeing in her mind all at once the times she'd walked in here to see Ross making a face while on the phone, or with his feet up on that desk, slurping noisily on purpose from a coffee cup, or any of a number of things that had endeared him to her and to all of the others in Bell Street.

How would he have handled all these latest developments, she wondered? She blinked away the sensation.

Marsh was watching her, and cleared his throat. "So, you went to see Donna last night," he stated. He tapped a pen on his desk. "How is she?"

"She seemed settled," said Alice.

"Did you discuss the security breach with her, and what her plan was?"

"What do you think?" Alice snapped. "She's settled, but she doesn't know if it's New York or New Year. There's no way she'll be able to discuss any of this any time soon. We're going to have to come up with our own plan."

"Alright, keep your hair on," said Marsh. "I was only asking."

He flicked through some papers that were in front of him. "Forensics have confirmed Evanton wasn't in the flat in Arbroath." His tone gradually softened. "And the lads have gone over the CCTV and all of the statements from the football park, so there's no doubt about Burly McKinnes having killed his father. That rules out any connection with Evanton, which means we've nothing to go on from either of those angles."

"I'm going to have a chat with Mo Skinner later on today," said Alice. "She might have a suggestion or two up her sleeve."

"Well, I suppose it's worth asking her," said Marsh, "but don't tell her about the security breach. I don't want that getting into the public domain. Can you just bloody imagine the news coverage then?"

Alice and Fran glanced at one another.

"I won't say anything about that," Alice promised.

"Good," said Marsh, suddenly looking very tired. "And the Cobra meeting is tomorrow morning, so we might even get some decent news after that."

They sat for a moment in silence, then Marsh shooed them off. "Go and do whatever it is you have to do."

Alice realised she had plenty to do. It was going to be a difficult discussion with Mo, and she would have to be back here at five to meet Bruno. Time was getting short.

Chapter 64

Claypotts Place had never been so busy. The bungalow at the end of the cul-de-sac was thronging with reporters and cameras. Voices called through the letterbox, asking Libby if she had any comment about the exposé in the Sunday papers about Donna having mishandled the investigation into Evanton's whereabouts. Others knocked on the downstairs windows, demanding to know if Donna's mental state had been covered up by the police all along.

Libby sat on the hall floor, her back against the wall, sobbing into her arms. When was this all going to end, she wondered? Was she ever going to get Donna – *her* Donna – back, and could they ever live a normal life? Do normal things like visit friends and go out for drinks? Was it always going to be like this, or did she have to make another choice? Should she just pack a bag, jump onto a train, and start over somewhere else, a new life? But it would be no life at all, she knew, without Donna. How could this mess ever be over?

She sensed a change outside, a shift in the commotion. It sounded as though someone had turned up outside the house, and the reporters had switched their attentions to the visitor. She checked on her front door security app, and saw Natesh running the gauntlet to her doorstep.

She sprang to her feet, and quickly opened the door to let him in. The instant he was inside, with the door locked behind him, she threw her arms around him and let the tears continue to fall.

"What am I going to do without her?" she wailed.

Natesh led her through to the living room and sat down with

her on the settee, making soothing noises.

"It's going to be alright," he told her. "It's really going to be alright."

"How do you know that?" Libby demanded.

"Because I know Donna," said Natesh. "And so do you. She'll get through this, and we're going to help each other while she does. Okay?"

Libby's sobbing came to a halt, and she nodded her head, sensing a strength in Natesh's voice that she'd never heard before. She blew her nose, and leaned into him.

"You know what we're going to do?" he said. "We're going to go up to Arbroath to Danny's. I bet you haven't seen Sally since she got here yesterday? Let's go and have some baby chat, get used to the idea that we're going to be aunties, and not mention any of this stuff."

Libby's breath caught. Natesh was right. She'd been in such a mess since Donna's hospitalisation that she hadn't even called her brother to make sure Sally had settled in okay.

"Yes, you're right," she told him. "That's exactly what we'll do. And you know you'll be an uncle, not an auntie, right?"

"If it's a boy," said Natesh, with a twinkle in his eye.

Chapter 65

DCI Marsh was pacing the floor of the team room when Alice arrived in Bell Street.

"Quick, everyone together," he waved towards the evidence board as soon as he saw her. There was hardly anyone in the room yet, still being very early on a Monday morning, so it didn't take long.

PC Stephen Morrison walked in as Marsh began. "The Cobra meeting has just ended. They're taking a watch and wait approach."

"Bugger!" said Alice. "So, we're being left to pick up the blame on our own when it all kicks off."

"Then, let's make sure it doesn't all kick off," said Marsh.

"Evanton's managed to have a body stolen from the morgue –

during a murder investigation," said Alice. "Managed to have it burned in the woods, set up a bogus hostage situation, shot the hostage in the city centre in broad daylight, derailed a fucking train and murdered our DCI, right under our noses! How the hell is that not kicking off? Do you know something I don't?"

"Remember your place, Sergeant," said Marsh, keeping his voice ominously calm. "You're starting to sound like Donna Davenport."

Alice gave him the finger. He ignored the gesture, and went on. "Now, we have more information since yesterday." Fran was finishing an update of the evidence board while he spoke. "John Ogilvie confirmed he was blackmailed, and told us it was all done by telephone. His caller had an Eastern European accent."

"Have we been able to talk to the train driver yet?" asked Alice.

"No," said Marsh. "But Ogilvie's wife was held captive until the body was stolen, so we might able to get some more from her. Seemingly she's gone to stay with her sister in Bristol or somewhere, but we'll get a hold of her. And – and now we seem to be getting somewhere at last – ballistics have confirmed that the bullets in the Dundee sniper shootings came from a gun we know to be associated with Abrim Kozel's gang. Also – this is new in – we've heard from Kozel's daughter's school that she hasn't been seen during all of last week. They tried to contact her father about it, and haven't been able to get him, either."

"We're just finding this out now?" Alice said, although she did wonder how early Marsh must have started work this morning, given this amount of new information.

"At least it sheds some light on what we might actually be dealing with," said Marsh. "Here's my working theory: Evanton has taken Kozel's daughter hostage in order to coerce Kozel into doing his dirty work. Making the phone calls, lifting Marnie Whyte, moving and burning Archie McKinnes's body, and all that."

"That works," said Alice. "And it fits with Evanton keeping himself one step removed while still controlling the show."

"But how does this actually help us?" asked Morrison.

"I've got Aberdeen checking CCTV for any sighting of Kozel's daughter being taken. We've got teams up there visiting all of the remote farmhouses across the area. It's only a matter of time before we find where he's been keeping her."

There was a moment of silence in the room while the officers digested the new information.

"It's made me realise the key to putting a stop to this is direct dialogue with Jonas Evanton," Marsh went on. "We're not going to be able to outwit him, but making direct contact will bring him out of his comfort zone. Has there been any communication with him since he phoned Donna?"

"None," said Alice.

Marsh looked defeated. "We need to get him to talk to us."

"I have an idea," said Alice. She was encouraged by Marsh's instant attention, and went on. "You know I went to see Mo Skinner yesterday?"

"Yes, how did that go?" asked Marsh.

"She made a suggestion. That she make an appeal at a press conference," Alice said. "She asks Evanton to get in touch with her directly. The contact could be done by phone, so she wouldn't be in any danger."

Marsh seemed to think this over. "I like it."

"Mo still cares about him," said Alice. "I think that's why she'd prefer to be the one to speak to him. And it's probably our best shot at getting Evanton to begin a dialogue," said Alice.

"I agree," said Marsh after a further moment's thought. "Set it up straight away."

Chapter 66

"Well?" Kozel demanded. "What are you going to do now?"

Evanton shot a glare at the gangster. As usual, the girl was hanging around at his back, listening in on everything while being shielded by her father.

He didn't have an answer for Kozel. He stared in at the embers of the dying log fire.

Loch Kinord sat black and frozen not far from the cottage.

Large snowflakes were beginning to settle on the window ledge outside, and coming down faster.

There was a chance, he thought with a fleeting panic, that they might end up stranded out here. While being snowed in meant that nobody could make their way here and find them, time wasn't on his side now. Davenport had figured out he was using a StingRay device. It wouldn't be that long before their IT Security managed to close it down, and then he would be in the dark while they worked out how to get to him. He couldn't let that happen.

Everything had been going smoothly, even to the point of having correctly second guessed Davenport's reaction in the Ethie Woods.

"You just had to go too far, didn't you?" Kozel went on, sneering.

He was right, Evanton knew. He should have known that killing Angus Ross might have pushed Davenport over the edge, fucking nutcase that she was. He hadn't taken that into account. Now that she was locked up, there was nothing he could do to get to her. He was going to have to think of a new plan. He was sick of this.

"Well, at least they still don't know where to start looking," he growled. "I'll think of something."

"Why don't you let Alexandra go home?" Kozel began. "Things have changed now…"

"The girl is staying here," Evanton snapped. He felt the rage rising. "If she goes, you'll just fuck off, too, and I might still need you."

He saw the look of pity that Kozel threw to his daughter, and again felt the sting of never having had that sort of bond.

Then he was distracted by an alert on his phone. There was something going on with Mo Skinner. Without saying a word to Kozel or Alexandra, he sped off to his surveillance room and fired up the screen that was linked to Mo's phone. He had to find out what it was he had missed the last time. What had made her cry?

It took him a moment to figure out what he was looking at. Mo was walking along beside that police sergeant, Alice Moone. It looked like they were inside Bell Street. He turned up the volume to listen in. They knew he might be listening, of course, so they were going to be careful about what they were saying. Still, he knew Mo, and could read her well.

"We're just about set up," Alice was saying to Mo. "You can take a seat in the canteen until we're ready. We'll go over everything with you first, before we take you through to the press room."

So, Mo was going to be taking part in a press conference, Evanton realised. Clever of them. *But not clever enough*.

Chapter 67

Standing just inside the media room, Alice busied herself with all the last minute details of the press conference, having seen Mo to the canteen, then tasking various officers with looking after the journalists and liaising with their own press office, meanwhile keeping a suspicious eye on PC Morrison.

The call had gone out at very short notice, and it was all hands on deck to make sure the large numbers of reporters coming into Bell Street all had the correct ID on them. One of them had to be turned away, having forgotten his pass in the rush to get there. Alice felt sorry for him. He was a *bona fide* journalist, one they'd worked with often, but security was tighter than usual this time, and they couldn't allow any exceptions.

In the flurry of activity, she was surprised to see Fran standing back and watching her.

"I thought you were against getting Mo involved," Fran whispered.

"That was then," said Alice. "Come on, we'd better go and see her now."

She cast a glance back around the room to satisfy herself that everything was in order, then she and Fran left and made their way towards the canteen.

When they got there, Alice could see DCI Marsh already seated right in the middle with Mo. He had brushed his hair and put on an even smarter jacket, she noted. Aiden Moore was there, too, having accompanied Mo from Arbroath. Alice and Fran weaved between the tables and sat down beside them, making a huddle of five in amongst the general din going on around them.

"Shall we go over the plan?" Marsh said, once Alice and Fran were seated. For their benefit he said, "I've expressed our deep gratitude to Mo for coming in," then turned to Mo. "We need to lure Evanton out of hiding, get a dialogue going. But we know he's unlikely to speak to any of us. His most likely candidate would have been Donna, but she's... well, out of the picture at the moment."

"Yes, I heard about that," said Mo. "How is she?"

"Not great," said Alice. "But she's in the right place."

"Tell her I'm asking for her, will you?" said Mo.

Marsh cleared his voice. "We agreed Evanton might be most likely to respond to an appeal if you were the one to make it, Mo."

"Your safety, of course, is paramount," Alice said, with a sideways glance at Fran.

"Yes, of course it is," Marsh cut in, sounding annoyed. "Once you put out the media appeal, you'll remain here under our protection until we can locate Evanton. Did Aiden explain it all on your way here?"

Mo sighed, and stared at her hands for a long time before answering. "Yes he did, and of course I'm here because I'm willing to do this, but you'll understand if I'm a little sceptical about your ability to protect anyone right now."

Gawd, thought Alice, *just as well she doesn't know about the phone hacking!*

Marsh's face went red, and Mo continued. "However, I don't believe Jonas would hurt me. Granted, I haven't spoken to him for some time, and I've no idea what his state of mind will be like."

"Do you think he'll get in touch with you?" asked Marsh.

"Yes, I think he will," said Mo. "Like I told you the other day, he will be wanting something, and I'm probably one of the very few people he'd trust. But... this will probably be a difficult thing for you to hear…"

Bated breaths around the table while Mo paused and then went on, "… I know what he's done, and there is no excusing any of it. Angus Ross was a good man, and a lot of innocent people are at risk while Jonas is at large. But we went through a lot together, and despite everything, I don't think he's a monster."

There was a silence, eventually broken by Alice.

"Well, you'll understand that to us, he is," she said. At the same time, she thought about Donna's *insurance policy*, and that she had been right to worry about Mo.

Mo conceded with a slight nod of her head.

The police press officer stuck her head in the door and gave a thumbs up.

"That's us all set to run," said Marsh. "If you're good to go?"

"I'm ready when you are," said Mo, standing up. "I'll read out whatever your press office wants me to read out, and I'll stay here for as long as it takes."

Marsh, Alice, Fran and Aiden stood up too, and they all began to make their way to the press room.

Inside, the room was heaving. Alice thought their last couple of press conferences were filled beyond capacity, but this one was bursting at the seams. And that was without having the spectacle of Donna, she thought.

Alice watched as Mo Skinner and Harry Marsh took seats at the liveried table at the front of the room. Camera flashes made the room pulsate, and gradually the loud chatter began to quieten down. Those that could find a seat sat down. Plenty of others crammed into the room, squashed shoulder to shoulder and pressed against walls.

A row of three TV cameras sat in front of the table, and another one was perched on a high pedestal towards the back of the room, all blinking at Mo and Marsh.

Marsh waited for the signal from their press officer, then stood up.

"Thank you all for coming at short notice," he said. "As you know, we've faced an unprecedented level of criminal activity during the past week. Our investigations have led us to believe this has been an orchestrated plan by Jonas Evanton to do as much damage as possible to Police Scotland at a time when our resources are particularly stretched. In order to restore public confidence in the police, we've decided to take this step today, to offer a communication channel with Evanton."

Alice could see he was almost choking on his words.

"So, now I'd like to introduce you to Mo Skinner, who'll be familiar to many of you. Mo has known Evanton for some time, and has kindly offered to speak directly to him."

He gestured for Mo to begin.

Mo straightened the papers that sat in front of her on the table, then set them to the side and removed her reading glasses. She was a pro, Alice observed, a seasoned lawyer who knew how to work an audience.

The hum from the overhead lighting was the only sound in the room as everyone waited for Mo's words.

She leaned forward, as far as she could towards the nearest camera, and stared into it for a few seconds, before taking a breath, and beginning.

Chapter 68

Alexandra took a sip from her can of Irn Bru, ignoring the look of scorn from her father. They were both standing side by side with Evanton in front of the large TV.

"Pathetic," Evanton spat at the images being relayed from the press room at Bell Street. Alexandra watched him closely, trying to figure out what was going on this time.

"Who is that prick?" Evanton went on, pointing a finger at Marsh on the screen. Marsh was talking about restoring public order or confidence in the police, or something. Alexandra couldn't quite make out his words above the torrent of expletives being hurled at the TV by Evanton.

Then the TV camera zoomed out, revealing the table that DCI Marsh was standing behind. Next to him sat a woman. Alexandra watched in fascination as the sight of the woman stopped Evanton in mid-profanity. He fell completely silent, staring at the woman on the TV.

The camera now focused solely on the woman, and came in close so that her face almost completely filled the screen.

"Jonas, I want you to listen to me," the woman said. She leaned forward, her eyes piercing the room. Even Alexandra found herself transfixed. The woman on the TV went on. "You know I've always been here for you. I know the things you've done, and I've still been here for you. You know that, don't you?"

Out of the corner of her eye, Alexandra was astonished to find Evanton nodding in agreement at the woman's words. The woman continued. "You're backed into a corner, Jonas. I know you hate that, and I know you would do anything to get out of the trap you've gotten yourself into. But you must be exhausted. You're tired, aren't you?"

Alexandra turned to see what Evanton's reaction would be now. He was reaching out his hand to touch the screen, and his face was beginning to contort.

The woman kept talking. "This can't keep going on, and the police don't have the resources to keep fighting you. Let's end this, Jonas, before anyone else gets hurt. I know you well enough to realise you'll have thought of the conditions you want to set in order to put a stop to it all. You need to tell me what it is you want."

Evanton was standing stock still, with his hand on the screen.

"I'll be honest with you," the woman went on. "I don't know how much bargaining the police will be willing to do. But we at least need to begin talking. Can you do that, Jonas? Will you ring the number that's on the bottom of the screen? You'll get through directly to me, and it's only me who will speak to you. Talk to me, Jonas, please."

Then the woman seemed to glance at the police officer nearest to her as though she was about to say something she shouldn't. Then she added, speaking more rapidly, "And there's something I need to tell you about, Jonas. Something I should have told you about a long time ago, but I was too ashamed. It's time you knew. Phone me…"

The police officer seemed to gesture for the TV cameras to move away, and suddenly the screen went blank, before coming back on with some other cop standing there.

Alexandra saw tears, she was sure, in Evanton's eyes, and watched agog as he sank to his knees muttering, "What did she mean? What has she been keeping from me?"

Kozel looked at his daughter and shrugged his shoulders in bewilderment.

Chapter 69

In the team room at Bell Street, a number of officers sat around a large desk, headphones in place, poised over the telecoms equipment, ready to instruct Mo Skinner the instant the call came in.

It had taken a lot longer than Alice had anticipated to get the journalists back out of Bell Street, so much so that she'd worried they might miss Evanton's call. They all wanted to know what Mo had been hinting at, but she had remained tight lipped about it, saying only, "It's a private matter."

Alice and Fran had had to bat Marsh off several times. He seemed to sense they knew what Mo was talking about, and it was obvious he wasn't happy about being kept out of the loop.

But they had finally made it back to the team room.

Tension was running high.

Mo was pacing back and forth, sipping occasionally at her coffee. There was an unusual hush, the normal buzz of chatter now absent as the officers waited anxiously. Many of the desks that normally accommodated a pair of officers busy on tasks had been pushed to the walls of the room to create more space for the telecoms team.

"What if he doesn't call?" Fran whispered to Alice.

"Why are you whispering?" Alice whispered back.

Fran's face reddened slightly as Stephen Morrison chuckled softly. Despite Alice's attempt, the nervous silence continued.

"He'll phone," Mo commented. "I'm certain he will. He has no other choice, really."

"She's right," said Alice. "Let's stay calm and…"

The piercing shrill tone of a phone ringing made her jump and emit a short squeal, despite her best efforts.

One of the officers at the large table looked up, and gave the signal that this was it. This was the call coming in on the line they'd set up to receive the call from Evanton.

Mo's face blanched as she set her coffee down carefully and sat next to the officer, as they had agreed during the drill earlier that evening. Rehearsed whispers and hand signals from the comms officers guided her into action. Her hand trembled slightly as she picked up the receiver. The room fell silent as she took a deep breath before speaking. "Jonas?" she said. "Talk to me."

Ready to run
Tuesday
Chapter 70

Alice wondered if she could get any more exhausted than she was right now. She'd been shocked when she felt her head begin to nod while she was driving. But if they got this right, then it should all be over soon. Possibly within the next few hours.

She had taken a circuitous route here to the psychiatric hospital, so that she could park at the rear of the building without passing the staff parking that surrounded it on three sides, and there was plenty of shrubbery so that her car could be well hidden.

Burly McKinnes was sitting hunched up next to her in the passenger seat, and he'd remained silent during the drive. Like Alice, he was dressed in black from head to toe.

Alice switched off the engine, also stopping the car heater.

There was thick cloud cover, bringing the temperature up just high enough for it to rain rather than snow. Visibility was very poor, which suited Alice just fine.

"It's freezing," said Burly. "Can we not just keep the engine running?"

"Sorry," said Alice, "but nobody can know we're here. It's not that bad."

"It's two in the morning in December," Burly growled. "It's fucking freezing."

Alice agreed with him, but wasn't prepared to say so. They had enough to think about, and she needed to stay fully focused. This was their one shot at getting Evanton. They couldn't balls it up this time.

They both froze when the figure of a man came into view not far from the back of the car. Then they saw a small flashing light dancing around at his knee level.

"A dog walker," said Alice. "Who the hell walks their dog out here in the middle of the night?"

They waited in silence, never taking their eyes from the man, until he passed by and out of sight. Seemingly he hadn't noticed them, or if he had, he hadn't thought anything of it.

Alice stole a glance at Burly. Hardly out of school, and he'd had just about the most awful start in life that anyone in this country could have. But Donna seemed to trust him. She had certainly been keen to give the lad a chance, and although Alice didn't want any part in letting him away with murdering his father, she was prepared to go along with Donna's wishes for now. She would work on her after they'd dealt with Evanton.

"This is the exciting thing about being an undercover cop," she told Burly. "You get to sit in freezing cold cars for hours on end, watching nothing and with nothing to keep you entertained."

"What do you mean, *hours on end*?" Burly looked mutinous.

"Okay, I exaggerate," Alice shrugged. "On this occasion, we should only be here about an hour. Two, max."

Burly still didn't look impressed, but sat quietly brooding.

Alice thought back to earlier that evening, when Mo Skinner had made the TV appeal. Mo had seemed to genuinely want to tell Evanton about Sarah. She was sure it wasn't just a tease to push Evanton into making the phone call, although her hint that she had something personal to confess to him certainly did the trick.

Evanton had phoned quicker than they'd expected. He had also agreed to meet with Mo, at a location specified by him. A remote cottage by Loch Kinord. He had made Mo promise to attend without any police. He reminded her that, as they knew, he was watching them and would know if they planned to accompany her, and told her that he had Alexandra Kozel. He wouldn't hesitate to pull a knife across the girl's throat if there was any hint of a police presence anywhere near the cottage.

Mo had agreed without any protest, and seemed remarkably calm at the prospect of making her way to Loch Kinord to meet Evanton face to face on her own. The police would follow, but not until later, giving Mo around an hour with him so that he would drop his guard. Now that she pondered it over, Alice began to wonder if it hadn't been a little too easy. Again, she trusted Donna's hunch that they were going to have to use their secret *insurance policy*. Her stomach began to heave at the information they'd found, but she hoped to God it would work.

She checked the time. Donna should be good to go by now, she reckoned. She brought out the red mobile and keyed, *Ready?*

Burly watched with interest now. She sensed in him a new alertness. He knew it was almost time. A few moments later, a text came back from Donna: *Ready to run.*

Alice nodded to Burly, signalled for him to sit tight, then eased open the car door and melted into the night.

Keeping a careful watch all around her, she crept towards the building, aiming for the thin line of light that she saw from the bottom of one of the doors. She pressed herself into a wall, waiting to check the door wasn't going to open. The last thing they needed now was for a pile of nurses to come out for a fag break.

When she was reassured that everything was okay, she reached into her pocket and brought out a security fob. True to his word, Bruno had been able to reproduce it from the serial number in the photograph Donna had sent by text.

Alice stepped forward and pressed the fob to the key pad. The door lock clicked, and she pushed the door open a fraction. As soon as it opened enough to see the person standing on the other side of it, she was relieved to see Donna looking alert and like her normal self again. The two briefly embraced, but exchanged no words. Then Alice slid inside the building, while Donna went outside and ran towards the car.

Chapter 71

While Alice and Burly had been sitting outside, Donna had been constantly checking the time. It was all so close now.

She'd managed to fool the nurses into thinking she had been taking her medication for four days now – or was it five? She'd lost track – but she wasn't sure how much longer she could get away with that. And one of them had almost found the red mobile earlier, when she'd forgotten to move it from under her pillow. That was a close call.

But her mind was clear now, alert and on the job. She just wished her body felt the same. All of the theatrics over the last few days had left her feeling stiff and below par.

She checked the details again that Alice had texted to her. They had Evanton's location. Mo was to meet him there at eight in the morning, with police back up arriving around nine, but Donna had other plans. She was certain that Alice and Burly would have arrived at the agreed spot by now. She would have enough time to get dressed and prepare the room as best she could.

Just around the time Alice and Burly had spotted the dog walker, Donna slipped out of bed and tip-toed to the bathroom, all the while listening out for any signs that one of the nurses might look in on her.

Nothing.

The coast was clear.

As she splashed cold water onto her face, she felt the dirt of this investigation begin to fall away from her. For the first time, she felt a glimmer of hope that this could be all over in the next few hours, once and for all. And that she and Libby could focus on moving into their new home, and look forward to the arrival of the new baby.

At the thought of Libby, she felt a stone drop into her stomach. The turmoil she had put Libby through, and at what should have been one of the happiest times of her life, brought a bitter taste to her mouth. The lies she'd had to tell her to protect her ate at her conscience.

Donna bit her lip and stared into the small mirror before her. She had to end this thing, get justice for all those people who had died. Justice for Angus Ross. Anger stirred in her chest. Justice for all the Agneses of the world. But more than anything, Donna was tired to her core. She needed to see Evanton brought to justice, so that she could finally give Libby the security that she so deserved to have, and the life free from worry that they needed together.

This job, she thought yet again.

And now time was starting to speed up.

She rubbed her face dry on a towel, and tip toed back into the room, where she silently extracted her clothes from the bedside storage unit, the black ones that Alice had brought on her previous visit.

Tying the shoelaces on her trainers, she wobbled and hit the plastic chair that sat beside the bed. The scraping sound it made as it slewed across the floor seemed to fill the room and echo for an alarming length of time. Donna froze. She heard footsteps approach.

Thinking quickly, she jumped back into the bed and under the covers, just as the door opened. Then she realised she'd left the bathroom light on.

"You okay in here?" the nurse asked.

"Mm," Donna tried to sound sleepy. "Just got up for a drink of water."

The nurse hovered by the door for a moment, then came into the room.

"You forgot to switch the light off," she said. "Let me just get that for you. You get back to sleep."

Donna kept quiet while the nurse switched off the bathroom light and left the room again.

When she was sure the nurse would have returned to her station at the other end of the ward, Donna got back up, taking extra care this time to make sure there would be no more noise. She checked her mobile. There was the message from Alice that she'd been waiting for.

"Ready?" it said.

Donna keyed back, "Ready to run."

She felt her adrenaline spike as she silently crept out of her room and made her way to the door where, if it was all going to plan, Alice would be waiting.

Paul sat in the coffee lounge sipping at a strong one and flipping through the day's newspaper. He was enjoying his late night chats with Donna. It wasn't every day you got to spend time with a murder detective.

He felt the sink of disappointment as their usual meet-up time came and went, with no sign of her. He sighed. There were another five hours left on this shift. Five long hours before he could get home, cast off his uniform and dive into bed. He had been doing nights for a long time now, and it was beginning to tell on him.

He took several gulps to finish the coffee, and tossed the newspaper onto the nearest table. Then the thought occurred to him that perhaps something was wrong with Donna. When he'd spoken to her earlier, she had certainly intended to join him for a chat. He'd better check on her, just in case.

He toyed with the keys in his pocket and whistled softly to himself while he made his way through the ward to Donna's room. Opening the door, he peered inside. He saw that she was in bed, and heard her grunt as she shuffled round onto her other side, then he closed the door quietly again and returned to his work station. He would be on a back shift next week. There would be plenty of time for chats while she was fully awake.

Chapter 72

The log fire was out. Abrim Kozel had watched the last of the embers turn dark and grow cold hours ago. Alexandra was curled into him, like she used to do when she was a little girl. He sorted the blanket that he'd wrapped around her, and stroked her hair. She'd been dozing on and off, but was awake now. She yawned, and looked up at him, as if she sensed he was about to get up.

He put his finger to his lips. This cottage had been their prison for more than a week now, and he had to take his chance to get them out. Evanton was losing it, and there was no telling what he might do next. But he also saw the opportunity.

"He is obsessed by the thought of meeting this woman in the

morning," he whispered to Alexandra. "He is no longer focused. I'm going to take a look around while he's distracted, find a weapon or a way out. Put a chair up against the door, and only open it if it's me."

For once, Alexandra nodded her head in instant obedience. It took him right back to her very young years, to when he was her hero. He felt a brief flush of pride in his chest, and he offered a smile, before waving his hand again to reinforce the instruction.

Kozel listened carefully, making sure he had correctly judged Evanton's location in the cottage. The rantings and ravings, and the thud of hurled objects didn't seem to be coming from the room with all the screens that Alexandra had caught a glimpse of. Evanton had guarded that room closely during the whole time he'd been keeping them here, making Kozel think it the most likely place to find a weapon.

As he inched his way in its direction, he paused after every few steps to listen, and was relieved to find that the din was getting further away from him the closer he got to the room.

With a band of sweat beginning to form across his forehead, Kozel grasped the door handle and slipped silently into the room that had, until now, been so fiercely shielded by Evanton.

As he stepped inside, he gaped in wonder at the line of large screens that covered one of its walls. Alexandra hadn't been exaggerating, he thought, when she had described it to him.

It took him a moment to realise that each screen had a desk below it. He went to the nearest one and looked at the handwritten notes that were sitting on it. The screen above this desk was dark, but not switched off. Kozel squinted more closely, and saw that it appeared to be showing the inside of somewhere dark, like a cupboard or a locker or something similar. The notes on the desk were headed up with the name "Burly McKinnes."

Kozel listened carefully again, satisfied himself that Evanton was still at the other end of the cottage, and tried to understand the notes on the desk. It seemed to be a timeline relating to the arrest and imprisonment of this Burly McKinnes. Kozel had no idea who this was, or why Evanton would be taking an interest in him, but clearly the ex cop had set up a very detailed surveillance. Kozel studied the screen again. It was definitely a display from some kind of camera sitting inside a dark storage area.

A movement on one of the other screens caught his eye. On this one, the picture was of a large room containing lots of desks. It looked like an office. But no ordinary office, Kozel saw. The movement that had caught his eye was of a uniformed police officer walking past. Excitement gripped Kozel's throat, as he studied the notes relating to this screen. Sergeant Alice Moone, the notes told him. And they, too, appeared to show a timeline of sorts. Kozel looked back up at the screen. Another officer arrived centre stage from a side room, and the two cops began to talk to one another. Kozel flinched when the sound of the voices in discussion came loud and clear into the room. A tick of anxiety made him look towards the door again, fearful of Evanton's attention being broached.

Tearing his eyes away from the screens and the desks, he remembered what he had come in here for. He needed to find a weapon. And fast.

Chapter 73

The ward sprang to life at 6am. The night shift were beginning to pack up, having a last coffee before the final check round.

The nurse opened Donna's room door, and sprang back in alarm.

"Morning," said Alice from Donna's bed.

"Who are you?" the nurse gasped.

"I'm Donna," said Alice. "Don't you remember?"

"You're not Donna," said the nurse, a terse expression fixing her face.

Alice got out of bed and went to the bathroom, while the perplexed nurse looked on.

"Oh my GOD!" Alice yelled at the top of her voice when she was standing in front of the mirror. "What's happened to my

FACE?"

The nurse was on her radio in a flash. Alice turned to her.

"Get the doctor in here," Alice told her. "I believe Dr. Novak is on call this morning?"

While she spoke, holding the nurse's attention, Alice reached under the pillow and brought out her warrant card.

"Police business," she whispered. "Get Dr. Novak."

The nurse continued to look perplexed, but followed Alice's instruction, and made an urgent call on her radio for Dr. Novak.

When she arrived not much later, Dr. Novak looked a lot younger than Alice had expected. The medic stared for a few seconds at the scars criss-crossing Alice's face, as everyone did upon meeting her for the first time, then sat tentatively on the arm of the visitors' chair.

"What's this all about?" she asked, her English perfect and with only a hint of an accent in it.

Alice held out a sheaf of papers. "You should read the letter on the top," she said.

Dr. Novak took the paperwork from Alice, and read from the letterhead, "Dougal Clarence, criminal lawyer and public notary. What is this?"

"Read it, please," said Alice. "Then I'll explain everything. There isn't much time." Alice saw the look that Dr. Novak gave her, and added, "I am actually perfectly sane, you know."

The doctor skim-read the contents of the letter, and flicked through the remainder of the papers, finding the necessary signatures, and nodded her head, ready to hear what Alice had to say. "An undercover operation?" she prompted.

Alice sat on the edge of the bed, facing Dr. Novak.

"Donna and I have been part of the ongoing investigation to find Jonas Evanton," she began. "It's all linked to the mayhem of the last few days – the stolen body, the shootings, the train derailment."

Dr. Novak stared at Alice, and nodded her head to go on.

"We couldn't figure out how he was managing to orchestrate all these crimes and still stay hidden," Alice said. "Then Donna began to suspect he was using our phones to spy on us."

Dr. Novak looked sceptical. Alice continued, "She ran her theory by our tech guys…"

Donna saw Bruno, an officer she'd worked with before, coming in through a door at the far side of the office.

… "and sure enough, the technology Evanton would need in order to use our phones to watch our every move is available, tried and tested. So she set up a trap."

"A trap?" Dr. Novak asked, her eyes grown wide. "Now I'm beginning to feel a little foolish."

Alice smiled. "We had to make Evanton believe Donna had had a breakdown and was locked in here."

"But if this Evanton could watch everything she was doing, how could she tell you about this?"

The shopkeeper barely registered her when she made her request, simply confirming in a bored voice, "Five of them?"

Alice held up the red mobile.

"We've been using these pay-as-you-go phones, and leaving our own ones in places that would fit with the picture we wanted Evanton to see," said Alice. She saw Dr. Novak's growing alarm. "Time's running out now," she told the medic. "I need you to phone DCI Harry Marsh at Bell Street and explain to him about this letter. I need him to authorise a full response to this address." She showed Dr. Novak an address in Deeside. "That's where Evanton is, and Donna will be arriving there just about now."

Dr. Novak's face blanched, and she reached for her own phone to follow Alice's instructions.

Chapter 74

"Are you not worried about getting caught?" asked Burly.

He and Donna were tearing along the A92, already past Arbroath and coming to the wide bend in the road at Inverkeillor. If it wasn't pitch dark they would be able to see the sands of Lunan Bay to their right, one of Donna's favourite places on a nice day. But she was keeping her eyes fixed on the road ahead, gripping the wheel of Alice's car.

"Nobody's going to catch us," said Donna.

Burly shook his head. "You're mental," he muttered.

Donna laughed. It felt good to be taking action at long last, and if she was honest, the risk of getting caught speeding through the countryside dressed like a Ninja added to the excitement. Burly seemed less enthused, but sat stoically beside her.

Donna glanced at him for a split second. She was glad to have his company, and she knew that if things didn't go to plan when they got to Evanton's cottage, the lad would have an important role to play in getting the message out to her fellow officers. She hoped it wouldn't come to that, though. She had other plans for Burly McKinnes. There was no way she was going to leave him to the law now.

They drove on, mostly in silence, and eventually Donna slowed the car and turned off the main road, heading inland.

It was pushing five in the morning now, she noted from the dashboard display. The driving was becoming harder, crawling across country at a snail's pace in the dark, until the satnav had them fairly close to the cottage, at last.

She stopped the car, and switched the headlamps off to get her eyes used to the dark. It was still a little too far to finish the journey on foot, but close enough for car headlights to be noticed. She had to get closer without advertising her arrival.

As the sinister shapes of the birchwood branches began to distinguish themselves from the pre-dawn blackness, Donna decided she could see enough to continue driving. She found the rough woodland track off the A97 that would take them towards Loch Kinord and to the remote cottage. She elbowed the slumbering Burly.

"Mmfff?" he grunted, managing to open one sleepy eye.

"We're here," said Donna. She switched off the engine again. "This is as close as we can bring the car. See the cottage across there?"

226

Burly tried to follow her pointing finger with his bleary eyes.

"We need to go the rest of the way on foot," she said, wondering what on earth might be awaiting them.

They left the car, both gasping at the shock of cold air, and pulled on their balaclavas. These would help keep them invisible in the dark, but were also a lifesaver in the freezing temperatures.

There were patches of snow underfoot as they went, and Donna was concerned about the loud crunching noise it made, having iced hard during the night. But they kept their course towards the cottage, making steady progress despite the odd stumble over hidden tree roots on the track.

Then they were almost upon it.

Donna crouched in close to a hedge that lined a field, and tried not to think about what creatures could be making the scurrying sounds. Burly was hunched down behind her, but he still cast an ominous figure in the twilight.

The cottage sat some 200 meters ahead of them, the lights at all of the windows blazing out towards the surrounding countryside, with no neighbours to bother. Some way in front of the cottage there was a small brick construction. A coal bunker, perhaps, Donna thought. She pointed towards it now.

"You're going to have to wait in there," she told Burly. "And do not come back out until I come and get you."

"I can't let you go into that house on your own," Burly growled.

"I'm a highly trained police officer," Donna said, "and a little crazy, so I can look after myself."

At her signal, they both scooted forward. Keeping almost on all fours, they quickly reached the coal bunker. Donna listened at its door to satisfy herself there was nobody inside, then pushed it open.

In the ever lightening twilight, she could see the coal bunker was empty save for an old wooden stool.

"There," she said to Burly, "it's even furnished."

The big lad grunted.

Donna studied his face. He looked so tired, she saw. Scared, too. And very young.

The red mobile in her hand buzzed, and she saw a message from Alice. "Operation Novak success. Go!"

"It's time," Donna said. "I need this closure with Evanton. On my own. Now, are you clear about your role? The police will start arriving here in around half an hour. Sit tight. If I don't come back out, you need to stop them here and warn them. If they don't appear either, that's when you phone your lawyer for me, okay?"

Burly began to put up something of a half-hearted protest, but bundled himself into the coal bunker.

"I'm not expecting trouble from him," Donna reassured the youngster. "As long as he thinks I'm here on my own, I'll be alright. Half an hour, remember. Start the clock now."

Burly nodded his understanding.

Donna closed the coal bunker door and moved off towards the cottage, keeping well into the shadows. It was time to face Jonas Evanton in the flesh.

Chapter 75

Barely ten minutes after Dr. Novak's phone call, DCI Marsh hurried into the psychiatric hospital, his face red from exertion.

"I could have you all for this insubordination," he said to Alice, out of puff from running. "But, bloody hell, this is brilliant! I'll drive. I want to know everything by the time we get out of Dundee. Ev. Er. Y. Thing."

As they raced up the A92 through Arbroath, then past the wide bend at Inverkeillor, on by Montrose and finally cutting inland at the small fishing port of Portlethen, bringing the rising sun to their backs, Alice brought DCI Marsh in on Donna's plan.

"How long have you known what she was up to?" Marsh wanted to know.

Alice thought back to the interview room, when Donna had charged Burly with his father's murder, and Dougal Clarence had blown a gasket.

"This is unbelievable!" Alice remembered Clarence protesting as Donna had roughed him from the room. She went on to tell Marsh what had happened next.

"There's an unused office just next to the interview room," she explained. "I really thought she'd lost the plot, but she whisked us in there and told us she had taken advice from Bruno at IT Security, and he had told her about the StingRay device. She told us about her plan to use our phones to show Evanton what we wanted him to see, which was a team falling apart and an investigation getting nowhere."

Alice checked that Marsh was following, then went on, "She wanted me to tell the team about the security breach, just when she got herself whisked off to hospital."

"That was all staged and part of her plan?"

"Of course it was," said Alice. "Then, because they all knew they were being watched, they wouldn't be faking how helpless they were feeling, so we didn't have to worry about anybody slipping up and giving the game away to Evanton."

"Genius," Marsh whispered.

"Got to hand it to her," said Alice. "She knew nobody was really going to be surprised at her having a breakdown, so she played that card well. She gave us these pay as you go mobiles," she held up the red mobile for him to see, "so we could discuss what we were really doing, without Evanton knowing or suspecting a thing."

"That's why you asked me to put my mobile in the boot," Marsh twigged, smiling.

"Yeah, the last thing we need now is for Evanton to find out the whole plan just at the last minute," Alice confirmed. "He could be watching on your phone."

"And who's been in on all of this?" Marsh asked.

"Just me, Bruno, Dougal Clarence and Burly McKinnes," said Alice.

"Burly McKinnes?" Marsh looked astonished. "But why on earth…?"

"Part of her plan," was all Alice would say about that. "And she

229

wanted Dougal Clarence to witness her plan before she got admitted to the psychiatric unit, as an extra precaution. It was imperative that Libby and Natesh in particular believed Donna really had a breakdown. If they had been in on the plan, they wouldn't have been able to act convincingly enough to fool Evanton. So, it had to be restricted to just the five of us."

"That argument you both had outside the press conference," said Marsh. "Was that…?"

"All part of the plan," Alice confirmed. She thought back to the press conference just after they'd charged Burly with murder.

For God's sake, Alice, she remembered Donna snapping at her. *Can you follow an order for just once in your life?*

"That was an order, was it?" she had shouted back. *"Well, fuck you, DI Dickhead."*

She told Marsh how she and Donna had made a show of walking into the press room side by side, exchanging angry looks, like two boxers squaring up before the fight. How they'd been sure to place their mobiles on the desk at the front of the room, where all of the commotion would be seen clearly by anyone who might be watching in. Then how she and Donna had used the general melee and confusion in the room to sneak out through a side door for a few moments to check with one another on how the plan was going.

"Donna was really worried about the effect it was going to have on Libby," she said. "But there was no other option."

As they drove on, with Alice relaying this story, Marsh nodded his head, impressed. "But how on earth did you manage to get into the locked ward?" he asked.

"Easy," said Alice, holding onto the door handle with the way suddenly becoming rough. "Donna photographed the keys and security pass bar codes, and I gave the images to Bruno, to have replicates made. Donna got a routine going whereby she would have supper in the middle of the night with one of the nurses she was friends with. She gambled on him checking in on her when she didn't turn up last night. By that time, we'd swapped places and it was me in the bed, and all I had to do was make some sleepy sounds and the nurse thought it was Donna all tucked up, so there would be no alarm to raise."

"I have to hand it to her," said Marsh. "She really does understand how people behave."

"Well, most people," Alice concurred. "But she might have met her match this time. I just hope she's played things right with Evanton. I don't have a good feeling, though."

As they hurried on across country, they could see from all angles closing in, but still at a distance, flashing blue lights. The cavalry was well and truly on its way. But, Alice wondered, would they get there in time?

They missed the woodland track that led off the main road, and had to double-back to find it. Then eventually they spotted the lights of the cottage, and it was time to leave the car.

Just then, from the direction of the cottage came the unmistakable sound of gunfire.

Two shots.

Instinctively, Alice brought out her own gun. Marsh looked at it, horrified. Then the police radio burst into life, and all hell seemed to be breaking loose around them.

Chapter 76

Donna stood facing the cottage front door. Could this really be it, she wondered? The moment she'd waited almost two years for. Finally coming face to face with Jonas Evanton.

She took off her balaclava, now barely feeling the cold. Her adrenaline must be at an all time high, she realised.

A sound at her back made the hairs on her neck stand on end.

She spun round.

Jonas Evanton stood before her, shock momentarily flickering across his face. "They've sent you in as the cavalry?" he sneered, quickly recovering himself.

"They don't know I'm here," said Donna, levelling his gaze and forcing her breathing to slow down. "So it's just you and me now. Isn't that what you wanted?"

Evanton looked her up and down. Her skin crawled.

"Gone all maverick again, then, Davenport?"

He drew a pistol from his back pocket.

Donna felt her heart sink. She glanced around in every direction, but there was no sign of help approaching. Perhaps she'd mis-timed the whole thing. After all, the chances of that were pretty high. And of her colleagues arriving to a murder scene instead of a rescue.

"Get inside," he ordered.

Donna followed his instructions and the pressure of the gun at her back, and they made their way through the cottage until they came to a kitchen. A dark, modest one, furnished old-style. Donna scanned it for potential escape routes, but wasn't optimistic at what she saw.

"I'm not an animal, you know," said Evanton. "We can sit down and work out some kind of deal." He gestured towards a small rustic table that sat in the far corner of the kitchen.

Donna glowered at him, not trusting her mouth, as she sat down. He sat down, too, their shoulders almost touching. Just what was it she had hoped to achieve here? Now she sat trapped, with Evanton blocking her way to the door. How could she have gotten herself into this position so quickly?

"Or did you think you were going to be the one to bring me in?" Evanton was going on.

Donna shrugged. "It's hardly a level playing field, is it?" She nodded to the gun.

Evanton stared at her. He placed the gun on the table between them, but not letting it go. "You know," he began, "I've been on the run all this time because of you."

"And you want it to end," Donna said, meeting his eye.

Evanton sighed, and toyed with the gun. "I want it to end, yes. But not just at any price."

"Give me a laugh, then," said Donna. Could she make a grab for the gun? "What is it you want?"

Evanton's expression grew dark. It made Donna think back to the MIC investigation almost two years back, to the way his mood and his temper could snap without warning. She found her body tensing, braced for an assault. She saw that Evanton had seen it, and he smirked again. Then he shook his head slowly, his mood changing once more. "I have to admit, I'm impressed you figured out the StingRay operation, and you even managed to play me at my own game. It's a real pity," he said. "In another life we would have worked well together, achieved a lot. But, back in the real world, I need to get out of here, and I'm guessing it'll have to be now." He moved the gun onto his lap.

"If you think I'm going to help you, you've got another thing coming," said Donna.

"You didn't learn a thing, did you, when I had Angus Ross killed?" he goaded her, standing up and beginning to pace around the small kitchen.

Donna knew what he was trying to do. But she was going to keep her cool and stay in control. "And if I refuse?"

"If you refuse," said Evanton, "then the nightmare you've been living this past week will just go on and on. And it'll be even worse for Libby Quinn – you're not going back home until I'm safely over the border."

"Says you and whose army?" said Donna, also standing up. She regretted the words immediately, when none other than Abrim Kozel walked into the kitchen. The surprise forced her back into her seat.

"Santa's little helper," said Evanton, standing aside like a music hall compere.

Donna noted the expression of contempt on Kozel's face. She also saw that he wasn't carrying a weapon. Was there something to be played between these two, she wondered? Her mind began to race. She was cornered in a room in the middle of nowhere by two of the country's most dangerous and wanted men. Her chances weren't looking good, she knew, but she was determined to put up as much of a fight as she could. She hadn't come this far for nothing, and even if she didn't make it out alive, she could at least buy her colleagues a little time to get here and give them a chance of capturing Evanton and Kozel.

"This is what's going to happen," said Evanton. "We're going to travel to the Irish border with Alexandra…"

"You are not taking my daughter anywhere!" Kozel burst out.

Evanton aimed his gun at the infamous gang leader. Kozel took several steps backwards into the kitchen, and found himself standing next to Donna.

"You will stay here with Davenport," Evanton said. "Make sure she calls this in as a false address. Tonight when we're in Ireland, I'll tell you where you can pick up your daughter…"

"You'd better not lay a finger on her."

We? thought Donna. Had she heard that right?

"Shut up!" Evanton's voice was beginning to rise, along with his temper. "You are following my instructions. When I call you, let Davenport go." He then turned his attention back to Donna. "You'll do whatever you have to do to clear up, then resign. Otherwise, I'll come for you. Maybe pay your little woman a visit in the night."

Donna felt sick. Now her head was swimming. Evanton would walk away, a free man, and live whatever anonymous life he wanted to live, while she and Libby would be forever more looking over their shoulders. She couldn't think of a way out of this one other than to follow his instructions. Except for the one thing she knew that she did have, thanks to Fran's efforts.

"You have a daughter," she said. "Mo Skinner had a daughter after the time you visited her in the States. That's what she wanted to tell you about."

Evanton froze.

There was a moment of complete silence. Donna felt her muscles tighten as she readied to spring up, to take advantage of the bombshell to get past Evanton and out of here.

But then she heard laughter.

Evanton's laughter.

234

"Is that it?" he roared. "Is that all you've got?"

Footsteps approached the kitchen, and a shadow emerged at the door. Donna's attention switched to it, and her heart sank when Mo walked in casually and took a seat at the table next to Donna.

"I'm sorry," she almost whispered to the DI. "But there are probably some things that should be left in the past. You pushed it too far, didn't you?"

"You're both going on the run?" Donna asked.

"You've done me a favour, in the end," Evanton laughed. "Now I'll have everything I ever wanted. You've no idea how delighted I was to discover I do, actually, have a daughter."

"Do you really think she'll want anything to do with you?" Donna spat.

"Perhaps in time," said Mo. "But Jonas and I have a bond that's different to anything you'd know anything about."

"Oh yes, the Bhopal thing," Donna cut in. Now it was time to cash in her secret *insurance policy*. Do or die. "About that…"

Both Mo and Evanton fixed their stares on her. Donna saw a flicker of fear cross Evanton's eyes.

"Do you remember being contacted by Sunil Sarang some years ago?" she asked Mo.

Mo went quiet, and eventually she looked at Donna and muttered, "Yes."

"Do you know who Sunil Sarang is?" Donna then asked Evanton.

"What are you going on about?" Evanton hissed.

Donna could see Abrim Kozel watching her, with a quizzical expression on his face. He looked as though he was weighing up which side to back. She went on. "I had an interesting chat with Sunil very recently. He lives in Bhopal."

Mo sighed, an angry sound. Evanton seemed to pale suddenly.

"He had a sister," said Donna. "Rashida, her name was. She died in the toxic gas cloud that night, although something terrible happened to her first. But you already know about that, don't you, Evanton?"

Evanton's eyes darted back and forth between Donna and Mo.

His breathing grew quicker, and he almost dropped the gun. Donna looked at him as she continued. "You know Mo always suspected what you'd done, don't you? She tried often enough to get you to confess. It's a pity Sunil Sarang couldn't get hold of the evidence when he contacted Mo for help. Was it a relief, Mo," she looked at the lawyer now, "to never have to face the truth?"

Mo remained silent.

"Well, you're going to have to hear it," Donna said, "because Sunil has the evidence now."

She was acutely aware that Evanton was positioned in front of the door, holding a gun, making all of them sitting ducks in this claustrophobic kitchen. But she could also see in his face the need to rid himself of the burden of his crime that he'd carried for so long.

"I am not a monster!" he yelled out suddenly. Donna felt Mo flinch beside her. "I was a fucking youngster! Everything was a mess…"

Donna could only imagine what horrors might emerge as he began to rant almost incoherently.

The young Jonas Evanton twisted away in disgust from the grasping hands of a woman whose eyes were opaque and weeping, her gaping mouth uttering silent screams of agony from lungs torn by the poisonous air.

The woman, Rashida Sarang, reached out, grasping desperately.

Donna watched Evanton rub a hand across his eyes, as though trying to bring himself out of a trance.

Evanton stumbled on, looking back at her with revulsion. The stampeding and the shouting, the screaming, terrified chaos in the blinding fog continued amok. He stopped.

Nobody was going to help her.

He turned back and looked at Rashida again.

"I am not a monster," Evanton repeated, staring at Mo.

Rashida heard his footsteps approach and she reached up for him, her rasping breath uttering incoherent pleas.

He saw her dirty fingernails, like those that constantly jabbed and picked at his clothing, those women in bare feet and filthy rags and their ceaseless laughing at him and his skinny, pale frame.

Well, they wouldn't be laughing at him now, he thought, as he felt the rush of blood in his veins.

With the first stirrings of arousal, he dragged the blinded woman behind an oil drum. Testosterone flooded his head at her shocked expression as he kicked her legs apart.

"You need to understand how sorry I was," Evanton pleaded with Mo. "I knew what I did was wrong, and I've lived with that guilt for all these years. But I've made up for it, haven't I? I stopped all the bloodshed when I took control of the gangs." He fired a look at Kozel. Kozel was looking back at him, with an expression of disgust on his face.

"Come with me now," he said to Mo. "We can put all of this behind us once and for all."

Mo shook her head, her eyes registering both fear and shock. Donna braced herself as Evanton brought the gun level to her head. She'd broken the bond between Mo and Evanton, and now he was truly left with nothing. She had, yet again, thwarted his plans, and although she wasn't going to live to see him brought to justice, at least she'd bought some time for her colleagues to get here and take him.

In that instant, Donna heard a noise by the door. Evanton began to turn back towards it, but too late.

A hulking figure loomed there, and moved with surprising speed. Burly McKinnes wrapped his huge arms around Evanton, pinning him to the spot, and placed a massive hand across his throat.

"Drop the gun," Burly growled.

Evanton struggled on the spot, but was unable to move.

Donna saw the swift action as Kozel brought a gun from his own pocket and aimed it towards Burly.

"Get the hell back out of here!" Donna yelled at Burly. But the lad's steady gaze registered refusal.

"Shoot him," Evanton told Kozel. "This is a fucking set up. I should have known."

237

Evanton's face grew purple, and it looked to Donna as though he might wrestle free of Burly's grip.

"Shoot him!" Evanton was shrieking now. "There will be others out there. They're not going to let either of us go."

Donna watched Kozel closely. She'd lost count of the number of rival drug dealers he'd killed. He certainly wouldn't be squeamish about shooting Burly. No, she realised. The gangster was weighing up his options. His daughter was in here somewhere, and he was open to negotiation.

"There's no-one else here," Donna said to him. "You've got surveillance all over the place. You'd have seen some kind of movement if there had been a full team out."

"She's lying," said Evanton, a trace of panic now in his voice as Kozel's gun came to point at him.

"Give me the gun and get the hell out of here," Donna said to Kozel. "Use my car to get away. Drive north and I'll send the cops in the wrong direction when they arrive. They'll be here…" The sound of approaching sirens began to filter through the morning air. "They'll be here any time now. Can you hear them?"

She saw that Kozel could hear the sirens.

"You stick to running your patch in Aberdeen," Donna went on, "and we'll give you a wide berth. All you have to do is give me the gun, and get out with your daughter while you can."

A gurgling sound suddenly came from the door, and Donna watched in horror as Evanton began to slide to the floor. Burly was panting with the effort of the stranglehold, and sprang away from the doorway as soon as Evanton fell.

Choking and retching, Evanton now lay on the floor, and without another second's hesitation, Kozel fired two shots into his torso. Evanton's body flinched at both shots, then fell still. A pool of blood oozed across the floor from underneath him, and the wall behind him was sprayed with blood and torn flesh.

The sirens stopped.

Kozel leaped over the body and ran from the door, shouting, "We've got a deal now." And he was gone.

Donna leaned forward onto the kitchen table, and closed her eyes. Mo was sobbing quietly next to her. It was over. It was really over. Jonas Evanton was finally dead. He would never have to answer for his crimes. But he was dead. He could do no more harm.

She felt huge arms surround her. The arms that had choked Evanton were now consoling her. Burly McKinnes held onto her until running footsteps grew louder and louder, and Alice Moone burst into the room.

One month later
Chapter 77

Donna and Libby walked slowly together out of the cemetery, hand in hand. A mound of flowers still sat atop Angus Ross's grave. A tear rolled down Donna's cheek. They walked in silence to the car park. A gull was sitting on top of the car, waving around a Gregg's bag in its beak.

"I swear that's you, Ross," Donna said to it, and she felt herself let go a laugh of relief. "Fly free, old friend."

The gull cawed, and flapped its wings, and took off, still hanging onto the bag.

"You could be right," Libby laughed with her. "I'm sure I saw it wink."

From the cemetery, they decided to make their way on foot to Ninewells Hospital, a twenty minute walk along past the housing of Ninewells Avenue and up the hill. Mid January, and the sun was shining. It could be the calm before the storm, Donna thought, or perhaps a new beginning. She felt the bitter sting of losing Ross, but she was at last able to rest, knowing she didn't have to look over her shoulder and wonder if Evanton was watching her.

More than that, she could rest her conscience at last. She'd never been truly comfortable with policing, when she could see how often the lines between right and wrong became entangled. And her career had taken enough out of her and Libby's relationship. Things wouldn't have been the same at work any more, anyway, she knew. Ross gone. Morrison sacked for leaking information to the press. John Ogilvie starting over with Cerys in Bristol while awaiting trial. No, nothing would be the same there.

Harry Marsh was alright, after all, she decided, and she felt a little bad as she thought of the shock on his face when she'd handed over her warrant card and her letter of resignation. But she did worry about what could be next for her. What would she do now that she was no longer a cop?

Then the memory of Agnes visiting her in hospital, and the idea

240

of the *Mad Cows* group came back to her. It stirred something in her heart. Maybe, she thought, as she walked along beside Libby, just maybe there was something in Agnes's idea.

She had an urge to phone Alice, to talk to the General about all of it. Just to check it was actually real. But Alice was in Turkey now, sunning it up with Efe Demir, and she smiled at the thought that they were probably going to be seeing a lot more of Demir from now on.

Good for you, Alice, she thought.

Inside the hospital grounds, she and Libby followed the signs to the maternity unit. As they walked, Donna found herself wondering about Burly and his girlfriend and their baby, due in the next few weeks. She felt a wry smile cross her face, wondering how life on the road with the Travellers was suiting them. It had been a stroke of genius on Fran's part to have suggested asking Sarah Cooper to help hide the pair until the Abrim Kozel trial was done and dusted. It wasn't quite witness protection, Donna thought, but probably just as effective, and it gave Burly and his new family the option of starting afresh somewhere else, away from the shadow of his father. He would never be able to come back to Dundee, though, wanted as he was for Archie McKinnes's murder. But Donna had a feeling Agnes would be making frequent visits to wherever he decided to set up home, and would get to know her grandchild.

When they reached the maternity ward, they found Danny in the corridor, talking rapidly into his phone. From the seating in the waiting area, Natesh suddenly sprang out, a cheesy grin all over his face.

"It's a girl!" he beamed. "I'm an auntie! Danny's just phoning to tell your folks, but isn't that just the best thing ever? I mean, EVER?"

Suddenly Donna spotted a No Smoking sign on the wall, and she turned to Libby, a realisation striking her like a thunder bolt.

"I haven't had a smoke for over a week!" Donna and Libby looked at one another and laughed.

It was true now, more than ever: one chapter had ended, while another had begun.

The End

Acknowledgements

Writing a book is a labour of love, usually over a lengthy period of time. I'm indebted to everyone who has stuck with me during the marathon it's been.

Most of all, I must say a special thank you to my partner Allison. Aside from putting up with all sorts of strange conversations during the course of my research, she always encourages and always supports my writing endeavours. She also reads an early draft of my work, and never fails to make suggestions that dramatically improve it. More than all of that, she's the love of my life, and she is stuck with me forever.

I have a number of specific credits to make, without which Run could not have been completed. Firstly, to Alison Findlay for inspiring me when writers block took hold. Her insightful questions and suggestions got the plot going again.

I also have to thank Arbroath Football Club (c'mon the Lichties!) for their enthusiasm at being the location of the book's opening murder. I thoroughly enjoyed my trip to Gayfield and the Club's generous invitation to take my notebook around behind the scenes. And I did promise to mention Tuttie's Neuk – so, hello! Thanks also to Drew Herbertson of the Scottish Football Association for his good humoured answers to my dubious questions about referees.

For the equation in chapter 51 I'd like to thank the Mathematical Association, who answered my Twitter cry for help. Visit them on m-a.org.uk

During the course of writing this book, the family went through a particularly stressful period, and I am thankful beyond words for those friends at work and in the wild who helped see us through it. Angela Wallace, Kelly Lacey, Victoria Logan, Jacky Collins, Amanda Fleet, Tana Collins, Ian Skewis, and so many others, your words and encouragement have meant so much more than you'll ever know.

I'd also like to thank my Advance Readers Group for their support. In addition to others mentioned, they were Alfred Nobile,

Alison Cairns, Christine Sharp, Louise Fairbairn, Mary Picken, Neil Broadfoot, Olga Wojtas, Sharon Bairden, Shirley Whiteside, Tami Wylie, Wendy H. Jones, and Laura Nelson.

As always, my heartfelt thanks to ThunderPoint Publishing Ltd and to my t'rrific editor Seonaid, who work so hard to make this writing dream a reality. Getting the thing written is just the beginning.

Mwa, mwa, mwa, everyone.

Enough slush, now. Importantly, to Kelly and Amanda, I have to say – I did it! I got egg on a pizza into the storyline!

About the Author
Jackie McLean

Jackie lives in Glasgow and has a varied background, including being a government economist, a political lobbyist, and running a pet shop in Glasgow's Southside (ask her anything about pets). She currently works with East Ayrshire Council, where until recently her job involved frequent visits to Kilmarnock Prison.

Her first novel *Toxic* introduced DI Donna Davenport, and was shortlisted in the Yeovil Literary Prize. The sequel, *Shadows*, was published in October 2017. Run is the third in this series.

Jackie has appeared at crime writing festivals Newcastle Noir, Crime at the Castle and Literally @ Newbattle, and regularly appears at Noir at the Bar events (including Edinburgh, Newcastle, Dundee and Dunfermline). She also forms part of the Dangerous Dames and Murder & Mayhem along with a number of other crime writers, and has appeared at events in libraries and bookstores across Scotland as part of these. She is also a Bloody Sotland 2019 Crime in the Spotlight author.

Jackie has run the writing group at Waterstones Braehead, and has also run creative writing sessions with the men in Kilmarnock Prison.

Jackie can be found online at:
https://jackiemcleanauthor.com
Twitter : @JackieJamxx
Facebook: www.facebook.com/WriterJackie/

Also from ThunderPoint
Toxic
Jackie McLean
Shortlisted for the Yeovil Book Prize 2011
ISBN: 978-0-9575689-8-3 (eBook)
ISBN: 978-0-9575689-9-0 (Paperback)

The recklessly brilliant DI Donna Davenport, struggling to hide a secret from police colleagues and get over the break-up with her partner, has been suspended from duty for a fiery and inappropriate outburst to the press.

DI Evanton, an old-fashioned, hard-living misogynistic copper has been newly demoted for thumping a suspect, and transferred to Dundee with a final warning ringing in his ears and a reputation that precedes him.

And in the peaceful, rolling Tayside farmland a deadly store of MIC, the toxin that devastated Bhopal, is being illegally stored by a criminal gang smuggling the valuable substance necessary for making cheap pesticides.

An anonymous tip-off starts a desperate search for the MIC that is complicated by the uneasy partnership between Davenport and Evanton and their growing mistrust of each others actions.

Compelling and authentic, Toxic is a tense and fast paced crime thriller.

'...a humdinger of a plot that is as realistic as it is frightening' – crimefictionlover.com

Shadows
Jackie McLean
ISBN: 978-1-910946-29-9 (Kindle)
ISBN: 978-1-910946-28-2 (Paperback)

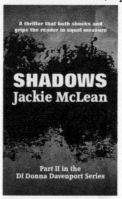

When DI Donna Davenport is called out to investigate a body washed up on Arbroath beach, it looks like a routine murder inquiry. But then the enquiry takes on a more sinister form.

There are similarities with a previous murder, and now a woman connected to them both has also gone missing. For Donna, this is becoming personal, and with the added pressure of feeling watched at every turn, she is convinced that Jonas Evanton has returned to seek his revenge on her for his downfall.

Fearing they may be looking for a serial killer, Donna and her new team are taken in a horrifying and unexpected direction. Because it's not a serial killer - it's worse.

Moving from Dundee to the south coast of Turkey and the Syrian border, this is a fast paced novel about those who live their lives in the shadows, and those who exploit them.

"With sensitivity and honesty, Jackie has written a thriller that will shock and grip the reader in equal measure."

The Peat Dead
Allan Martin

Shortlisted for the 2019 Bloody Scotland McIlvanney Debut
Scottish Crime Prize.
ISBN: 978-1-910946-55-8 (Kindle)
ISBN: 978-1-910946-54-1 (Paperback)

On the Scottish Hebridean Island of Islay, five corpses are dug up
by a peat-cutter. All of them have been shot in the back of the head,
execution style.

Sent across from the mainland to investigate, Inspector Angus
Blue and his team slowly piece together the little evidence they
have, and discover the men were killed on a wartime base, over 70
years ago.

But there are still secrets worth protecting, and even killing for.
Who can Inspector Blue trust?

"A mystery so redolent of its island setting that you
practically smell the peat and whisky on the pages." –
Douglas Skelton"

This atmospheric crime novel set on Islay gripped me from
the start. A book that shows decades-old crimes cast long
shadows." – Sarah Ward

In The Shadow Of The Hill
Helen Forbes

ISBN: 978-0-9929768-1-1 (eBook)
ISBN: 978-0-9929768-0-4 (Paperback)

An elderly woman is found battered to death in the common stairwell of an Inverness block of flats.

Detective Sergeant Joe Galbraith starts what seems like one more depressing investigation of the untimely death of a poor unfortunate who was in the wrong place, at the wrong time.

As the investigation spreads across Scotland it reaches into a past that Joe has tried to forget, and takes him back to the Hebridean island of Harris, where he spent his childhood.

Among the mountains and the stunning landscape of religiously conservative Harris, in the shadow of Ceapabhal, long buried events and a tragic story are slowly uncovered, and the investigation takes on an altogether more sinister aspect.

In The Shadow Of The Hill skilfully captures the intricacies and malevolence of the underbelly of Highland and Island life, bringing tragedy and vengeance to the magical beauty of the Outer Hebrides.

'...our first real home-grown sample of modern Highland noir' – Roger Hutchinson; West Highland Free Press

The Deaths on the Black Rock
BRM Stewart

ISBN: 978-1-910946-47-3 (Kindle)
ISBN: 978-1-910946-46-6 (Paperback)

It's been a year since Rima Khalaf died in a fall from the Black Rock, deemed to be a tragic accident by the police.

But her grieving parents are dissatisfied with the police investigation, so DS Amanda Pitt is sent north from Glasgow to the small town of Clachdubh to re-examine the case.

Despite the suspicions of the distraught parents, all the circumstances seem to confirm Rima's death was indeed a tragic accident, until another woman is also found dead in the town.

Frustrated by the lack of any real evidence, DS Pitt pushes the limits of legality in her quest for the truth.

Stewart writes with a gritty intensity that places the reader in intimate contact with the darker side of society, in a way that forces you to empathise with the uncomfortable idea that sometimes the end justifies the means for those who are supposed to uphold the law.